SCHRÖDINGER'S GOAT

SCHRÖDINGER'S GOAT

A Quantum Suicide Love Story

Book I of the

WARDENCLYFFE TRILOGY

DANA REYNOLDS

Wardenclyffe Tower Books ™

WTB

WTB

Paperback Edition
ISBN 978-0-9884380-8-8

19627 W Vanzant Rd.
Springdale, AR 72764

Cover Art by Dana Reynolds
You may contact the author at:
author.dana.reynolds@gmail.com

∞

If *Many-Worlds Theory* is true, events, locales or persons, living or dead in this book are a certainty somewhere, but resemblance to the universe you reside in is such a long shot, you may consider it entirely coincidental.

For my son, Zac
—Who inspired this book and encouraged me to write it

CHAPTER ÖNE

"My medium is time. It is as immense as the uncounted 'verses evermore expanding. It is as immense as love."
—*The Artist*
A retrospective of 4D works from the Wardenclyffe Foundation

∞

In the year 2123

Sergei leaned against his machine to steady himself. Dismayed by the slamming in his chest, he sucked air deeply into his lungs and wondered if his old heart could take it. There were surely limits to bio-enge'd longevity, and if anyone had ever pressed the boundaries of that threshold, it was himself and now. The exertion of his imagination winded him. It was fear. Just fear, pure and simple. He felt as though he tottered on the railing of a bridge, about to jump from such a height he could not see the bottom. Well, he *was* about to jump. Not from a bridge, but from the world.

He used to joke that his machine was just a broken calculator where the function was division, but the product was multiplied. It was the old loaves and fishes shtick: Break bread and pass it on and never come to the end of it. Jesus fed five thousand this way. Sergei fed roughly eleven billion, not counting alternate populations. Whether or not it was miraculous depended upon one's grasp of multi-dimensional physics. And faith, of course. Sergei had faith in himself, to be sure, but it was hard won, a long time coming and still, not quite enough.

Having come to it at last, he tried calm himself in the recollection of standing with Lilly so many years ago under the gentle beam of the first proto-type. Its only effect back then was that water had condensed and beaded on them, but it was enough to fill her with wonder and cause her to believe. She'd looked up at him, lashes dewed and pupils wide. Her lips had pulsed with warmth beneath the rain collecting on their skin. He could remember how the droplets felt, growing heavy as they broke their surface tension to track down the length of his arms and drip from his elbows, while his hands cupped Lilly's face, his attention on the firm press of her kiss. The memory was as clear as if it had been yesterday, and not nearly a century ago.

Sergei let his aged hand rise. He drew a finger across his mouth and then dug at his eyes.

His machine was now a small chamber, a booth perched over a trapdoor that would open at the touch of a button and drop him into pure theory. It was a one-way trip and he wouldn't be back to publish the results. With luck, he might find himself suspended by a safety net of rarified mathematics. He hoped to hell it would hold.

It was a Quantum Suicide Machine, but not like those Trans-Dimensional portals the kids these days were calling *shunts*. This new one didn't split the universe to calve off a parallel dimension. It didn't branch off, *it grafted on,* all the way back to the trunk. Back to what the engineers called the Point of Origin. *The past* —using layman's terms. As for himself, the only origin that mattered was the temporal horizon that defined the circumference of his original sin. That's where he was going. *Back there*: back in time to be with Lilly. To save her. To stop himself before he killed her.

Sergei shuddered.

The problem was, the past wasn't a place with an address. He couldn't point to a moment in time and say, "There. That bit right there. Aim for that." Time was merely a notion and a figment. An event was only one experience within all eternity, and the experience was different from 'verse to 'verse, parallel or branch.

Though he stood tottering on the brink, and though he couldn't see the bottom at all, he trusted his own experience and its singular vibe. The resonance he programmed into the Hadron cell was his own frequency of a particular sort: It was of him holding Lilly firmly in his heart and mind. Even underneath his fear, he felt the ever-present vibe of his longing for her. The pitch and tone of it rang clear as a bell, clear as it ever was. He fairly buzzed with it as he climbed into his machine and he imagined the harmonics of the tiny black hole quivering in sympathy with the enormity of his love.

The machine was tuned in and ready. And so was he.

He checked it twice. Then he checked it again. There was no margin for error. Once operated, and after a delay of one minute, its shell would assume its own resonance, requiring the machine to melt down in high-frequency liquefaction, leaving no trace of what he had done and no chance of anyone following. He would either be gone before that happened, or he'd hit the kill switch and shunt the hell out of there.

Inside the booth, Sergei paused with the door open, engulfed in an anxious anti-meditation. His ears reddened with embarrassment, though there was no one there to witness it. After having come all this way, after living this long, after working out every detail to perfection, he was not about to let fear get the better of him, and yet there it was. Any way he looked at it, he was at the end of his life, and screw what-all probability and parallels, it was *scary*.

Quivering like a shunt-virgin, he took a deep breath and reached out to close the door.

If only the Wholly Rollers could see me now, Sergei thought.

CHAPTER TWÖ

"The desire that guides me in all I do is the desire to harness the forces of nature to the service of mankind."
—*Nikola Tesla*
The Wardenclyffe Foundation Archives

∞

In the year 2123

Lauder squinted into the rising sun at the farmhouse from the edge of its back garden. The house belonged to the Murderer of the World, the Un-Maker, the Father of Shunts and one of the last of the First Generation of the Undying; an old man and forever old, amen. A *Geezer*, as far as Lauder was concerned, but the worst of the lot: The house belonged to the esteemed Sergei Elder-Enge, the chief engineer who first split the world with his unholy and un-wholly machine.

The light seemed wrong. It seemed weak. Lauder glanced up, certain that the sun speared his pupils with less vigor than it should have done. He let his eyes drift, observing the unwholesome afterimage, black and blue and bruised. All the evidence he needed was right there: The wounded sun was one more sign of the universe rent asunder.

Lauder shuddered and burrowed into his nostalgia. He longed for a whole and singular world. He wished mightily he could un-shunt himself and go back to his origin. He wanted desperately to reunify the 'verses to the One True Universe, as did all Wholly Rollers, but he was no longer in fellowship with that congregation. He was fed up with their moaning, *Going,*

going, goners! and not doing a damn thing about it. Lauder was different; he was resolved to act. So, act he would. Indeed, he was giving it his *undivided* attention.

Lauder wet and pursed his lips and whistled. The sound echoed feebly between himself and the house and died.

Nothing.

He held a canister of *Sleep* out in front of him like he might graffiti a wall, took a deep breath and called, "Here, boy!" and suffered hallucinations of snarling dogs jettisoned across the lawn.

But, no dogs came. Gradually he accepted the house was unarmed and he lowered his wavering can of *Sleep*. He took in the quiet. *Was the Geezer even home?* As far as he could see, the agri-animals were goners too. No geese sifted the shallows of a pond that was as smooth as a mirror. The shed was silent, where should-wise be a goat.

The keep is down, he realized, and his heart fell. Mayhap the gig was up. He'd been careful of pings, but it looked like he'd tripped the Geezer's instincts anyway. He'd been sussed out.

Geezers weren't patched in as a rule, being too old the take the goog implant without paranoia. But old folk had rich experience to guide them. They had dark thoughts from way-back-when, teeming with over-ripe memories of nefarious daring-do. This one especially kept to the old ways and more than most: The World Murderer stayed whole. He was neither divided nor split. Unparalleled, you might say, and among that elite politic of geezers who never stepped into a shunt, never relieved the world of his upkeep to sojourn in alternate dimensions. It was a special hypocrisy for him that first opened the door to that machine and said paradise awaited all who stepped through. —For all, except himself, of course.

Lauder was mulling this over when he saw movement through a window of the house. His heart leapt and he sprinted across the lawn, keeping the *Sleep* canister at the ready. Bounding up to the patio, he was astonished to see the door wide open. He didn't hesitate, because *he who hesitates is lost.* He stepped through the doorway and made directly for the nearest wall, to press flat next to an old bookshelf. He saw it was a lawyer's case, with leaded glass doors wedged open by books stacked haphazard-like and spilling out onto the floor. The dining table in front of him was likewise a jumble of books. He focused on the title of one on top, *"Tesla, Man Out of Time"*, and his goog auto-relayed, *Null: creative domain expired.*

Lauder clicked off his goog with annoyance. He didn't need the distraction.

He moved quietly into the main room across threadbare carpets. Aside from an armchair, a mechanical piano and more stacks of books, the room was spare.

Lauder could hear faint music playing but discerned it was only coming from the greenhouse. Behind the glass wall he could see the hydroponic cradles slowly rotating, but oddly, they were empty. He glanced at the room's readout to learn the music was a composition by Bach; whoever that was. He'd bet his creds Bach was expired too, but he didn't bother his goog to find out.

An ark opened off the greenhouse. It was a small one, a micro-ark meant to carry only one man without surplus. From where he stood, Lauder could see the hutches and coops were empty, too.

Lauder exhaled so deeply his shoulders dropped and he let the can of *Sleep* hang loosely at his side. Things were looking up. It seemed the old man was preparing to leave, and that bought Lauder some time. With the luxury of time, he could properly orchestrate the media, and on his own terms. Lauder could spin the Murderer's dispatch as an act of righteousness: *A premeditated act of righteousness.* He'd have time to post several good takes on his goog before he was arrested. If it got out and the right people gave it a look-see, it might make enough people think twice about shunting themselves before it all drained away; then his life was not null. That was the dealie-o.

A hallway lead from the great room, and Lauder crept along it, gripping his sandal thongs with his toes to steel his nerves. He tried to ignore the shakes that loosened his joints and made him need to pee. *The worst that could happen was already happening,* he told himself. He was here to double-delete it.

Then he heard the least expected thing: from the room down the hall a high-flux generator whined and stressed with the familiar power-up sequence of a shunt.

He had his own shunt!

Of course he did. Why wouldn't he? He invented the accursed thing; it was the knife by which the world was dying the death of a thousand cuts, and it was for the offense of that unholy contrivance that Lauder had appointed himself the old man's executioner.

Lauder mulled this over for a couple of blinks. *The Geezer wasn't just leaving; he was going to* split!

Lauder launched from where he stood, and pounded down the hall. Shoving aside his fear, he burst through the door. Across the jumbled room he caught the motion of the vault of the shunt closing and the Geezer sitting within. Their eyes met only briefly. They met for only the time it took for light to play across their pupils – for just the time it took for the Geezer's expression to register surprise, then alarm. Both Lauder and the Geezer telegraphed the thought, '*Stop!*' but for entirely different reasons. And then the old man pulled the door closed with the inside handle.

If Lauder wasn't running and yelling he'd have heard the *click*. Because he was busy dodging tables and equipment he also didn't hear the vacuum lock engage with a suck and a *sssomp*. So, the shock wave hit him by surprise. —Hit him right in the solar plexus; hit him mid-leap towards the vault door. The silent *whoomp* made his bones flinch and his terror bloom. The room rattled around him. His hand closed around the shunt's door handle at the same time as he heard the *crack!* that normally precedes a lightning strike, least-wise when it is not made by a shunt.

Déjà vu, Lauder thought. *Like that time with Arlee.*

But there was one critical difference: During the trip across the room, he noticed something off about this shunt. It was cabinet-like, not coffin-wise, with the apparatus affixed to the top, not underneath. Being homemade, it was clunkier than the public utilities, crowned with a jumble of routers, mods and god-knows-what-all. A stepladder stood next to it, at the ready, and the outer panel was off, like it had just been serviced. But most importantly, it wasn't coupled to an incinerator like the public shunts were. It was freestanding.

So Lauder didn't wait for the hiss and roar of heat jets. He gamed there weren't any, and this is what saved him, because when he pulled open the door, and was confronted with the empty chamber, he saw the readout, saw it was counting down. Next to the readout was a simple toggle switch. He toggled it. The countdown stopped at 09.

He stood stupidly, now that he had time to. The Geezer was goners. Not there to be observed as dead or alive, but *goners.*

Somewhere Schrödinger's cat was —or was not —turning in its grave.

The blank look on Lauder's face twitched, his fear eased and a different expression started to take shape. He clicked his goog by the lobe, and opened his retinas to scan the shunt inside and out. In a slow care-wise motion, he turned around and did the same eval of the room, googing as fast as his jack would take. Googing everything. The feedback compiled and he found himself a stool and just sat there, his grin getting bigger by the gigaload.

CHAPTER THREE

"Everyone wants to know what it was like 'the first time around'? —But the thing to understand about time is: there is no 'first time around'. The question makes about as much sense as if I handed you a ball and asked you to show me where on the surface was the first part of the ball?"
—*The Artist*
A retrospective of 4D works from the Wardenclyffe Foundation

∞

In the year 2010

Lilly smelled the ozone right before she heard the *crack!* of lightning. She felt the lag before the light, felt it right down to her bones. She sensed a lift as the plasma exploded up, then down, as the bolt struck the top of the feed mill's silo across the street.

Lilly pressed her back against the window of Neat Stuff Pawn Shop. She held her breath, held it as hard as she could to push down the shakes as she concentrated to lift her wrist to see her watch. Her arm raised slowly, dragging through air gone syrupy and thick and let out her breath in a slow deliberate count.

"One-one-thousand, two-one-thousand, three-one-thousand." She was not counting seconds before the thunder; the thunder was upon her. She was keeping time, keeping it like it was a thing she might hold and possess.

The thunder was still pealing from its first crack and it rattled the window behind her. The glass pulsed in a slow *nudge*

nudge nudge against her shoulders while she focused on the second-hand that crawled reluctantly around the face of Hector's old watch. The watch hung loose from her forearm on a silver band heavy with turquoise and memories. From her first glance it showed only two seconds had passed, yet her count was at five and she counted steadily on. The second-hand arrived at three as she reached eight. It stuttered at four and as she deliberately recited "twelve-one-thousand." In that instant and without the intervening sweep of the hand, it caught up. *Caught up*: Four to twelve just like that in a surge of here and now.

She grabbed sanity by the tail and hung on. It whiplashed back with a roar and a downpour that was sudden and drenching.

Move.

Lilly burst through the entrance of the pawnshop, relieved to find it open this late in the evening. The rain barged in right behind her, along with a frantic bird seeking shelter. Its wings beat around her head before it veered off. Lilly stood amazed on the threshold until a gust of wind and rain reminded her to close the door. Before she could act, a sucking drop in pressure slammed it shut, ruffling fliers taped on its backside like so many feathers, mimicking the harried bird.

An antique black enameled fan turned and blew musty air in her direction.

"Hoo! Lilly! There you go!" Shorty slapped the newspaper spread across the glass display case that was his sales counter. "That was a close one!" he bellowed. "Nearly gotcha out there, didn't it?" The only answer he was really looking for was whether or not she was a customer.

Lilly was not a customer. Not today. She was at that moment gripped with the awful realization that she was literally in the process of having the shit scared out of her.

"Bathroom?" she squeaked.

He thumbed over his shoulder. "Back there where it's always been. Watch yourself. Lots o' junk."

She bolted *back there* and flew down a narrow path between stacks of junk, just as he said. The bathroom was a cinder-block cell in the far corner and she was relieved —in more ways than one —to find it in time. The light operated with a tug of a flyspecked cord knotted around a one-inch washer. She pulled it, shut the door, and worked the button fly of her jeans pretty much simultaneously. She hit the seat squarely as her bowels let go. Sweat and goose bumps peppered her skin and nausea swept up, demanding new and urgent attention, and a decision to be made.

Misery is the cure for panic, she decided, pulling the cold wastebasket onto her trembling knees and purged all of her digestion at once. *How does this serve fight or flight?* she wanted to know, and not for the first time.

Outside the thunder rolled and the rain roared on the metal roof, neutralizing the wretched sounds she made in the bathroom. A small casement window stood ajar and let in a fine atomized spray of rain-fresh air and Lilly was grateful for it. It was dark beyond the glass. Twilight was swallowed up by the storm.

In time, that queer euphoria that comes after being sick revitalized her a little, and gave her hope. She located the can of Lysol under the sink, next to a water-stained and bloated roll of paper towels. There was pressure in the rusty can and she strafed the air before wiping surfaces with the stiff towels.

Satisfied she'd done the best she could with the tools available, she leaned over the sink and cupped handfuls of water to her face and over her head. She rinsed out her mouth. She gave herself a bracing look in the mirror, assembling some dignity. "You are still here," she told her reflection. With shaking hands, she fished her cell phone from her jean's pocket and hit '1'.

"Lilly?" Sunner answered. It was difficult to hear his voice against a throbbing whine in the background. Static screwed with the reception.

"God, I can't believe my luck. You actually answered your phone. Can you come and get me?" She hoped she didn't sound as pathetic as she felt.

"In Fayetteville?" he asked.

"No, I'm just here in Decatur, at Neat's."

"You're *here?*" he asked. There was a clatter and a squall, and then silence.

She thought the call was dropped.

"Sunner? Are you there?" She was answered by a crackle and pop, and she heard thunder roll out of it and over the building. She shut her eyes.

"Lilly? I can hear you. Can you hear me?"

"Yeah. Still here."

"I thought I lost you."

"I thought I lost me too. I'm not feeling so good."

"Don't move! I'm on my way!"

She heard his phone tick off the line before she had a chance to explain or say goodbye or tell him to drive carefully, but he was like that.

A renewed spell of weakness overtook her and Lilly sat in the only place she could with the vaguely alarming sensation of sitting on a toilet fully clothed. Breathing in and out, she felt hollow, which was better than feeling crazy. As she steadied herself, the storm that came out of nowhere went back again and the rain eased off to where she could barely hear it. She saw the light shift to a soft glow through the frosted glass, like dawn was approaching instead of twilight. At last she felt able to navigate back out through the dingy back room. She wanted to avoid Shorty if at all possible, because he seemed bored enough to be interested, and uncouth enough to ask questions.

As she threaded through the junk, she set her face in an expression that made it clear it was *not okay* to pester her and *too much time had passed* in the bathroom for it to be decent to mention it at all.

She was relieved to see that Shorty was occupied with a customer who leaned on the counter with his head down.

As to be expected, Shorty was short. He was a stout barrel of a man who moved wincingly as though he'd recently been thrown from a horse. He was the kind of man whose belly arrived on the scene before the rest of him did, and who was always looking around on the off chance someone might be sizing him up. With his chest puffed and his arms stiff and ready for whatever might come of it, he was delivering a lecture to his hapless customer.

"This here is a pawn shop. It ain't no post office. You want to send a package; you go to the post office. You want storage; you go rent yourself a bin. This here is a pawn shop."

The old man he addressed appeared to barely possess the strength to hold himself upright. He hung his head as though his neck had just let go and maybe the rest of him would follow if he didn't get what he needed. He certainly wasn't getting what he needed from Shorty.

A thick flat package wrapped in brown paper lay between them on the counter.

Shorty took a deep breath and swelled up a little more, yawping out his words as though the old man were deaf.

"You want me to hold it, you've got to pawn it. I pay you — let's say like twenty bucks, and you pay me back with interest. Once't it's paid for, then you get it back. If you don't pay, I sell it. That's how it works, see?" Shorty punched the air with a stubby finger. "You don't pay me just to hold it here. That would be *storage*. This is a *pawnshop*." He paused when he saw Lilly from the corner of his eye and shot her a look that she didn't like.

The old man was shaking his head.

"Keep it. Just keep it safe for me. Just for a while." His voice clotted as he wrestled with an uncooperative tongue, though its burden seemed more emotion than age.

Lilly picked her side and moved into the room to back up the old man, with whatever sort of backup he might need. At her approach, he jerked up suddenly as if he'd reached the end of a drop with a noose under his chin, and he looked at Lilly with so much anguish it paralyzed her. It was a nursing-home face, gaping with the shock of a lucid moment, where fog lifted to a horrific realization.

He gasped, *"Not yet,"* in answer to nothing and then dissolved into confusion, turning this way and that, trying to get his bearing. Tears wobbled down his face.

Shorty was put out. He wanted no part of this.

"You want me to call someone? You want someone to come and get you?" He picked up the phone. *"Son,"* he said, and waved the phone receiver at him, a kind of warning. The looping chord waged in sympathy. "You tell me who to call or I'm going to have *them* to come get you now. You hear me? You got people? You just take it easy now and tell me who to call or I'm going to call *them*."

The old man wasn't taking it easy. He was taking it hard.

"No?" Shorty prodded.

You're not giving him time, Lilly thought. *All he needed was some time. Anybody could see that.*

"Then I'm calling Sue. Sue is with the sheriffs, but she's a real nice little gal. She'll take care of you, *hear?* —Get you where you belong." Shorty punched numbers into the phone.

"Don't go!" The old man reached a hand toward Lilly. It was trembling, but not with the palsied tremor of the aged. It was as though he held his heart out to her and could barely manage the weight of it. Lilly came closer to steady him. He took her hand like an old lover might. He seemed to just want to hold on, and as he did he stared at her with an intensity that made her blush.

The old man flinched, and his gnarled hand clutched tighter. "Ah, no. No. No. Not yet." His voice quavered as some fresh anguish filled his eyes.

"I'm so sorry," she offered. "Have we met before?" She hoped her voice was soothing, she hoped he didn't see how uncomfortable she was. She did her best to deliver what solace he required, but she was wrung out and wanted nothing more than to sit down and wait for Sunner.

A sorrowful thought occurred to her, "Are you —*were you* a friend of Hectors?" As she asked, she glanced at the big wristwatch hanging loose on her forearm.

"Don't bother that gal, now," Shorty interrupted. "See?" he tapped the receiver on the countertop. "It's ringing. They'll send someone right off. That little gal just came in out of the rain, that's all. She ain't no one you know."

"It's okay," Lilly said, speaking to the old man. "It's no trouble. My name is Lilly. Hector was my husband. Did you know him? Hector passed away, did you know?"

"*Lill.*" His whisper turned her name into a prayer, and he slowly lowered her hand, letting it go like one might release a small animal.

With his eyes locked on hers, he retreated several paces, taking each step with no regard to what might be behind him. His movements had a weird grace that kept Lilly transfixed, but when he stopped he dropped his gaze to the floor and his face went blank.

Alzheimer's, Lilly concluded. She didn't know what to do, but at this moment, she was the only one to do it because Shorty was talking urgently into the phone:

"Yeah. Here at Neat's. For godsakes, can't you come right along?" Shorty wasn't happy with the answer on the other end of the line. "What do they pay you for?" he wanted to know. "Can't you send Sue?"

Meanwhile, the old man seemed so forlorn and lost, Lilly was compelled to go to him again.

"Hey," Lilly said, and gently touched his shoulder. "Hey?" He looked up and locked on, eyes panning her face.

"Help me, Lill," he said.

She nodded without hesitating. "Okay."

He gazed at her. "I'm sorry. I'm just so tired."

"It's all right. Everything is going to be okay," she offered.

"Jesus," he whispered. "Damn-it all to hell." He hesitated a moment, then reached out to enfold her face in his woody hands. For a moment she thought he was going to kiss her on the mouth, and shied her face away because she had just been sick. He tipped her head forward instead and pressed his lips on her forehead; The better part of valor.

His tenderness so reminded Lilly of her lost husband, a profound sadness overtook her. She felt weak again. Dizziness swarmed behind her eyes. Tinnitus sang through her head.

The old man leaned down and whispered intimately in her ear, "Can you hear it?" he asked. "It's almost over. Can you feel that?" But Lilly was fully employed in the business of managing the unexpected renewal of her grief, whose accounts came due without warning, though not as frequently as they once had done. She knew if she didn't step back and regain her composure, she was going to sag against the old man and he wasn't a candidate for shoring her up. She took a deep breath, cooling the shards of glass in her throat. *There.* That was better.

Thunder peeled anew, beating the storefront window with a fresh burst of rain.

"Damn that boy!" the old man burst. "Were you afraid? You were caught in the storm!" Then just as abruptly he turned his attention to the floor where he seemed to find the stains on the cement as confounding as the weather.

Gone again, Lilly thought. This was heartbreaking to watch. She wished Sue or whoever would hurry. Lilly was out of her depth. She wondered how the old man had made it here on his own. Someone must be looking for him. Some distraught daughter who left the door unlocked was right now frantically searching in the rain.

"About time..." the old man started to say.

Lilly offered a quizzical smile.

He lifted his eyes to her, watchful. "Ah. Saved by the bell," he sighed.

Next to them the door banged open. It tinkled the bell suspended on bailing wire over the sweep. It was Sunner. Sunner was here to rescue her. He swept into the shop and wrapped his rain-specked arms around her and gave her a long fortifying hug.

"You're wet," he told her.

"And I probably don't smell the best," she agreed, feeling heat rise to her ears.

Sunner pulled back, taking inventory.

"Are you okay?"

She looked away. "There was this lightning strike, like, right there, and I don't know, I just freaked. It was so stupid."

"I say screw that!" the old man barked. "Fear is the mind killer. You do what you have to do."

Sunner's response was tempered by a touch and a look from Lilly.

"Sometimes it's smart to be scared," Sunner responded carefully, sizing up the old man in exactly the way Shorty wished to be sized up.

Sunner pulled Lilly a step further back. The old man stood too close, but that wasn't it. There was something else.

"I don't need help," the old man huffed. It was obvious he was in his own world, having his own conversation.

Lilly deflected Sunner a second time and lifted her eyebrows to recruit him into the conspiracy of compassion. Sunner enlisted at once.

"Look. I've got a pickup. Let me run you home?" Sunner's concern was genuine, but he seemed perplexed, like something was tickling the back of his mind. Lilly knew that look. Sunner had a peculiar genius that resolved the world in complex patterns of numbers. She didn't understand it, but she could tell: Whatever was going on here, for Sunner, it just wasn't adding up.

From his post behind glass counter, Shorty tried to regain control of the situation. "You just stay out of it, Sonny!" He advised, getting Sunner's name wrong like he always did. "They's on their way to come and get him. Don't muddy it up now by getting him all confused. He's confused enough as it is. They'll handle it. They'll take care of him."

Sunner and Lilly exchanged another look, but their moment passed as the door banged open. A plump woman hurried through. She was squeezed into a khaki uniform and trailing a dripping umbrella.

"Sue!" Shorty demanded her attention. "That feller there is scaring my customers."

"Angels and ministers of grace defend us," the old man muttered.

Sue looked at her feet as she stomped the rain from her shoes and tapped her umbrella on the floor. It was a calculated move to get the old man's attention. She kept her eyes down and moved slowly, the way you might approach a dog you were unsure of. She reached out carefully and put her hand on his shoulder and offered him a beaming smile. It was the kind of smile usually reserved for toddlers.

"Hi hon! My name is Sue! What's your name?"

The old man was clearly annoyed.

"Do you remember your name?"

"Oh for Christ's sake," he sighed.

"My name is Sue," she repeated. "Are you out for a walk? That's quite a storm out there, isn't it? Did you get caught in the rain? Is there somewhere you were going? Can I help you get there? Where do you live, sweetheart?" The questions were rhetorical as she had taken his arm and was already backing him toward the door while fumbling with the umbrella.

"Sergei Elderidge," he said.

Sunner blinked.

"Is that your name, hon?" She asked him.

"Aloha," he replied, agreeably enough.

Sue said, "Well! How about that!" and patted him on the shoulder. It's hard to know what to say to 'Aloha' when you are a deputy in a small town in Arkansas. Nevertheless, she kept him moving through the door. There was some difficulty on the threshold where he seemed to want to exit backward.

"Mr. Elderidge, aren't you frisky this evening?" Sue said, and gave Shorty a wink as she shook her umbrella open. She finally managed to raise it over the old man's head, pulled him across the sidewalk and press-ganged him into the back of her sedan. She shut the car door and hurried around to the driver's side, trying to outrun the raindrops.

Shorty stood his ground, safe behind his counter.

"Well goddamn!" Shorty said. "Poor old som'bitch." He gave Sunner the once-over to see if there was a challenge coming. There wasn't. He cleared his throat. "So what ch'you lookin' for?" he asked.

"Found it," Sunner said and he tightened his arm around Lilly and turned his attention to her. "It's really coming down out there, and it's nearly dark," he told her. "Do you want to wait it out, or what?"

Shorty tried to find a handhold on some business. "Sure! You all wait an' stay dry. I'm open for as long as I need to be! Sonny-boy, you should see the old Compaq what just came in. She's a beaut! An Lilly, I ain't got no new pictures, but I got this one picture book you might..."

"No," they both said together.

Lilly peered through the door at the dim outline of the feed silo where the lightning had altered her state. Its rain-slick metal flickered in reflection of lightning more distant. It appeared not quite there between the flashes, like it was struggling between two worlds. Just looking at it gave her the willies and made the world feel slippery, made her brain feel like a hive of bees. She tamped it down.

Don't think about it, just look at something else, just do something instead. Keep moving. Keep it together.

To Sunner, she surfaced a grin. "I won't melt," she told him, "and dark doesn't matter. Let's get moving." Lilly took a deep breath and pushed through the door and out into the rain, with Sunner right behind her.

∞

Sunner kept his hand lightly between Lilly's shoulder

blades, steering her toward his truck, which was parked askew across the street, with one front tire deeply creased by the curb. He paused at the centerline, and looked up the street where the police sedan's taillights flashed briefly at the town's only 4-way stop. Lilly kept going, and his hand felt cooler as it was deprived of its place on her back. He frowned, and then he followed her.

She ducked into the truck's cab on the far side without his aid. He pulled open the driver's-side door and hitched one foot up on the running board, and paused again, starring after the cruiser. It was gone now, but not past pondering. As he stood there, he didn't care that he was getting wet. His concern was divided equally between Lilly, and the fact that Sergei Elderidge had come back.

CHAPTER FÖUR

"Because it is our nature to experience time from our first moment of consciousness onward, we think that is how time moves. It isn't. That is how we move."
—The Chief Engineer
The Wardenclyffe Foundation Archives

∞

In the year 2010

Settled into the backseat of the city's police sedan, Sergei steeled himself against the tides of time that sucked and pulled at him in the turbulence of the car's passage. Time always had this effect on him when he moved too quickly. Even a brisk walk had its hazards. But a car ride? *Intolerable!*

He held onto the bench seat like it was a life raft and ignored the road and all possible routes receding ahead of them, unrolling before the windshield as though they were speeding in reverse; but that was only his own perspective. Things weren't going backward. Things weren't moving at all. Only he was. He closed his eyes in meditation and dropped away to find within himself the eddy he was looking for; that still, deep place that went neither back nor forward but ran dark and bottomless and silent. He floated there, resting and weightless. He needed rest. He sensed a *beginning* bearing down on him.

For days the vagaries of it had chirped at him like crickets in the grass, nagging and warning and throwing him off his bearings. The ground beneath him was even more uncertain now, the going trickier than usual. He had to place his feet so carefully. Shift back, toe, heel, lift, balance; wait for the path to rise up to meet his feet.

Increasingly, he was surprised, and surprises had to be negotiated, examined and carefully backed through until he was weary of the careful way of going. He found the pauses, the little footholds. He read the signs and portents while all the time running the numbers. Always the numbers. It made him bizarre, calculating the mathematics of her attention. But what did it matter?

Lilly barely recognized him. Wariness replaced her warmth, and even though he spent precious time examining each moment upcoming, he saw the reflection of himself leaching from her eyes. Soon they would be entirely empty of him, and he a stranger. Before him was the oblivion he bargained for. It was where she and he pulled apart and they no longer were, forever and never again.

Too soon, he thought. Not enough time. Had he told her what she needed to know? Would she take actions to change the outcome? He couldn't tell. The hell of it was, he would never know if he had made a good bargain. He —this aspect of himself at least —would never pass this way again. *And other aspects of himself?* Well, that didn't bear thinking about. He would leave those speculations to the philosophers.

Just now, he focused his mind to concentrate on the package he must retrieve from the pawnshop while the vagaries of shifting pasts and futures chirped and swarmed. It was a trilling, buzzing, drilling, shrieking, roaring distraction. He could hardly hear himself think. He could hardly keep his pitch and tone. Soon it would drown him out entirely and he would fall through. Time would open up behind him and he would tumble back. No hold, no hum, no place to be anymore. There was no way to know how deep he would fall or where he would find himself or how long it would take to tune in to a new way of things. Only one thing was certain: He knew when he next surfaced he'd be like a leaf on the water, rushing toward unknown rapids.

And she would be lost to him forever.

CHAPTER FIVE

"There is always some damn fool who wants to find the exit from Eden."
—*The Chairman*
The Wardenclyffe Foundation Archives

∞

In the year 2123

"Tag it and bag it," Lauder commanded his goog. *"Show all."*

Info-balloons billowed into his sight line, filling up the World Murderer's laboratory and half-maxing the short-term memory of Lauder's goog. It was a ridiculous way to proceed, but he liked the way the tags swam and bobbed across his augmented vision to keep their orientation facing him. It was like a halo of worshiping fish, swollen with advertising, begging to be chosen to erupt their roe of *learn-mores* and *buy-nows*.

He listed the price tags, and the results were staggering. All this booty made him whistle in awe as the accelerating numbers kept nudging the totals column sideways.

Ludicrous results. Ridiculous.

With the Geezer gone, Lauder was only briefly tempted to Craig the gear from the abandoned lab and turn a profitable score. But avarice wasn't his deali-o. These expensive antiques were stinking with too much juju. Better to leave the genie lamp lie. Get out with your skinny and live! Besides, he wasn't a sneak-thief. He was a zealot and above petty crime. As far above as an assassin was to a shoplifter, although he'd not killed anyone yet.

The ozone of the recently operated shunt made him uneasy. It triggered deep-seated memories, of course, but that was only the half of it: It was the unexpected absence of its operator. The unoccupied space where the Geezer *should have been* reached out and formed a cushion around Lauder's ears. In that terrible absence his breathing was amplified. He heard his heart race as he considered what it might mean.

Factoid: the Murderer of the World rigged the shunt to blow, so there was no looking back. Wherever he'd gone, he was goners for good. The machine he left behind was now fair game, but just what the hell was it?

"Scenarios," Lauder commanded his goog. "What's all this dreck for?"

He felt the drag behind his ears as the scenarios lagged. A command prompt to patch his location came in on a fade over his right eye. He refused. He declined a bio request as well. —His or the Geezer's. Context? What could he say? *Suicide?* Not a word he wanted floating around his intel. *Illegal departure?* Not unless he wanted a security prompt. He insisted on minimum disclosures and went with what he had, snapping the link and going dark on any new parameters.

"Resident resources only," he insisted.

The trouble was, there were archaic mechanical jobbers spliced in the Geezer's machine. It complicated his search. Most of the booty was unmanufactured, and pre-etheric by the looks of it. Wire! Routers! This anachronistic vanishing cabinet was a puzzle, and the absence of the World Murderer dead or alive proved it was not a shunt. So what was it, and where did he go? Lauder did a 360 from four different locales to reverse-engineer and fill in the blanks as best he could.

In the end, he tabulated only one option other than a shunt with above 46% probability: Trans-dimensional entanglement tracer.

That old chestnut.

Lauder frowned. He doubted the Geezer was another kook trying to communicate with the departed, and Ouija boards were not in the habit of making the players disappear.

Nevertheless, he gave it a half-hearted Wik, and his goog

landed him hip-deep in Trans-D Ether theory with an un-purged wire-punk entry for phone booth (whatever that was), a scholarly tag to Alexander Graham Bell (vaguely familiar) and finally a post-creative-domain 2D pop-cult reference to Tardis, which browsed him to the colloquialism of tard or retard, something that caused him to snort up shortly, but it was an obvious dead end.

He took another tack and queried: "Trans-dimensional Entanglement Tracer" plus "shunt". And without waiting for results, he refined: "Schrödinger/Tillman Effect" or "STE" and "Trans-D Ether."

His goog got helpful finally, and recommended he add "Hadron cell."

"Quite likely," he sneered. Even if the Geezer shit diamonds, there was no way he had a Hadron cell. *No way.*

Except he did: apparently he had *two*. Because as soon as he allowed, two blue pegs bobbed in his inventory. His eyes darted to where they floated from within the open door of the not-a-shunt.

"No way," he whispered in awe.

Lauder followed the balloon's tail and found it tacked to the interior control panel. He let a question mark tic his mod.

No precedent found, his goog told him. For starters, shunts didn't have control panels. They were operated from the exterior, simultaneously executed by a lawyer, a shrink and a clergyman in a hands-on triad fail-safe ignition sequence. (*Overkill,* he had thought the first time he shunted and emerged weak with hysterical laughter over his own pun.) Shunts simply didn't employ Hadron cells.

Speculate, he ticked.

No precedent found.

"Stupid-ass goog," he muttered, going to audible. "What mayhap ist das?"

No precedent found. His goog wanted badly to go back to speculating about the ghost-phone, but he wouldn't let it.

Lauder popped the panel and right away the two blue markers ticked down to one.

"What's the deali-o?"

There were two cradles. The one that was helpfully labeled

'spare' was occupied, and fully charged. The one labeled 'primary' was empty. The tally sagged and the totals column contracted, decreased in value by nearly half. At least now he knew what accounted for that astronomical price tag.

"End tag-it," he snapped. He was growing tired of the distractions. The balloons tanked, and he proceeded on bios.

Next to the primary cradle was, in fact, a Trans-dimensional Entanglement Tracer, just as his goog had said. In short order Lauder found its memory, jacked in and sent for help. Help, it turned out, wasn't much; which is to say it jawed his ears off with tech-specs floor-to-ceiling.

Water, water, everywhere, and not a drop to drink.

He needed to sit down. Not in the psudo-shunt, of course, but on the floor next to it, where he could keep an eye on it.

"Engrish, please," he sighed. Data weary, his eyes started to burn and he rubbed the plants in his temples. "It's been a biggy day, old son," he complained.

But all he got before switching to dark was the old axiom: *Jump in a hole and pull the hole in after.* His goog offered no ref-ID what the damn-hell that meant.

CHAPTER SIX

"How would you think about life differently if I said, 'let art govern your actions'?"
—*The Artist*
A retrospective of 4D works from the Wardenclyffe Foundation

∞

In the year 2010

It wasn't a long drive from the pawnshop to Sunner's secluded farm where Lilly rented a cabin, but in the dark slanting rain it seemed like it to her, especially when lightning turned the rain into spears of light and thunder shook the truck. When Sunner finally pulled into the gravel driveway she expected to be relieved. Instead, she said, "Uh oh."

"My folks are here," Sunner sighed. Every light in the cabin was blazing. "I guess they figured you could use the company."

"I can take care of myself." Lilly was embarrassed by evidence to the contrary and that her phobia of lightning was public domain. She missed Oklahoma where the storms tramped down like angry prophets, and you could see them coming from a long way off. It gave you time to say your prayers and be three sheets to the wind with a bottle of whiskey down in the hidey-hole before they hit. Here, they mounted up over the hills without warning, all wrath-of-god and took you unawares. *Ozarks in June. What was she thinking?*

"They worry about you," Sunner said of his parents. "You should have gone down to Fayetteville like you planned. It's not storming in Fayetteville."

"You sure about that?"

"Yes, I am," he said firmly. He stared at the cabin "You could have called and let me know. I'd have come hung out with you. Helped you keep a weather eye out. Phones these days; they are portable, you know."

"I called you, didn't I?"

"After the fact."

"Emergencies only. I drain batteries."

"So you say."

"I don't like surveillance."

"That I can understand."

When she snorted, he grinned at her. "Turn about is fair play," he said. Before Lilly, Sunner had used his phone only as a convenience for himself. He used it to call, not take calls. Most of the time he kept it off, with its battery in the other pocket. But that was *before.*

He absently pressed the phone in his pocket and frowned.

Lilly misread his pensive expression. "Don't worry about your folks. I'm being a pain in the ass. Your parents are sweet and company is good." His frown deepened. Realization slowly crept across her face. "You were hoping to have me all to yourself, weren't you?"

He looked blank for a moment, then recovered with a grin. "Yes, and now my evil plan is foiled. I was going to have my way with you." He bobbed his eyebrows and twiddled an imaginary mustache.

"No, you weren't," she said, and peered through the wipers slapping the windshield of his old Chevy truck. She looked up at the lightning rods on either end the roof, decorative and unnecessary, but comforting nonetheless. The storm was quiet, the rain steady, the wind gone, the thunder distant, *but still...* She considered the motionless whirligigs and the windsock mourning in the downpour. On sunny and breezy days they were all camp and cheer. Now, not at all.

They both sat staring at the attic loft, at the window to the room that she considered her studio, which, even now, Sunner thought of as his bedroom.

"It's still coming down," he said, to pull her back. He turned off the truck. It held on for a few stuttering seconds until the rain replaced the engine noise, soft and encasing. She felt him shift in his seat toward her.

"*No,*" she said, but not against the weather. It was a ward against the clear and present danger in the truck. Sunner's shift toward her crackled the air and spun her moral compass.

I am too old for this. And he is too young.

Lilly pulled the latch to where it clunked open and she launched herself through the door. Each year was one of a decade of arguments that made her bolt out of the truck and into the rain; each splashing footstep was an indictment against her inclinations. He was so young... But oh, he was easy to be with and depend upon. He was easy to talk to. It was easy to finish his sentences, as if they shared a secret language infused with little intimate understandings that darted between them like bright flashing minnows.

The rain baptized her the Ecumenical way: by sprinkling, not immersion, and she fled with her better judgment held tight to her breast.

∞

Sunner watched her beeline to the house. When the screen door slammed, when she was safe inside, he shifted his gaze to the barn. He was sorry to waste such perfect weather for his work, but with Lilly here it was impossible.

Before she came, he had the cabin to himself. His parents had finished the house on the other side of the property and moved there without him. Finally, the barn was his as well. He liked being tucked away down a lane so remote it was hard to find, even with a map. He wished it were *impossible* to find and if he didn't need the electricity, he'd take it off the grid entirely. The idea appealed to him, but not the way it did to his parents. They wanted to live off the land, on their own resources. He wanted to *make* his own resources. And that's just what he was doing: scouring Internet junkyards and taking deliveries of heavy boxes funded by his knack for tinkering. He repaired things: appliances and electronics and power tools and cars and computers. Sometimes he *failed* to repair something, but only when it had just the thing he needed, like a resistor, or a motor that turned a rod just the right size.

And then Lilly arrived. She had knocked at the door, asking if he knew of any places to rent for the summer. He was taken with the sweet inflection in her voice that pegged her as not-from-around-here. He answered immediately, "You found it. The guy who lives here is just moving out." It just so happened, that guy was himself and he only just decided.

He moved all his gear to the loft of the barn that afternoon and introduced her to her landlords. His parents, bless them, just took it in stride and played it cool, but he could feel their eyes on him, crinkling up with fun.

Lilly didn't travel light. She enlisted Sunner and his truck to fetch her things from the U of A, where she was in residence at the Fine Arts department, preparing for her Masters. She was one of those anachronistic die-hards, refusing to trade up for a GrafX tablet tricked to a Mac. Yeah, she was old school: canvases, easels, pizza boxes full of paint tubes and bouquets of brushes in coffee cans. It took careful packing and slow driving to keep these from blowing out of the back of the truck. He was glad-hearted to drive slow; she perfumed the cab of the truck with the scent of her hair, the sweetness of her breath, the undercurrents of other odors that pricked his imagination. *Yes, pricked was the word.*

He was mesmerized by everything about her. The way she moved as she packed her supplies, the careless brush of her hand has she handed him box after box. The nude sketches, *oh hell yeah,* that were scrawled on butcher paper and had to be rolled and secured with rubber bands so as not to rub out the charcoal.

Oil and turpentine and mineral spirits... Aphrodisiacs, it turns out. *An artist.* Oh yes.

But mostly, mostly, he was enchanted by the sum of her. By that shape sublime which rose in his calculating brain. He looked at her and saw crystalline geometries gone hazy around the edges with a hum in the upper registers of his imagination. Her numbers, they sang to him. His skull trilled with her harmonics. The breadth of her pushed against the scales and defied measurement. When he looked at her, his math failed him. It was at once a relief and a deep mystery he must solve.

They were both dabblers of the arcane. Dilettantes. Adepts at anachronisms, and he hoped to discuss that with her someday. Already he was nurturing the fantasy of giving her a tour of his workshop in the barn, showing her his great secret engine, the turbines, the motors, the Tesla coils... and then showing her the loft with its oak floor polished to a dull shine from the abrasions of a hundred years of hay stored and stacked there, scrubbing it smooth, season after season. He'd show her his living space. He'd show her his bed.

If she was not blind to his intentions, she was cool to them. It didn't discourage him. He was patient, trusting the way of making, finding familiars in the process. Building their rapport piece by piece as with his machine, with faith in his labors. There was nothing he couldn't suss out when he applied himself. And she was such a pretty problem. That she was pushing thirty made the prospect more intriguing.

But his machine needed attention. Tonight. Sunner wanted to wind up the turbines again. This storm came in cascading fronts, which allowed him to coordinate the power surges with lightning and not cause alarm with the electric company.

—But she had called him when she was afraid.

—But his engine wanted to run under the cover of lightning. July and August loomed with hot clear weather and no way to test and tinker.

After August she would move on.

He pondered that, looking for loopholes.

In the end he climbed out of his truck and headed for the house, not bothering to run in the rain, as he knew he'd be no drier for it.

CHAPTER SEVEN

"There is a first time for everything, though it has yet to be proven if there is such thing as a last time for anything."
—*The Artist*
A retrospective of 4D works from the Wardenclyffe Foundation.

∞

In the year 2010

The happy funk of fresh-baked banana bread made the air inside the cabin golden with sweetness.

"Wow," Sunner said. "Smells like mom left us a little something." He entered the kitchen through the back door and saw Lilly investigating the warm bread left on her kitchen table. She'd made a quick change since he saw her a few moments ago.

"It smells like heaven," she said. Sunner agreed, but he was inhaling peppermint toothpaste and the results of her splash-and-dash while he was dithering in the truck.

"Food raised with loving kindness is all the medicine you need, Mom would say," he said. He was grateful to see his mother wasn't here to say it. Apparently, his folks had come and gone. *Yay.*

A roll of thunder rumbled over the cabin and the rain picked up again. Sunner was watching her carefully.

"Company is good medicine too," she offered.

"Uh huh." He was unsure if he was getting the drift just right.

"—If you could just hang with me here for a while," she clarified.

"Sure thing." He *was* getting the drift just right.

"It's safe in here?"

"Absolutely. Couldn't be safer," he assured her.

A clap of thunder offered a different opinion and the lights went out.

"You know if you hear the thunder, the danger is already past," he said in the dark.

"Of course I do," she snapped.

"Right."

He heard her pull out a chair and sit down. He did the same and found her hands across the table. They were trembling. He squeezed them.

After another stretch of flickering silence, he tried another tack.

"This cabin has weathered a lot of storms. It's at least a hundred years old. You know those logs are at least a foot thick..."

"You don't have to do that," she said. So they just sat and listened to the wind buffet the trees and watched the flinging shadows against the window. This didn't seem to bother her at all, but the elderly trees with their heavy branches were a bigger threat than the storm. Sunner kept this to himself but listened intently. He willed the walnut trees to stand, especially the one next to the barn. He couldn't bear to cut it down, but every wind was *worry, worry, worry.*

He hid this from Lilly. He hoped she felt grounded holding his hand. He didn't move until the space between the lightning and thunder opened up enough for her to breathe normally.

"If you're good for a moment," he tried, "I'll go get my sleeping bag."

"Sure." She had no problem with that, so he hurried before she could change her mind. He could hardly believe his luck.

The tree stood. The barn was whole. While working the padlock, he could hear Watch snuffling and whining on the other side of the door. When he got it open, she forgot her manners and jumped up on him, planting two big paws on his chest and jabbed a cold nose under his chin. He gave her the ear-scratch she was looking for and she dropped to the ground and wagged circles around him. In spite of the happy German Shepherd, Sunner made his way just fine in the dark, past his machine, which stood in mute accusation.

He mounted the ladder to the loft and pounded up double-time. In the loft, he rolled and strapped his sleeping bag by the light of his phone. Then he thumbed the back panel off the old Zenith radio and fetched the baggie from among the tubes. He threw his bedroll down the ladder hole, taking care to miss his dog and climbed down, his hands and feet fitting in the divots, with the baggie in his teeth.

His machine loomed sullenly in the dark. He tried not to think about it.

"Go lie down," he told Watch, and she trotted off to her wad of blankets on the floor. Always careful, he slammed the bar of the padlock home, spun the dial and gave it a good jerk to be sure. All this took less than three minutes.

When he got back, Lilly was busy in the living room, working in the dim halo of one oil lamp. There was a thick quilt doubled over on the floor for padding, a pile of pillows thrown down. She was making up the couch.

"I'll sleep in here too," she said.

"Sweet! A slumber party!" He threw his bag on top of the quilt and followed it, landing with a thud on the floor. "And I found something else you might appreciate..." He held up the baggie and shook the contents. "Food raised with loving kindness is all the medicine you need," he quoted his mother.

"That's not food. Please tell me you didn't raise that."

"*Medicinal* purposes." He bounced his eyebrows at her, "and yes I did."

"Oh really. *Medicinal purposes*: You're not having any then?"

"Manners prevail. The lady must not smoke alone."

"What would your parents say?"

"My parents would be the first to tell you 'Ozark gold ain't banana bread' and this ain't any-old weed. It's a sacrament in offering to the god of thunder."

"I don't smoke."

"You call yourself an artist?" He filled the paper, licked and rolled. Lighting up was a ritual he concentrated on. Presently he leaned back on his sleeping bag, cocked an ankle on his other knee, held his breath and exhaled slowly.

"It will calm you," he said seriously, holding the joint out to her.

"No."

But as she sat on the edge of the couch, a fresh peal of thunder prompted her. She reached out and took it from his hand. He saw how awkwardly she handled the joint, not sure how to hold it, trying it between her fingers one way, then another.

"Wow," he observed. "You're not kidding."

"Here's to the god of thunder," she saluted, and put it to her lips. Sunner hoped it was slightly damp. His kiss by proxy. He hoped she'd notice, hoped she'd like it.

"Hold your breath," he told her, but her throat and nose rebelled and she erupted in a fit of coughing and laughing.

"This is supposed to make me feel better?" she asked. "I want a do-over. I'm going back to 'just say no'. For the record, I wasn't in my right mind. I was seduced while in a compromised condition."

"Were you?" he grinned. He liked the sound of that.

Lilly heaved a theatrical sigh as she lay back on the couch and put her feet up on the armrest, oriented like he was. She passed the joint back to him on the floor. "You can keep it," she said.

"Too bad." He was sincere. "It would make you feel better." He took another drag and saw her watch his ember glow and hoped for her it was a guilty pleasure. His thoughts slipped a notch and his horizons narrowed around her. It was a perfect circle and she was sitting at the center of it.

"I'm supposed to want some banana bread now, right?" she wanted to know.

"Is that what you're really hungry for?" he asked her. He was languid and rakish at once, his gaze steady. Smoke spurted out of his nose with silent laughter when her eyes widened. He made sure there was no mistaking his meaning.

"No. Not banana bread," she said.

To his surprise, she reached for the joint with an impatient gesture. He handed it over, but she didn't put it to her lips. She just studied it, deeply pensive.

Lightning again. There wasn't room for a thought between

the crack, the flash and the crash of thunder.

"Better?" he asked, but she didn't answer. He was up in an instant. She was rigid on the couch, her hands pressed flat over her ears and counting. The joint between her fingers was singeing her hair, but she was unaware.

"...*Two-one-thousand, three-one-thousand...*" She rocked back and forth with each number, putting her all into each second.

He immediately went to her, took the joint away, pinched the ember in her hair and pulled her into his arms.

"Hey, hey, no need to count. It was right on us but the rods did their job. It's okay."

Her eyes bobbed over him, up and down, back and forth.

"Am I still here?"

"Where else would you be?"

"Where's my watch? Where's Hector's watch?" It had slipped down on her arm. She cranked it around, the face toward her. "I can't read it in the dark," she said. Her voice was lost and sorrowful. "I've lost count... But I'm still here?"

"You are still here."

He held her for a long time. When he pressed the joint to her lips, she turned her face away, so he let it go out. Moving carefully so as not disturb her, he pinched the ash and tucked it behind his ear. There was more lightning, but it was in the distance.

Some time later she murmured, "It's not about the lightning."

"Okay," he said, and held her until time stretched out and she fell into a tense sleep. And then he kept on holding her.

∞

She awoke to a dark and silent house. Cool moonlight dimmed and rose behind scuttling clouds. The lamp had gone out. She could tell by the controlled cadence of his breathing that he was awake, his arms loosely around her, her head against his chest.

"Well, this is awkward," she whispered.

"No. It's not."

She didn't move. Instead, her awareness reached out like radar and she traced the length of them, where they touched, where they didn't, the aspect of his skin, his warmth, his presence... solid. So solid. So... *young*.

Sunner might have felt her gathering up for an observation he wasn't going to like, so he interrupted her.

"How much do you sleep? Every night—how many hours do you sleep?" His voice had that keen edge of having waited a long time for the moment to ask her this. It was clearly a rehearsed question.

"What?"

"Humor me."

She turned it over, looking for booby traps. "I'm a lazybones," she said cautiously. "Eight-nine hours. More on weekends, if I can get away with it."

"Really." He seemed pleased. "So not accounting by birth dates, I would say by life actually lived, we are about the same age"

"How do you figure?" Her cheek drew up against his chest and presented an enigma: smile, or grimace?

"I've never needed more than four hours of sleep."

"That's not healthy."

"I am the very picture of health," he assured her. "I'm just wide awake, like it or not, twenty hours a day. Line that up with your fifteen-so hours, over the course of our respective lifetimes... what is your birth date?"

She told him.

"See there. By actual conscious experience, you are only 1.19666 years older than I am. That's no bother at all."

"Is it really? That's a lot of sixes."

"Do you need a calculator, or could you follow along if I wrote it out for you?"

She ignored his teasing. "Less dreamtime, though. Dreamtime counts."

"I almost never dream."

"That's the saddest thing I've ever heard," she said with total sincerity. Her own dreams were important to her. She looked forward to them every night, and left them reluctantly in the morning. In her last year with Hector, they were a sanctuary from his suffering. "To not remember your dreams..." she felt genuine pity.

"I remember everything," he assured her. "I just don't dream."

"Of course you do. Dreams are how your brain assimilates your day. See? Not only have I had more experiences, I've assimilated them. You may be younger than you thought."

"Oh, very clever."

"I am."

"But I don't dream. I assimilate my experiences as they happen, thank you very much. Except for those four hours, I give it a rest. All that real-time assimilatin' is hard work."

"A life without dreams is half lived," she said, and she meant it.

"It's not the length of a life, it's how the time is spent."

"My point exactly, Sunner..." she sighed and gathered herself up to say what had to be said. His argument was sweet, but only underscored the age difference between them. "I've been through a lot. A lot. I've been married... You still live with your folks –well, on their property, at least, and you've never even been to school, as far as I can tell..."

"School's expensive. Learnin's free," he said, nonplussed. "And we have this thing now? Called the inter-web?"

"Not the same."

"MIT. School of Engineering. You've probably heard of it?"

"Massachusetts Institute of Technology."

"I've taken in every lecture online. Every one. I can quote them to you. I understand them. Hell, most of the time I just use them for validation."

Lilly tried not to wince at his defensiveness. It only made him sound younger.

"I get it. You're a smarty-pants. But that's not my point. Sunner, I've been through this before." She was taking inventory in her head, trying to decide what baggage of hers to unpack for him. "I know all about the complications of differences in age. Hector was quite a bit older, you see..." then she stopped, seeing no way to proceed from here to her advantage.

"Tell me about Hector," he said.

She wrung the heavy turquoise watch around and around her forearm.

"It really has nothing to do with us. It's not important."

"It is to me," he said softly and waited.

After a time she faltered: "I was fourteen..." she stopped when she heard the intake of his breath. "No, Sunner, hear me out. At that age there are two kinds of girls, those that want to ride horses..."

"...and those who want to ride boys," he finished for her, laughter in his voice. When he saw her look he laughed outright: "Let me guess. You were a horsey girl."

"'Fraid so. At least at first..." Sunner's interest was palpable and she tsked herself for dropping an innuendo. "...and there was this riding academy nearby," she course-corrected.

"Hector worked there? Hector was your stable boy?" There was laughter behind the words.

"It *was* Hector's. Ever see The Horse Whisperer? Hector was like that." She paused and when next she spoke her voice had gone soft. "He could make a horse dance in place. Just dance. –You couldn't even see him move. It was like magic. Watching him made you believe in centaurs."

Sunner let her remember.

"You could say he did something similar with me" and she paused again, not for effect, but for courage.

"Two years later I was old enough —according to the laws of the State of Oklahoma —to marry without my parent's permission."

"Okay," he said. "So you married young to an older man."

"Decades older," she stressed.

It seemed to pain her, but he couldn't help asking. "How many decades?"

Lilly remained silent.

"So, a lot of decades," he surmised.

"You are shocked, of course."

"Surprised. And in the interest of full disclosure, a little bit turned on."

"I'm not a slut," she said evenly.

"Now that really is too bad."

"That's grossly inappropriate. I was a widow at 25."

Lilly felt him sigh. He had assumed she was going to tell him it had all been a mistake; that they divorced and her ex-husband was fair game for good-natured ribbing. This put a different complexion on things.

"I'm sorry," was all he could manage. He gave her a little squeeze to show he meant it.

"I was 23 when the... when he was struck."

"Struck?"

"Struck by lightning," she said.

"Oh." Sunner sighed again.

If he thought he had it all put together now, he didn't. Though Lilly told him it wasn't about the lightning, it was only partly true. It was about the moment right after.

They'd been out to gather the horses before the storm rolled in. Hector didn't like the horses out in bad weather, but the storm came up faster than they expected. Trying to outrun it, they loped across the back pasture to where the small herd was. The horses were already standing huddled with their backs to the wind, their hindquarters backed up all the way to the barbed-wire fence that stretched a quarter mile into the gloom. Lilly had never been particularly worried about storms, but she'd never been caught out in a treeless expanse as one bore down.

Hector got in behind the herd, to move them off the fence, but he pulled up short with a terrible realization; The wind had suddenly stopped and they were dropped into a pocket of stillness. Lilly felt the hair on her arms start to rise. It felt like someone was rubbing a balloon along her skin. The hair on her scalp lifted too.

"Get down!" Hector had yelled, just as her horse wheeled out from under her and she was fell to the ground so hard it knocked the wind from her lungs. She struggled to sit up, gasping and afraid the other horses might run over her. But what she saw instead filled her with terror. Blue static ran like mad fairies down the fence wire and arced across to anything it could reach: the odd high blade of grass, to the random thatch of scrub, to any errant twig trying to grow out of the horse-cropped earth. When it got close, it arched across to the bit of Hector's horse, which reared, and the blue fire erupted from its iron shoes and leapt up the reins and exploded like a cracked whip off the top of

Hector's head.

And it held him there. He and his horse hung suspended from a noose of light, motionless, soundless, while Lilly waited. And waited.

Nothing moved around her at all. Only her, and though she felt her heart had stopped beating, she struggled onto her hands and knees, then to her feet. It was as if the world hung motionless in the balance. And then Hector slipped a notch in a thrum of noise that cut off again as he froze a second time. Only the lightning was moving and its lazy whipcord eased around Hector like syrup falling through cold water.

She took a step toward him, moving stupid and slow, her voice sounding like a lowing cow to her own ears. And then they were on the ground together, and the ground bucked and tried to throw them off in convulsion of noise that included a sudden drenching rain.

"It didn't kill him," was all she said of it. "But it would have been better if it had."

"Three years," Sunner realized. He was sorry to imagine Lilly in her early twenties confined to nursing an invalid husband. Such a waste.

"That's when I started to paint: Because..." She shrugged. "All those pretty horses. I wouldn't go riding, not without Hector; so I painted them instead."

In the long silence that followed Sunner stroked her hair. It was a sad story and he wished it wasn't hers. He regretted that his clever banter about their age difference had led to this, but it also made him tender toward her in a way he hadn't expected.

She continued her story, stepping over the obvious. "Later, I found out he had money put aside for me to go to school. *After...* So I did."

"He took care of you," he said aloud, and to himself he thought: *But not the way you needed to be.*

Sleepily and without malice she agreed. "He took very good care of me. You can't even begin to compete..."

"I'm not trying to," he lied. "But maybe I can give you something he couldn't." He was worried as soon as he said it, but she seemed to take no offense.

"You have no idea..."

He sensed playfulness in her tone, so he pressed on. "I beg to differ. You'll find I'm quite imaginative."

"Well, I suppose if the brain really is the largest sex organ, you may have *something* to offer."

When words failed him, she smacked his forehead with the palm of her hand.

"You're an idiot," she said, but he was pretty sure she was grinning when she said it.

He just sat there. She'd managed to put him off his footing for once. He cleared his throat. Pointedly. Dramatically.

"I may not have Hector's experience, but I assure you I'm old enough," he tried. He let her chew on that while he traced little circles with his finger on the back of her hand. When too much time passed and she had no comment, he gave up and asked her, "Do you want to finish that joint?"

"Which one?" she managed, and he laughed, and tightened his arm around her.

"You are so... very..." Lilly sighed. "But I don't want to be your Mrs. Robinson."

"Who?"

"See?!" she cried with exasperation.

"Kidding. Mrs. Robinson. Anne Bancroft. Dustin Hoffman. Coo-coo cachoo. And that was way before your time as well, so don't get all ageist with me."

"We watched a lot of old movies."

"I can imagine."

"We did other things as well."

"So you say."

"Things you and I will never do," she admonished.

"So you say."

They both had a lot to ponder. After a time he pointed out, "The storm cleared off."

"Then I guess you'd better move back onto the floor," she said softly.

"Yes ma'am." It wasn't what he wanted her to say, but he was satisfied he'd gained some ground overall. He eased out from under her and rolled off the couch.

"—Because there is more room on the floor," she surprised him, and rolled off the couch and onto the floor after him.

"When the student is ready, the master appears," he laughed.

"*Mistress,*" she corrected, and stifled his astonishment with her mouth.

CHAPTER EIGHT

"You will forgive me if I demure. Even in my public works, there remain private moments."
—*The Artist*
A retrospective of 4D works of the Wardenclyffe Foundation

∞

In the year 2010

"...And all this time I thought young men were impulsive and unskilled," she said.

"I'll have you know I've been in training for years."

"Virginity ain't what it used to be."

"Huzzah for the inter-web."

CHAPTER NINE

"What is done is done, until you do it again."
—*The Artist*
A Retrospective of 4D works of the Wardenclyffe
Foundation

∞

In the year 2010

Memories were a bitch.

Moving as he did, Sergei suffered a constant retrospective of himself and it was easy to lose his thoughts in a landscape of recollections. So dense was the screen of his past that it seemed impenetrable, and he was confounded at how it blocked his way like a wall of hoary greenery, like a feared and ancient forest, like a wilderness over-run with brambles and mystery. Memories of the aged ran riot, and in that regard he was Methuselah making his way back to boyhood haunts, seeking trails that hadn't known his tread in close to a century.

Except for memories of her: She was an open glade. A teeming meadow. An oasis in the tangled old-growth that opened up and let in the light.

When he thought of himself with her, he was not old. He was as evergreen as she was, because she'd not been permitted to be anything else. And it was this younger self, this true self, the ageless observer in his mind that dwelt with her in that tended garden of his inner life. So accustomed was he to her company there that when he saw her now, restored and in the flesh, his imagination utterly failed him. The woman of bone and blood and flashing eyes did by every comparison bankrupt the vault of his imagination. He was humbled by the failure of his fantasies. The facsimile of his dreams was dry and brittle paper in comparison to her living form. And yet even that simulacra had been enough to ignite the homing instinct and keep him beating his wings for a lifetime to return.

Lill.

For all that labor railing against time's machinery, she'd been his only for the briefest span of days before she was swept away. Now, from a different vantage point, all he could do was watch. —Watch as she dwindled, diminishing by degrees into the distance and ever beyond his reach. This night, this fortuitous night, he was reminded that all suffering was attachment. He suffered bitterly, and he suffered absurdly, and he suffered most of all because all of his jealousies were of himself.

CHAPTER TEN

"Even when you hide your light under a bushel, it's still a light."
—*The Artist*
A retrospective of 4D works from the Wardenclyffe Foundation

∞

In the year 2123

In the end, Lauder opted to bury the Hadron cell he took from the Geezer's psudo-shunt, because what else could he do? It's not like he could Craig it or drag it to a recyc shop, and time was ticking down. He nested it among the roots of an old growth tree, because no one would disturb the tree until it died of natural causes. He buried it only a few inches down because he was exhausted by the time he carried it that far, and an inch or a mile wouldn't make a hu-hu bit of difference if it were being swept for.

It was safer there than in the lab; The Murderer of the World had no next-o'kin, yet scavengers would show up PDQ when his geo-pegs signaled goners. Then the recyc would take over, and bye-bye booty. Well, it depended really on how patched-in the Geezer was. If he was running dark it may take an hour or two before he was pegged missing. Maybe longer. Geezers had special clauses. *Grandfather*-clauses, as it were, that gave those so inclined an opt-off the grid, and it would stay that way until Geezers thinned out enough that they lost their Senate majority. On the other hand, if the Murderer were altogether sans-GPS, then Lauder had all the time in the world.

Was the Murderer an opt-off? It didn't take a long think to suss that out. It fit, just peachy. Why wouldn't he be?

In spite of the nice satisfying rush of adrenaline, Lauder knew only time would tell. He spent it lurking in the woods, worrying about losing the uncertain treasure of the psudo-shunt. He had the deconstruction specs in his head, so he could cobble together one his own if it came to that, but he'd never get a chance on another Hadron cell. Not in this 'verse.

If the cell made it go, then he needed it, because he very badly needed to finish what he started. He'd been *that close*. The Murderer of the World had looked him dead in the eye, and the Geezer had been afraid. Fear in another's eyes made Lauder feel more confident, somehow. Stronger. He felt it like OneUps quickening through his veins. But it also made him ashamed.

On toward afternoon, he executed an ears-open nap in the glade near the cell-hiding tree. It was a nice enough temp and he was beat. He didn't have the pearls to stay in the house or use its empty bed, even though there was no body, no crime, and so, no alibis needed. He was honest-to-god just a witness.

Poly that, Jack.

When he awoke it was mid-afternoon. His relief at not having to kill the old man contributed to his refreshment. He was surprised at how long he slept and how alert he felt. He rubbed the sleep from his eyes and settled in to watch the house some more, though he had the unsettled feeling that the house watched him back. When his alarm went off, he jumped.

Enough time. It was for certs; the Geezer was off the grid. Lauder broke his gaze with a snort, stood up, dusted his britches and retreated back up the lane, not keeping to the woods, and not threading through the orchard, but right up the middle of the bloody lane, as bold as you please. It was just like he owned the place. For all practical purposes, he did.

CHAPTER ELEVEN

"How is it people continue to argue that you can't change the past, yet believe you can change the future? The future is just someone else's past further on down the line."
—*The Artist*
A retrospective of 4D works from the Wardenclyffe Foundation

∞

In the year 2010

The violet light of dawn was on her. It cupped her in iridescence as if she lay curled in a seashell and was illuminated by its shining wall. Sunner thought her a mermaid in this light, sleeping in the still pool left behind by the night's tidal surges. She was tangled in the quilt meant to be his mattress, disarrayed in the aftermath of *them*. He had no firsthand knowledge of the ocean; he'd never stood on a beach, smelled the salt air nor listened to the rush and seep and drag of waves, but the recognition was deep and primal.

There were things he vaguely remembered wanting. Now, he simply wanted her. *Her.* He knew he was possessed by the idea and he was glad for it, in spite of the jealous opposition of his other big obligation. As daylight increased in the room, so did his understanding of the complications that snared him; He had to go check his machine. There were decisions to be made.

She was right about one thing; She was a lazybones. She didn't stir at all when he untangled himself and found his clothes and headed for the bathroom. It was a reluctant shower, and he was tempted to leave the crusty high-water-marks that tightened his skin here and there, just so he could continue to appreciate them. But she might not like that, later. And he wanted *later* to be soon and often and evermore. So he showered with a new fastidiousness, and stepped out to regard himself in the mirror. Unchanged, but entirely different in all the ways that mattered to him. It did not cross his mind at all how fleeting a thing was youth, and how often he would revisit this day in an endless recycling of memory. He was in that moment and in the past few hours as close to enlightenment as he would ever be: completely, mindfully, in the present.

But then he had to look in on her again before he left the house. He stood some minutes, imprinting the image intentionally for eternal recall. It was the beginning of sorrows.

As he approached the barn, a glance at the side door made his pulse stumble. Something was wrong. The padlock he set last night with a double-jerk to check the rod's engagement looked exactly as it should, and yet he was certain it had been breached. It wasn't one of those cheap locks that can be cracked by applying formulas listed on the internet, and he was the only one who knew the combination, which he changed both frequently and randomly. It looked fine.

And yet...

His brain cramped with the idea it was not as it should be. It was hard to explain but it didn't add up. Perhaps he was alerted because he didn't hear Watch snuffling inside the door like she usually did when she heard him coming, or maybe it was something else. When the vast sum of his perceptions was off by a tick, the missing digit could be anywhere. He didn't feel like he had time to look for it. He only afforded himself a couple blinks to adjust his accounting before he did the combination on the lock, flipped it open on the hasp and pushed open the door. Fear for his dog and his machine fought for the upper berth inside the cabin of his skull.

The room was dim just as it should be. The banks of lights had not been switched on. He stepped inside the doorway, to the right and into the gloom in one fast motion. Watch did not rush up to greet him, but he heard her tail thumping deeper in.

"Who's here?" he asked. Whoever it was, had made friends

with his dog.

"It's just me. No need to be alarmed," a gravelly voice said from the center of the space. "I have unpredictable ways, sorry to say." And after another moment's pause he added, "You're going to want to leave that lock undone, or give me the combination. Saves on too much speculation. Don't forget the lights!"

Sunner flicked the light-switch and saw Sergei Elderidge, the old man from yesterday, sitting on the wheeled stool at the center of the array of equipment. Watch leaned adoringly on him, her nose in his lap. Until this moment, Sunner had completely forgotten him and their strange meeting the night before when he fetched Lilly from the pawnshop. His name, Sergei Elderidge, presented itself with importance, and he felt a pang of guilt.

"How did you get in here?" Sunner asked. Was it possible he had slipped in last night and Sunner had unknowingly locked him in? Did Deputy Sue drop him off here? Did he come in the barn looking for shelter from the storm when Sunner went upstairs for his sleeping bag? Why hadn't he just come to the house? The questions kept popping up and the answers seemed too complicated to be plausible, yet here he was. One thing for certain, it appeared the town had a new character they were all going to have to adjust to. He wondered if bumping into him was going to become a habit. He hoped not.

"Again?" Sergei asked. He tapped his ear to make his point.

"How did you get in here?"

The old man ignored the question and turned his attention to Watch, speaking with a peculiar cadence. "*Good dog*," he said. "What a good girl. You *are*. Are you? Here, now girlie. Right *here*."

"Bad dog," Sunner muttered, annoyed. She whined, looked up at Sergei and took his leave only when he waved her on. She trotted happily over to Sunner and shoved her nose into his hand in greeting, but then bounded back to Sergei.

Well then.

"Mr. Elderidge..." Sunner said cautiously. He was unaccustomed to saying 'Mr.', but it seemed the right thing to do, considering the age of his uninvited guest. People of a certain vintage liked their honorifics. "What are you doing in my barn?"

"You know who I am," Sergei either stated or asked, but

saying it seemed to relieve him.

"My folks told me about you," Sunner replied. But that couldn't be right. That was too long ago. His scalp prickled like it did when he first saw him at *Neat's Pawnshop*. Sunner couldn't catch the sum of him. He did his calculations over. His numbers were wrong. Just wrong.

"You should listen to your mother. There is nothing to worry about."

That was random, Sunner thought, but tried to pick up the thread to follow it. "You helped my folks when they were starting out," Sunner acknowledged. "—Gave them a place to stay. But then you took off." He waited for an explanation, but didn't get one, so he pushed on: "They've kept the place up, all these years," he said pointedly. "They just built a house." He hoped his meaning was clear. He was starting to worry the old man had an agenda, and hadn't just come home to roost.

Sergei seemed to register his mistrust. "You don't trust your own dog?" he asked.

"Dogs are better judges of intention, than of character."

Sergei sighed and ruffled Watch's ears, just the way she liked it. "I guess I'd better be going," he said. But instead of leaving, he looked long and hard at the machine. "Well, I see it's still here," he said. "It appears they are right. A paradox is an enigma wrapped in a... how does that go?" he shook his head. "Maybe *you* can tear it down, but I doubt it. I was going to do it myself, you know. Tonight. But here it is and here I am, so I suspect I didn't. Or couldn't. You know what I mean."

All of Sunner's internal alarms went off.

"It was just the perfect crossroads," Sergei sighed. "Such a fortuitous night." He looked up at Sunner with a wistful smile. "Even so... a good night for *you.*"

The claxons in Sunner's head were making it hard to think. The old man couldn't be talking about him and Lilly, not if he'd been locked in here all night. The alternative was hard to imagine, and it pierced him with a sharp embarrassment that flared into pure anger.

Before he could put his indignation into words, they were interrupted by a plaintive bleating outside, followed by his mother's voice.

"*Pi! Come back here!*"

A large white nanny goat scrambled through the door, her enormous milk-filled udder swayed beneath her. She skidded to a halt, surprised, and turned her amber eyes on Sunner, bleating a complaint that clearly ended in a question mark and then shook her horns and sneezed.

Watch jumped to her feet and started barking furiously, as Donna burst through the door with murder in her eye.

"*Pi!* This isn't your barn anymore! Now get back here *and I mean now!*"

Sunner's mother was an ample woman with a wild fringe of henna-dyed hair that seemed to catch its fire from her ruddy cheeks. She had the look of someone altogether capable, if a bit perplexed, and ready to yank the slack out of any situation. It wasn't just when she was chasing goats. That was how she was all the time.

Sunner groaned. Until this morning, Sunner's barn was his sanctuary. One dog in particular was the exception, but no guests, no goats, and most of all, no parents.

"Mom... for Christ's sake..." Sunner started, but Sergei interrupted him.

"Donna! Aloha!"

She pulled up short, astonishment and disbelief on her face. "Cheese and rice! Sergei, look at you!"

"Donna!" He repeated, and jumped up to met her in a few mantis-like strides, clapping her around the shoulders. "Here you are, all grown up!" He cackled as though that were terribly funny.

"Oh my god!" she said. "You look so... We didn't expect..." Her voice trailed off, but she recovered. "This is going to knock Zip out —just knock him right off his feet! I just can't believe... Zip'll go nuts when he hears you're back!"

"I doubt it," Sunner muttered. He grabbed Pi by the collar and hauled her to the door. Let mom sort out the old man, and good luck to them both. "Lock up when you're done," he snapped.

If Sergei really was his parents' benefactor, that complicated things, but it didn't change how he felt. He thought of Lilly asleep in the house and considered his privacy —*their* privacy— violated just the same. But that was not the half of it.

Tear down the machine...? Did Sergei have the right to do that? Maybe he did. The property was his; Sunner's family was just... what? Squatters? Caretakers? Now that he was back, they might have to leave.

Sunner would have to negotiate with Sergei for time to dismantle his machine and move it to a safe location. But that would take time. Maybe weeks. And to what safe location exactly? Where would he go?

Why did things have to fly apart just when it was coming together, just when he and Lilly...

He hardly noticed he'd dragged the reluctant goat all the way up the hill to the new milk house. His father was there, hosing down the parlor. He looked pleased to see Sunner had Pi in tow, and shut off the nozzle so as not to frighten the goat.

Before he could speak, Sunner blurted, "Dad. Sergei Elderidge is back! Down at the shop. Mom's with him. You'd better go see. He wants me to clear out of the barn."

"Well," Zip said, pulling off his cap, to scratch his spotted scalp. "That's hardly likely, is it?"

"Really Dad, It's him. Mom knew him. I think you should check it out."

His father frowned, gazing down the hill at the old home place. "Sergei's okay. He's a good old boy..." but he didn't sound convinced. "You sure it's him? He'd be old as the hills by now."

"Dad. Yes. I'm sure. *Mom knew him.* He knew her. It's him."

"Damn," he said softly. "What do you think of that?"

"I *think* you should go talk to him," Sunner said impatiently.

"Reckon I will. You finish up here, will you? Pi wants her milking."

"Sure. Why not? I've got nothing better to do."

Zip gave him a meaningful look before he left, one he quite deserved. Sunner waited until his father was out of earshot before he kicked the door, expressing more frustration then he intended. The door banged into the casement like a shot, releasing a shower of dust. Pi sneezed and regarded Sunner with reproach.

Nevertheless, Sunner *did* feel better. He took three deep

breaths to further calm himself, and nudged Pi toward the stanchion. She hopped up on the platform and put her head through the yoke, but after his outburst she eyed him warily, refusing the grain he poured into the feedbox.

Sunner sighed and scratched her between the horns to make amends.

"Good old Pi. You need to meet Lilly."

Sunner reached for the milk pail and switched on the weather-band radio, part of his milking ritual. The mechanical voice spoke of days ahead that were sunny and clear. Good for Lilly. Bad for him. Would he have another chance at the turbines before he had to tear down his machine and clear out? He grabbed Pi's teats with a scowl on his face.

Pi humped her back and kicked at the bucket.

"Right. Calm down. Got it."

Sunner finished as quickly as he could. He jogged down the crooked footpath where it veered around rocks and hillocks of grass, wanting to get back to the barn as soon as possible. Goats tended to pick their way, and over the years, their people followed, even when in a hurry.

The door to the barn was closed. The lock was back in place and *felt right* this time. The cabin was silent. There was no sign of anyone now. He imagined Lilly asleep as he'd left her and let his worry melt away. He figured his parents had taken Sergei back to their house. The thought gave him ease. His folks were soft-hearted people, but strong where it counted. He began to think they'd find a way to hold on to the farm. And why not? In his whole life he'd never heard anything but praise and gratitude for the old man. But then again, they figured he was dead.

Sunner looked at the cabin again and hesitated. A moment longer wouldn't hurt. She wasn't going anywhere. But then, neither was the machine. Proximity won out. The lock was in his hand so he spun the combination and tugged it open.

The barn wasn't huge, not even by standards when it was built, but it was plenty big: Over 35 feet from the floor to the ridgeline. Only the front half was lofted. The back was open up to the gabled roof, and in that section the turbines stood, three spires reaching nearly to the ceiling.

His folks had kept it up over the years, but there was a league of distance between an old hay barn and... Well, Lilly called it a laboratory. She pronounced it like Peter Lorre might, with sinister inflections.

When Sunner spoke of it to others, he called it a *shop* to evoke the vision of a Chevy up on blocks, its engine suspended by a chain. A shop might have a broken welder in the corner. A derelict tractor, partially disassembled. An old redwood incubator abandoned and dangerous with rotten eggs. Such was a 'shop' in the local vernacular, and Sunner wasn't above a little sandbagging to shore up the notion. But his was not a shop in that regard. This was different. Way different.

The previous summer, he practically rebuilt the barn, making it 'tight as a drum', as his father would say. He striped the seams of weathered oak with narrow slats of golden cedar. He poured a cement floor; one heavy wheelbarrow at a time. He pried off the tin roof that was pin-holed with sunshine and put down decking, tar paper and shingles. He tied a rope around his waist as extra insurance as he inched along the toehold and nailed down the asphalt shingles in rows as he progressed. He'd only dangled once; *intentionally*, he insisted, *just to test the lines* –but he had to call for help on his cell phone, to the delight of his father who celebrated the incident with every guest and casual acquaintance thereafter.

Then, slowly and in secret, he began to build his machine to schematics fully formed in his imagination.

Sunner pushed the door open carefully, not sure what to expect. The interior was perfectly dark until he put the lights on. Watch wasn't there. The only chink in his armor was her doggy door, but it was hidden behind the cistern, and Watch didn't permit so much as a mouse to cross her guard. She positioned her blanket next to it, and slept with her nose to the magnetic flap. But she was out now. Taking care of doggy business? It was unlike her not to greet him outside or in, and it rankled how she had taken to the old man. Maybe wherever his parents had taken Sergei, she had tagged along. Let her try begging for a biscuit today. Just let her try!

Everything else in the barn seemed in place and in order,

and he was satisfied until a rustling in the rafters caught his attention. A heavy flapping followed and dust motes filtered down.

Great. They've gone and let a bird in.

Sunner caught a glimpse of it and moaned.

Worse. A pigeon.

The bird chortled softly, and the shadows shifted, but he didn't see where it went. He weighed his options. Once a pigeon settled in, there was nothing to be done but kill it, because it would always find its way back to make a mess. But fire a .22 in here? *Oh hell no.*

Sunner climbed the ladder and looked around his loft. No droppings, yet. No pigeon either. It was sitting quietly somewhere. He stomped his feet across the loft, waving his arms and yelling, but the bird, wherever it was, did not stir.

Sunner looked down at his machine. He looked at it the way an artist gazes at his canvas. Even from this angle it gave the effect of expanding the space it occupied. The idea of a bird gumming up the works was intolerable. There was only one thing for it. He'd have to cover the machinery until he found the bird. He had to afford the pigeon some time and let it settle in, establish a favorite spot, and then he'd lay a ladder up to the roost, and come back in the dark. Pigeons were helpless in the dark.

He'd gone squabbing with his folks in other people's barns before. You could just reach out and lift them from their ledge after dark; take their squabs right out of the nest. You wanted them nearly fledged, almost full-sized and indolent with fat. His mouth watered as he thought of his mother's roasted squab with the skin browned and crisp to perfection over the buttery dark flesh. For the older birds, there was pigeon pie with just a touch of white wine in a flaking golden crust.

Oh yeah, mister pigeon. You picked the wrong barn this time.

He went to get his tarps and plastic sheeting. Patience and culinary ambitions would will-out in the end. As long as the weather held, there wasn't much else to do anyway. And then he thought of Lilly, and had to admit that there was plenty else to do. The thought made him hurry.

He leaned out next to the last tower, standing on a narrow rafter with his shoulder steadied on a cross-brace and tossed the tarp out with a spin. The ends spiraled around the tower, and dropped, weighted mostly by the copper eyelets, and from each of these a bright yellow nylon cord hung in kinked weightless strands. Tented, the towers looked like three closed umbrellas.

He noticed the light shift as the door opened. Lilly's voice followed.

"Good morning, Sunshine! Are you in here? Do you want some coffee?"

He gave her a good-natured grimace. "Only my mother is allowed to call me that, and unless you want to be known as *Moonbeam* from here on in, you won't do it again. Stay put, I'll be right down. Don't move, don't..."

He cut himself off, surprised to discover he wanted her to come in. He wanted her to see the cleverness of his machine. He wanted to see her approval. However, he most assuredly did not want to see her like she was in the storm last night, terrified by the lightning. A small sin of omission, and everything would be fine. There was no harm in showing it to her, but there was no way he'd crank it up.

He cat-walked across the rafter and alighted on the loft floor, hurrying to the ladder.

"Oh look," she called. "A dove!"

"It's a pigeon!" he corrected. "Keep an eye on it, will you?"

"No, it's a dove. A pretty white one. Can we keep it?"

His head appeared in the hole at the top of the loft ladder.

"Yeah," he said and grinned. "Keep it in your oven for about 25 minutes."

"Oh, you wouldn't!" she said.

"Oh yes I would," he insisted as he came hand-over-heel down the ladder and landed smoothly in front of her. She was carrying two steaming mugs of coffee and handed one to him.

"But just look at it," she gestured up with her chin. "White doves are sacred. You wouldn't eat an angel, would you?"

"Don't tempt me," he looked at her askance until she realized his meaning. In spite of herself, she blushed.

"*That* is a *pigeon*," he told her. He looked up, fixing the roost in his memory. Figuring on where best to place the ladder.

"I'm sorry, but in the interest of saving your immortal soul, I insist: *No eat white bird.*"

"Every chicken you've ever eaten was white, except for those you've had for dinner at our house," he told her.

"I'm talking about doves, not chickens."

"Poor chickens," he observed, sipping his coffee. It was hot, with cream but no sugar. It would do.

"You know in art or religion – which is the same thing, by the way – a dove is a messenger of hope, peace, purity, longevity, fidelity... the Holy Spirit. White doves especially are off the menu."

"*Pigeon.* Doves are different. Well..." He corrected himself, "If you're going to get technical, *dove* is the species. *Pigeons* are the genus. So all pigeons are doves, but not all doves are pigeons, if you get my drift."

Lilly tried again. "Venus. Aphrodite –did you know the Syrian dove goddess was consort to the snake god?" Lilly bounced her eyebrows at him. "*Snake god,*" she repeated and let her eyes slide down with a devilish grin.

"Nice try," he smiled at her. "But that pigeon there is a common rock dove."

"A dove, then, however you look at it."

"Look," he said seriously. "It's crapping in my la-*bor*-a-tory." He said it the way she did, with the late-night-scary-movie inflection.

"Shit happens," she smiled sweetly at him. "Maybe if we catch and release, she'll just fly away."

"To heaven or something?" he asked sarcastically.

"Maybe."

"And I can keep my immortal soul?"

"Well. At least until it falls to other temptations." She leaned in for a kiss and he was happy to oblige. His coffee was sweetened after all.

Lilly had been surprised when she awoke this morning in the tangle of blankets on the floor. She lay few minutes to ponder what had happened, *what she had allowed to happen,* the night before. She was surprised she had no regrets, first of all. She rather liked the age difference. It was interesting to be the one with experience for a change. The difference was subtle, but it gave her a certain edge that made her feel powerful and sexy, in spite of the fact that he had seen her at her most vulnerable —not just in bed, but before: on the borders of a fugue brought on by the storm.

But he'd known about that before. When he first learned of her phobia, he'd put up the lightning rods to humor her, even though he knew and she knew they weren't necessary in a house grounded by its electric wiring. He brought her cheap gaudy whirligigs and weather socks as little presents. There was no mockery in these gestures. He made her feel cared for in a way she hadn't since before Hector was struck down. Last night Sunner let her take the lead, and he followed with enthusiasm. She felt like she'd snatched a prize away from him, though he was happy to wrestle her for it, and in the end he let her win.

She pulled away slightly from the coffee-flavored kiss. "So, which is it: Time machine? Death ray?"

"Doomsday device," he said. "No, wait. My mistake. I've got that hidden under my mattress. This here is a docking station for the giant robot buried under the milking parlor in my secret lair."

"So, what does it do?" she asked him. She was standing so close her breath caused a warm buttery slide through his brain as if he were inhaling the fumes off a snifter of rum.

"I'm not sure," he told her. Drawing out the word '*sure*' so his lips gave him a tactical advantage and he took it.

"Oh, c'mon!" she laughed, pulling out of the kiss.

"Well, that's not entirely true. I know what it does, obviously, I just haven't worked out what it's *for*."

"I'm not following you."

"All right. Follow this: Imagine you are in London, it's the 16th century and you are rubbing a copper rod with wool and silk."

"Sounds kind of dirty," she observed.

"Stay with me. It makes a pretty spark, right? But what's it for? Neat trick as long as the priests don't catch you, but it's a long time before someone says, 'Ah-ha! I can plug my toaster into this and brown my bagels.'"

"So, what does it do?"

"Pretty sparks, so far."

"Obfuscation," she sang the word and squinted at him.

"Maybe a little. You might be a spy and there might be poison in my coffee."

Lilly locked eyes with him and took a deliberate sip from his cup. He found it more than a little sexy, the way she did it.

"Do you want to see my paintings?" she asked.

"I've seen your paintings," he reminded her. "I helped you move."

"No, you've seen my schoolwork. Do you want to see *my* paintings?"

"I have a feeling you are going to say '*tough beans.*'"

"See, we understand each other perfectly."

Sunner bowed to defeat. "Well, seeing as how I've seen everything else..."

"Consider it tit for tat."

"I've seen those too."

"Would you rather drink this coffee or wear it?"

"I'm hoping," he said, "that it will turn out to be a water-maker."

Lilly regarded him. "Seriously?"

"Right now it's about as far away from that as a 16th century static charge is from lighting the eastern seaboard, but yeah. *Water-maker.*"

"But water is... free."

"Is it?"

She rolled her tongue and took that in, nodding slowly.

"All the same, I'd think you'd be percolating hydrogen or something."

He looked at her askance for a second time.

"*H* -two-O?" he said, with the emphasis on the 'h'.

"Oh."

"But I'm not doing it for the hydrogen."

"What are you doing it for?"

He took both coffee mugs, set them down on his workbench and took her in his arms. Her chin fit perfectly in the indention above his collarbone. She sniffed the neck-band of his white T-shirt, and turning her head slightly, she tasted his neck.

"This is going to sound arrogant," he said.

"And that will be different, how?" she laughed into the hollow of his neck.

"If you thought anything were possible –anything you put your mind to, what would you do?" He let her think about that for a few moments. "Pure water," he said, "is the absolute base requirement for life, with respect to air and sunshine, of course, and thousands die daily for want of it. That would be good, for starters, don't you think?"

"You're not just desalinating seawater, are you?"

"Not a lot of that in Arkansas," he pointed out. "Besides, that's no mystery. Neither is pulling water from the atmosphere. Ever run a dehumidifier? You can easily tank six gallons a day from thin air from a single unit. That's plenty for a small family, as long as you don't shit in it. But running a dehumidifier to any effective degree is hardly free, especially in dry climates. Desalinating also requires huge amounts of energy.

"Sweat the salt out at the coastline and transport costs eat you up. You can't lay pipes to refugee camps, because they are always on the move, and even if you could, you have to pump it. Uphill. From the coast. You can truck it, but water is heavy. Fuel is expensive. Well, now it is," he grinned. "A couple of H's for every O. The trick is, the Holy Grail is, a water-maker which powers itself."

"Solar power?"

"No. Not solar."

"How does that work? Is that some kind of rainmaker?" she looked at him apologetically. If that were so, her expression said, then she would feel very sorry for him, tiptoe out and close the door gently behind her.

He tightened his arms around her to keep that from happening.

"It's not a rainmaker." *Except as a by-product*, he thought, thinking of last night's storm. "Although, seriously, that wouldn't be half bad. Did you know that straight up the middle of the Sahara is —*was* —a Great Lakes basin like ours? It had a river near as long and wide as the Nile that chained them together. It also happens to be mineral-rich. A farmer's wet dream, and I do mean that just the way I said it. Green, wet, rich.

Forget Lucy at the Olduvai Gorge. A century or two of rain in the sweet spot and a shitload of compost might just bring us another shot at the Garden of Eden."

"But it's not a rainmaker."

"No. And neither am I. Just making a point."

"All right. Your heart is pure. Your intentions are noble. You are a good man, as mad scientists go..."

"Technically, it's a bastardized Tesla frequency resonator coupled to a Seari Effect generator..."

"*Derivative retro-dada deconstructionist schlock.*"

"What?"

"That's what they call my style of painting."

"Did you just change the subject?"

"Not really. Tit for tat. I'll show you mine because you showed me yours, but it probably won't make any more sense to you than what you just said did to me. You're a mad scientist, I'm a failed painter." She handed his coffee back to him and held hers up: "*Cheers!*" She tinked her mug against his. They both drank.

"Derivative retro-dada-whatsit: Is that good?"

"No. It's crap. It's derivative because it's too much like another painter —also failed —and it's schlock because it's just plain poor execution. The 'retro' is 'a do-over'. Dada is an anti-art movement from the nineteen-teens and mine is considered so bad, so very bad, it's anti-art, but not in the same blithely intentional way Dada was. It's just plain bad.

"But screw it. I like it. When I saw the first Pia Stiller — that's the failed artist I'm the derivative of —I was hooked. There was and is just something about her work that gets me, so I paint like that. She sticks out like a sore thumb, and she was *blithely and intentionally* painting in her own crappy way back at the turn of the last century, which means she was doing it first and therefore, she is *proto*-Dada. In fact, I'm doing my dissertation on her."

"Who is Pia Stiller? I'm afraid I don't know beans about art."

"And I have no idea what a Tesla-Seari-discombobulator is," she said happily. "But you can toast my bagels anytime, Sunner not-a-rainmaker."

"The best I can hope for is to make them soggy, Lilly paints-like-crap."

"All right. Soggy it is. And I'll do your portrait. A crappy portrait of you holding a soggy bagel."

"Sounds great."

"And maybe, just maybe, you can 'splain to me how you are going to make water out of thin air."

"Because air's not thin," he said. "It's chock-full of watery goodness."

CHAPTER TWELVE

"If the genius of invention were to reveal to-morrow the secret of immortality, of eternal beauty and youth, for which all humanity is aching, the same inexorable agents which prevent a mass from changing suddenly its velocity would likewise resist the force of the new knowledge until time modifies human thought."
—Nikola Tesla
The Wardenclyffe Foundation Archive

∞

In the year 2123

The psudo-shunt in the World Murderer's lab was sans-patent —at least in the current creative domain. That gave Lauder the currency to powwow with a chief engineer, and not just *any* chief engineer.

Engineering wasn't his bailiwick, but he could read a feed just like anyone else, enough to do a little bio-screening before he dangled his come-hither. The criteria was simple: he wanted an engineer successful enough to have vouchsafed a larcenous heart. Lauder knew success only came from nefarious daring-do, as his own recent successes and crazy-assed luck were proving.

The engineer he got was Chief Enge Nidhi Duginapali *G4*. See what crazy-assed luck? And all Lauder had to do was leak a snip of the schematics on the net, fake and then lame his IP-PGP so he had the look-see of a nice fat pigeon. It didn't take long for the foxes to sniffy-sniffy. In less than three hours he had sweet pickings. But, *Nidhi Duginapali!*

Her lackeys pinged him first. Lauder had the good sense to only allow them a peep at redacted bits of the specs. —More sheer dumb luck that it was the right bits. Whatever the psudo-shunt was, it gave them wood. He made his demands, with just the right mix of understated spin, insider jargon and threats regarding genuine comps. It got him an eyes-only access grant that he had to dress up for: Ascot, derby, the works. He even wore full-on gloves, a deceit of genteel modesty that hid the three bars tattoo'd on the back of his right hand.

Nidhi had clout and know-how, but she was a Gen4 goog-head. He figured she could shift the chips all day but wouldn't turn them over. That's how goog-heads operated: Strictly face-value. That's what came from getting 'plants before you went home from the crèche. He thanked his parents for his nature-boy kidhood that kept him an animal until his first day of conditioning, but that's how everyone did it back in the day. Now infants were googing before they could talk. Scary little bastards.

Nidhi's bio told him she had no crossovers with the Murderer of the World, which was surprising at first, seeing as how she was an expert in STE, Trans-D, etcetera, et. al., and for all practical purposes, she was his chief executioner. But as a Gen4, she was precociously patched while the Geezer had famously checked out decades before her natal day. He was ancient history. Done. She on the other hand was just beginning. She might have found the World Murderer an interesting dinner companion had she time for that sort of thing. She didn't. She worked 18/24 and sequestered her staff on per-project contracts. Some of them hadn't left the premises for months. She was that paranoid. She was perfect.

And she had market share. Municipal shunts were often-as-not stamped with the logo of her lab, but not always. There were up-and-comers. There were always up-and-comers. Competition baby. It made this weary old world turn 'round.

If the world were not already goners, Lauder would have thrown himself on a sword rather than unleash another of the Murderer's devices, and putting it into the hands of one of the chief executioners, no less, but that hardly mattered any more.

You can't hurt a corpse.

Nidhi's loco was in the GO suite atop the municipal shunt in Bangalore. To get there, he had to physi-link from the GO, local. Same brand, obviously. She ran her lab on exclusives.

The loco was less than ideal. Lauder grimly packed his meds and took a charter to his access point. Hiring a driver was frou-frou, but he was flush now, and had to look the part. He'd done his time in corp. He knew the speak. Posturing... well, it was like riding a bike, wasn't it? It was all about the confidink. He figured Nidhi's office copped he was bogus, but because she kept the appointment anyway, he took it as a given she was open to shenanigans, and exemplary shenanigans didn't come cheap. So he ponied up for the driver, going vertical all the way so as not to crease his pants.

He dallied before the pearly gate at the grand entrance, full of regret for breaking his promise never to enter a shunter again. He'd doped, but only a little. He had to stay sharp. Just one quick whiff. —Just enough to enable him to push through and aim for the desk on rubber legs. He wished for more.

Three uneasy steps into the lobby and he registered the commotion and saw there was a send-off party in the VIP room. Damn-it all to hell! The doors were open, and a tipsy crowd spilled out, laughing and sparkling the way people only do at christenings, weddings and public suicides. It was all-out: the band was live, and Lauder judged the music anticipatory (rather than celebratory or consolatory), which meant the guest of honor hadn't shunted yet. By the size of the crowd, it was likely a level-up. Well, goody for him. Or her. Whatever. They were dead meat, either way.

Lauder kept his face neutral and approached the front desk.

Before he could announce himself, the waiter said, "palm, please," and she scooted the veinal reader over to him.

"I'd rather not," he said primly.

"Sir, it's policy, I'm afraid."

"Yes, you should be afraid. Naughty-naughty. Surveillance is illegal, my deary: A mandatory security scan is a breech."

"Sir, contract validation requires..."

"I'm not here on contract. I'm not here as witness and I'm certainly not going to shunt today."

And never again, if I can help it.

"I'm here for a physi-link only, capiche?"

He saw the slight tick of her eyes as she consulted her mod.

"Name?" she asked blandly, dislocating from her unfortunate blunder.

"Not playing," he said.

She frowned. "What's your deali-o, bro?"

There was a round of cheering from the VIP room, and the crowd broke out in song: *For Auld Lang Sine.* It was almost time, then. He hoped to be in the elevator and out of earshot when it happened. He already felt the chills coursing up from his fingers to spread across his chest. Nausea contracted his stomach and his face felt hot and numb. He wanted to scream, *"Get out of there, you stupid cobber!"* but the host was several times dead already, so why should he care? Nevertheless, cold sweat buttered his skin and his ears began to ring.

"Get me the concierge!" he demanded. "I have an appointment with Chief Enge Duginapali, in the GO suite, pronto."

Her eyes ticked again, and now she tracked.

"Certainly sir," she crooned, and slid a pass-card across the gilded countertop. "Special elevator access. Use the gated..."

He grabbed the key and walked like he wanted to run, moving away from the lobby as fast as he could and maintain some dignity. But it wasn't fast enough. The crowd hushed, damn them, and he could hear everything. The turbine wind-up, the *crack!* which was just like the sound lightning made before the peal of thunder. Except, of course, no thunder followed. His ears strained. He couldn't help it. It was the penultimate moment, that split-second of anything-is-possible, and then he heard the *whoosh* of the heat jets, as the shunter's body was incinerated. Half a tick later the crowd cheered wildly, and the band opened up on its celebration set.

Lauder stumbled into the elevator, trembling with rage. When he hit the top floor, he managed to find the refresher in time to purge his lunch in private. With only minutes to spare, he emerged, squeaky and composed, spiffed-up and glad-hearted the physi-link was just a look-see, because in spite of his appearance, he reeked of fear and sick.

CHAPTER THIRTEEN

"Anyone with the intellectual wherewithal to time travel will lose sleep over unsubstantiated paradox. The possibility of going back in time and killing one's own grandpa, if only by accident, is enough to give anyone the willies."
—*The Chairman's Notebook*
From the Wardenclyffe Foundation Archives

∞

In the year 2010

Sunner's mother was as Sergei remembered her: a bit quirky and distracted, but altogether herself. Donna held nothing back and was completely without mystery. She looked Sergei square in the eye when he asked if she and Zip would go over the deed transfer with him. She was altogether skeptical.

She had an absent-minded mannerism of tapping the tip of her thumb with the tips of her other fingers as though she were counting. He had forgotten that. He also noted the thoughtful way she clucked her tongue before she started to speak. She even slightly pursed her lips at the end of each sentence, concluding each statement with a slight kiss of the air. So it went like this:

Tsk. "No offense, Mr. Elderidge, but I'm putting tomorrow's date on this because I want my lawyer to have a look." Tsk. "I trust that is all right with you?" *Kiss.*

It was all right with him.

Tsk. "Of course, *you* can sign today, in good faith," she said. "If you want it notarized, we can do it again, but I'm taking you for your word." Her air-kiss this time was a little coy.

You think you remember what's important, Sergei thought, but you don't realize what's important at the time.

He had to be careful around her. She wouldn't be easy to fool, although she seemed satisfied when he'd delivered his little speech and she didn't hesitate to sign the paperwork with the post-date scrawled in the margin. But afterward? She stared long and hard at him, tapping her thumb with each finger in turn, and plumbed his character for hidden agendas.

Sunner's father was another story. Sergei was surprised at how hapless Zip was. He rushed to put his own signature on the line (without the post-date) and then deflated with such relief he seemed to shrink in his chair. Yet, Zip was uncertain. He acted his part as someone who had forgotten his lines, and therefore repeated himself as though every moment was a rehearsal for the next. He said and then restated the same thing over and over, reassured by his own incessant talking. He wanted to believe he had done the right thing, but obviously he didn't.

After signing, Zip said aloud to himself, "This will set Sunner right. This will do it. This will set him square on his own two feet. I've always said all he needed was a door to walk through. Now he has one, and no mistake. This will set him right, yes it sure will."

Sergei found this endearing, and a little heartbreaking. He wanted to hug him, but of course he did not.

Deed or no, Sergei would look out for them. The mere fact that they were here now wasn't necessarily evidence they didn't need looking after. Times change. Oh yes they do. That was a fact.

So he added his signature to the deed even though his own linear experience was evidence it would make no difference. But he did it anyway, because it was less drastic than shooting his own grandfather, and who knows what might spin off behind him as a result? Not him, unfortunately. He would never know, but that didn't stop him from trying.

Sergei may have been the first to rig a shunt for time reversals, but he wouldn't be the last. Once a thing was done it would keep on being done, forever and anon. But if he could divert Sunner in the first place, there would be no shunt to reverse, and no reversal needed. Let someone else bear the burden of that invention. Let someone else be ever-after hounded because of it.

Sergei couldn't shake the sense of menace that had begun at the moment of his departure when he saw the man with 3 tats reaching out for him with murder in his eye. He'd known instantly that here was a Wholly Roller, one of that fringe sect of Unitarians who worshipped the One True 'Verse. Once converted, Unitarians didn't shunt. But they usually didn't kill either, at least not for the past couple of generations. This guy was different. He wore his murderous determination like a second skin. Yes, Sergei was quite sure what kind of man he was.

Even in a world where everyone's age was fixed in their physical prime, there were nuances the practiced eye could read. There was a certain cadence to his movements. A degree of weariness around the eyes. A fluidity to his manner that came from long and practiced habit. And then there was that indescribable stamp of generation. Just as you could tell a Euro-American from an Australian at a glance, in spite of their common roots, each generation had their look. Even in the split second that Sergei locked gazes with the man, he knew him to be Generation Two, though it belied the treble tattoo of only three shunts. He was not a youth. He was not inexperienced. Whoever he was, he had some years on him, and the fact he'd only shunted thrice in all his time marked him as a Unitarian. The look in his eye nailed him down as an extremist. Sergei knew from experience how extreme extremists could be. Such men didn't merely give up. Such men could only be stopped. Or, even better: *prevented*.

Since his arrival, Sergei hadn't stopped looking for him. He would never stop looking for him, or others like him. They were a mathematical certainty, and they could be anywhen. Anywhen at all. As if things weren't complicated enough.

Sunner's parents sat looking at him with relief as his pen came up from signing his name. He might as well as signed in blood.

CHAPTER FÖURTEEN

"The philosophers ask, 'what is art', and I answer 'art is love'. Even art that deconstructs is searching again for love."
—The Artist
A retrospective of 4D works from the Wardenclyffe Foundation

∞

In the year 2010

Lilly and Sunner were upstairs in the little attic room of the cabin, the one that Sunner still thought of as 'his room'. Against the sloped wall was where his narrow bed once was, Lilly unwrapped a framed portrait taped in brown paper to show him.

It was a large photograph under glass.

"This old calotype will be my next canvas," she said. "I paint over them."

The portrait was of a young woman in a high-necked Victorian blouse. The picture was tinted in places. Sunner presumed it was to make it more lifelike but it had the opposite effect. The ringlets of her hair were lemonade-yellow and her cheeks and lips were such an unnatural pink that, even faded, made the tinted print garish and comical. Her eyes were a slight blue, but the paper showed an odd gloss where the color was added and it made the irises appear to hover in slight foreground over the dead gray of the eyes. The edges diffused into mist and made it appear to be the likeness of a ghost, and he said so.

Lilly gave him a smile.

"She probably is a ghost by now. Most surely is. I don't

know what will become of her, though. She's not talking to me yet."

"She talks to you?"

"Well, no. Not yet. But I suspect she will, when she's ready to give up her secrets."

"That sounds ominous," Sunner said.

"Let me show you a painting that's done, so you can see what I'm going for."

When she peeled back the brown paper on the next one he found himself at a total loss for words.

First of all, he couldn't see why she called it a painting. Obviously it began its career as a photograph very much like the one he just saw. The picture bore the faint likeness of someone from the late 1800's, sitting stiffly and staring fixedly at the audacity of the camera. It too had been hung to ripen about a century but it looked like something had gone terribly wrong. It was scraped, streaked, stained, rubbed and drawn over. The various outrages it suffered nearly wiped out the subject, whoever it had been. Paint, as far as he could tell, had nothing to do with it.

While he was considering what he might say, she rummaged deeper in the box of portraits and took out an old magazine. Sunner was relieved to be able to switch his attention to something other than the painting. The magazine was old: so old, the black-and-white cover had yellowed considerably. The pages themselves were holding together just fine but they had an unnatural thickness and coarseness from the patina of age. The cover had a deep crease through the title which read "Architectural Digest, 1929".

Lilly carefully leafed to a page bookmarked with a Day-Glo orange Post-it note to an article titled "Remembering Stormfield." It showed what appeared to be an Italian villa, but across one corner was a super-imposed portrait of Mark Twain.

"Stormfield was Sam Clemens' last house, where he died." She glanced at him, "Mark Twain was Sam Clemens' pen name. You knew that, right?"

Lilly watched for his nod before she peeled the next page over. She showed him several interior shots of the same house. The last photo was of five chimneys rising out of charred ruins.

Each chimney had two hearths, one for each floor, but the one on top was suspended over nothing, the house having entirely burned away. Stormfield was no more.

Lilly pulled Sunner's attention away from the ruin by tapping on a different photo on the page, to get him to look at one of the interior shots. It was of a room that contained a hanging portrait that looked as though it had endured the same indignities as the one Lilly had worked over. The painting was the focal point in a parlor and hung over the mantle of one of the hearths that would later survive the fire. Wingback chairs were arranged to face it. Sunner studied it long enough to satisfy Lilly but he speculated that anyone who sat in that room might soon wish the chairs were turned the other way around.

The caption read, "The Devil's Portrait II, Artist Pia Stiller. Circ. 1909. Photo courtesy of the Wardenclyffe Foundation."

"Hmm," he said. The title at least seemed appropriate.

"Pia Stiller is my inspiration," she told him. "She worked in the late 19th - early 20th century. Other than that, she's almost entirely unknown, which is amazing because her work is so remarkable; so ahead of its time. But then, almost none of her work survived."

"Yeah. Fires and such," he said.

"Oh, this one might still be out there somewhere," she said. "The house had passed to different owners by the time it burned. It was years after Sam Clemens died."

"So it's missing."

"So it seems."

"And you've based your work on this itty-bitty photograph?"

Because of her enthusiasm, Sunner resisted taking the magazine and turning it on edge to see if it might look better that way. It looked just the mess to him, but Lilly saw miracles in it, so he bit back much of the commentary that wanted to bubble out of him. He had the sensation it might find its way out his nose in snorts if he didn't also hold his breath.

"When I came across this, it felt like God smacked me across the face," she said with wide and serious eyes. "I was just smitten. Two inches of a photo plate in a magazine sent me reeling. I had to see more but I only found one —and I did get to

see it. It was in a private collection in Kansas City. And get this:
It was titled 'The Devil's Portrait IV'. They didn't let me touch
it, let alone radiograph it, but they let me photograph it at least.
But the photos don't do it justice. Wanna see?"

"Sure. Number *four* you say. It begs the question."

"I know, right? Where are one and three?"

She dug out a large manila envelope and spilled out a pile of
8 by 10s. Sunner picked through them, trying to think of
something nice to say.

"I'm not great with a camera," she admitted. "Too much
glare off the glass, and it screwed with the focus, but it's a
memory trigger at least. It keeps it fresh in my mind."

She was watching him look at the picture.

"Recognize it?" she asked.

"It is kind of like the other one," he allowed.

"No, I mean the subject. Doesn't that kind of look like Mark
Twain?"

He frowned.

Lilly chewed her lip. She wanted him to see it, but he didn't.
Not really.

"Does it make a difference if it is?"

"It can make all the difference. If I can connect her directly
to Mark Twain, to Sam Clemens, then that may give her the
boost she needs to get her work recognized."

"I expect she's long past caring," he pointed out.

"*I care,*" she said.

"But you've already connected them. The painting in
Stormfield."

"There is a big difference between owning a portrait and
posing for one."

"But she could have done this over a photo of him at any
time." He tapped the 8 by 10 before him.

She looked at him queerly.

"You don't see it, do you? When I asked if you recognized
him, I wasn't talking about the photograph she did it over. I was
talking about the painting on top. The painting itself is his
portrait."

He looked again and was defeated.

"No. Sorry. I just don't see it." And then he looked at her

funny. "Are you saying Mark Twain *posed* for a painting called
'*The Devil's Portrait*'?"

She grinned at him. "He was an irreverent rascal," she said.
"Ever hear of 'The Mysterious Stranger' or 'Letters from Earth?'

Sunner shook his head.

"Books he wrote from the Devil's point of view. They were
so sacrilegious his estate refused to publish them until 50 years
after his death. One was a correspondence between Lucifer and
the archangels discussing Christians —and not in a very
flattering way. Funny stuff. Scandalous, back in the day. So
yeah, posing for 'The Devil's Portrait' isn't much of a stretch."

"*If* it's him." Sunner made it clear he didn't think so.

"Yeah, it's a long shot," she admitted. "Another problem:
It's a good 15 years before its time. It's sort of Dada, in a way.
But in the wrong country in the wrong decade. Yet here it is! Big
as daylight. Isn't that something? If I can 'out' her as a
precocious artist, then her work becomes valuable. If it is
valuable, people will start looking for them, and once the hunt is
on, they'll start popping up."

Even as she was saying it she had to suspend her own
disbelief. The truth was, Sam Clemens seemed to have gone out
of his way *not* to mention either painting. That in itself tweaked
Lilly's imagination, but it did nothing to support her arguments
to Sunner. It was the same point of contention she had with the
Art History department at the University. It always came down to
written provenance, and this one photo, which might have been
taken after Twain's death when the house was in other hands,
just didn't cut it. A painting by the same artist in Kansas City
bearing only abstract resemblance to the writer didn't help her
much either. The serial title only helped a little. Although it was
obvious to her, no one else had agreed it was a portrait of
Clemens.

"So you want to set the record straight," Sunner was saying.

"The record is never straight," she said. "I just want to see
them. Well, that, and write a killer dissertation."

"And your chances are better if you can show she was
important to Twain."

"Except I can't. There's no provenance on the painting in

Kansas City and Sam Clemens never mentioned Stiller. Not in his autobiography, not in letters nor in any of his household records And believe me, between him, his creditors and his housekeepers, there are pretty much records of everything. Everything, with one notable exception: This damn painting. That in itself is intriguing, don't you think?"

He had to admit it was.

"So you've only found the two?" he asked.

"Number three was listed in an estate sale in Colorado Springs, but there are no records of where it went or what it looked like. And there was a fifth in Serbia, of all places, on a list of Nazi war booty. It was likely destroyed as 'deviant art.' So I've only seen the one. I've found mentions of others, but no photos and no current records."

"That's too bad."

"But I might be fixin' to see another," she said with a big happy smile.

"How's that?"

"I believe one is buried beneath the Decatur Municipal Building. The Devil's Portrait *Number one.*"

"*What?*"

"I *know*, right?" Lilly wriggled all over, like a happy puppy, thoroughly enjoying his reaction. It was infectious, and he found himself grinning back at her even though it made no sense to him at all that a painting linked to Mark Twain might be buried under their little local municipal building.

"That's why I'm here!" she announced. "I'm trying to get first dibs. I've spent the last couple of months convincing the University of Arkansas that there is an extremely —*extremely* rare work of art, literally at their doorstep. Proof that a seminal artist began her career right here in the Ozarks, during a backwater time when Arkansas was just a bunch of Hillbillies living in the sticks."

"Hey."

"I'm just sayin'," she shrugged, grinning. "Decatur, Arkansas, in the 1880s wasn't exactly the Paris salon."

Sunner had to bite his tongue. It seemed to him Pia Stiller was hardly a candidate for the Paris salon herself. Not that he knew what the Paris salon was, but it seemed a safe bet.

Why in the world would there be a painting buried here? He wanted to ask. *By this artist or any other? How could she possibly know that?*

"Anyway," Lilly continued, "they finally saw reason and have provided a grant to purchase the painting from Decatur, provided I can talk them into digging it up, and provided I'm right and it really is a Stiller. If I'm lucky beyond my wildest dreams, it might even be the original Devil's Portrait, and if so, maybe I can get funding from Crystal Bridges to research the others."

"And if it's not?"

"Next stop, the Twain archives at Elmira College, New York."

"And if it is?" he asked softly.

"Next stop, Elmira." She said this softly too, and they spent a moment in silence, examining the complications and implications of what they might say next.

"Of course..." she tried to patch up the silence, "if it's here, and I'm sure it is, the University will give me all the time I need with it. It'll have to be to examined and cataloged. As far as my thesis is concerned, it's the cherry on top. It all has to be sorted out."

"That could take some time, could it?" Sunner didn't keep the trace of bitterness from his voice, and he ducked his head, embarrassed by it. For the first time his youth and inexperience felt like a thick custard coating his skin, matting his hair and making him look completely ridiculous. But he didn't know what to do next, and that was a novelty. So he jumped to his feet to get out from under the uncertainty that was descending and said, "Well, I've got to get back to work," and made for the stairs.

This new love had risen like the sun, blotting out all the stars he was used to navigating by. Now, suddenly, it seemed vulnerable and impermanent. He knew it was foolish to expect permanence in anything, and especially foolish to expect it of relationships. It showed a lack of sophistication, and he didn't want Lilly to think he was one of those hillbillies from the sticks with a moral compass pointing to the wrong century. He hadn't realized he was expecting her to stay with him. But there it was, looming like an unexpected mountain rising out of terrain he'd never seen before.

"Sunner—" she called after him, but she really didn't have anything else to say and they both knew it. Yet she followed him down the stairs and all the way to the back door. He stopped there, framed in daylight and looked at her.

He still didn't know what to say. His tongue lay thick and rebellious in his mouth, refusing to interpret whatever it was he was feeling.

"Sunner—"

He held up his hand to cut her off. Finally he came to it.

"I just need a grace period to figure out how not to screw this up," he said, "however long we've got."

"Sunner," she said. "*Me too.*"

"Okay."

"*Okay.*"

He thought she might then come to him and kiss him, and indeed she walked up to him, all soft, gentle, womanly, and her closeness pushed aside his worries just a bit. Given one moment more, they'd have it all figured out, but they were interrupted by the sound of gravel crunching under tires.

"Oh hell no," he whispered. She was so close the words puffed at her eyelashes. Her hand was on his chest, over his heart.

Sunner scowled and told her, "My folks are back."

If Lilly felt it was galling to be with someone so young that having the parents interrupt was a recurring theme, she had the poise not to show it. She looked amused, only. Her sigh was not condescending. Her regret was only that the moment was lost.

And then by mutual consent they decided it wasn't lost, and seized it. The full weight and knowledge of that mountain of certainty he had just glimpsed for the first time a moment ago passed between them. It took only one second more to sum up with a gaze and a kiss what might have taken the rest of the summer to circumnavigate and explore, but in that quick kiss their constitution was writ, voted, ratified and signed. He looked at her and marveled, even while doors were slamming, Watch was barking, and his mother calling.

Apparently, there was more than one way to consummate a marriage.

"That didn't take so long to figure out, now did it?" Lilly smiled at him. There was wonder on her face too. The rest was just details.

"I guess time *is* on our side," he said. But he couldn't have been more wrong.

CHAPTER FIFTEEN

"The best way to triumph over ignorance is to outlive it."
—*The Chief Engineer*
The Wardenclyffe Foundation Archives

∞

In the year 2123

Chief Engineer Nidhi Duginapali G4 stood serene on her side of the room. The solar wind proved quiet because her physi-link was pixel-perfect. Her age was fixed somewhen midway in her second decade, as was the fashion in Indiasia. She was small and plump in a girlish rather than womanly way. It was disarming and disconcerting. Lauder focused on her right hand, which she held posed, two fingers gently crooked, as if to grant a benediction, except she held it so he could see the back, rather than the palm. The point was to show off the moot-elite tattoo block on her hand. *Too many shunts to tally*, it meant. Stripes so numerous they formed a solid square. It was her rank and office: Moot-elites were post-50 to their credit, and had carte blanche, and yet she was just a Gen4. Were she a Euro-American, she'd be a determined Gen3 to have that many sanctioned shunts under her belt with the requisite waiting periods and peer reviews, and that would be with an unending cycle of reapplication. Gen4s just weren't old enough.

But they did things differently in the Cinosphere. Population crisis and all that. You could shunt every night of the week if you liked, even before your 50th natal day. Many did. It wasn't the most prosperous nation for nothing. *Cred junkies*. Lauder shuddered when he thought of it. A zillion shunts. A world a zillion times divided. It made his lungs ache. As soon as he was done here, it was off to the oxygen bar and spare no expense.

He smiled at Nidhi and tried to keep his shallow breaths from hissing through his teeth.

Though two generations older, his own three stripes marked him a neophyte, Level 1. Short but one shunt-cred for a level-up class C marriage contract; three more if he wanted procreation points on his license, as Arlee used to point out to him on a daily basis. With such dismal prospects, until Arlee came along, he'd been spared coercion from solo-partners, although over the years he'd been served several candidacies for a junior partner in a group marriage but he had refused. Junior partners in a marriage were little more than housekeepers, and there to thin the burden of rent. Hardly incentive to die. *Again.*

So until his recent windfall, he remained a singleton in a service hostel. *The old man on the block.* Except right now, in the Murderer's digs with the Hadron cell, he reckoned he was one of the wealthiest dubs on the Amerisphere, so he was doing all right, for a squatter. Too bad Arlee wasn't here to see it.

He was ashamed of his three tats that testified he had shunted only three times. Ashamed, but not for the reason you might think. He was ashamed he had any at all. He generally wore a fingerless glove on his right hand for privacy. Today he wore full dress whites. His three tattoos were strictly need-to-know. After the first shunt, it was all academic anyway. Too late for his salvation. Too late for the real world, back there somewhere, de-peopled and sorrowing and gasping for air.

With post-fifty, Nidhi was stretched so thin she hardly mattered anymore, at least by his reckoning. Most saw it the other way around, as though slide-stepping was a virtue with compounded interest. As though it wasn't assisted suicide. He knew the difference and that made what he was about to do easier. Funners, even.

"Trans-dimensional Entanglement Tracer? Forsooth?" She asked.

Lauder refused to be disarmed by her little-girl voice. He stayed focused on the black mark on her hand that may as well have been a black hood.

"Nay, Enge Duginapali? Methinks you know better?"

"Curious specs?" She agreed. "Shunt-wise, yes?"

"Somewhat?" It seemed safe for him to allude. "But not-a-shunt—?" He leaned close to her. It could have been a bow.

"Launch trial data is inconclusive?" When he added, "I need a capable engineer?" his meaning was clear. "A thorough decryption of the Hadron memory?" He splayed his hands in a gesture of deference to her superior analytic. "The effect is too startling to account?"

"How so, Mr. Lauder?"

"My pilot is missing," he whispered. Making the first drop of the rising inflections. He was watching her very carefully, and her eyes betrayed her. They flicked quickly to a point over his shoulder, to a point in her room on her side of the world, where she made eye contact with someone.

Exactamundo.

"I understood this was a secure conversation," Lauder said hotly. *"Terminate."*

Nidhi's gaze snapped back, appalled.

"Now wait just one minute!" she cried, and took a step forward, but her avatar winked off and he was alone in the physi-link.

Gotcha, he thought.

He sat and relaxed in one of the deep leather seats at the con, waiting for the uplink request to blink. It did, but not too soon. The pause was exactly right to denote conciliatory indignation. He paused back, arranging himself causally in the chair. Not even standing now. His pause was just right for guarded indulgence. He switched on, his rehearsed proposals on the tip of his tongue. He didn't even have to access his short-term for a prompt.

Yeah. This was going to be *funners.*

CHAPTER SIXTEEN

"No big laboratory is needed in which to think. Originality thrives in seclusion free of outside influences beating upon us to cripple the creative mind. Be alone, that is the secret of invention; be alone, that is when ideas are born."
—*Nikola Tesla*
The Wardenclyffe Foundation Archives

∞

In the year 2010

"So, let me get this straight," Sunner told his mother. She and his father were sitting across from him at Lilly's kitchen table, while Lilly herself hung back at the counter, discretely at the edges of the conversation. She was adding fresh coffee grounds into the filter as quietly and slowly as she could manage in a silent ballet, as stealthy as Tai Chi.

"Elderidge just signed the place over." Sunner regarded the deed that lay out before him on the table. "Well... that's just... great. Isn't it?" He was trying to reconcile this with the strange conversation he'd had with the old man in the barn this morning. Then, Elderidge seemed to want the barn back. He'd wanted the machine out of there and torn down as well. But Elderidge was erratic, and perhaps his parents had taken advantage of one of his generous moments. But that didn't sound like his parents, and Sergei Elderidge seemed more to Sunner than an addled old man.

"That's what I'm saying," his mother said. "You can see his signature right there."

"No strings attached?"

Donna afforded a quick glance at Zip. It was as loud as a shout. Even Lilly faltered at the coffeemaker.

Sunner's dad cleared his throat.

"Well, that's the damnedest thing. Your godfather did have one stipulation."

Sunner winced at the qualifier. He could tell his dad had said 'godfather' intentionally to add ballast to what he was about to say.

"He also wants to pay for you to go to school."

"*College*," Donna corrected.

"—If you start this summer, that is. He's pulled some strings at MIT, if you can believe it. Who knows what that codger is worth, and what connections he's got, but he says he can get you in."

"Don't be ridiculous."

"Summer session starts next week."

"No. Absolutely not."

"Sunner," his mother said, "MIT! We *agreed* and he signed it over, just like that. *It's our farm.* We've worked for it all our lives." Her words hung there going nowhere. She took in her son's expression and frowned.

"Oh, you are *not* going to screw this up!" She snapped.

Sunner stared at her in disbelief.

"We could never have afforded to send you to school, least of all, this school. Don't you see how great this is? Of course we agreed! Why wouldn't we? It's the opportunity of a lifetime."

"I never agreed," Sunner said evenly, "but if he signed, then you've got your deed and everything is square. *I have my own plans this summer.*"

He did have his own plans, but that was beside the point. He was appalled his parents could not see through such an obvious subterfuge. 'Square' was the last thing it was. This looked as crooked as a corkscrew to him. The old man had no interest in him, other than the need to get him out of his way, a need so urgent that it didn't balk at the price of tuition at MIT, nor the value of their little farm, such as it was. But that was taking it at face value and Sunner wasn't buying it. Elderidge's supposed connections at MIT only made Sunner more suspicious. You just didn't walk up to MIT and 'get in,' even if someone was pulling in some favors. The offer was likely an outright lie. Speculating what Elderidge expected to accomplish in the brief space between the time Sunner accepted and the time the lie was discovered made his stomach hurt. It suggested a strike that was quick and decisive.

Even if leaving didn't interrupt his work or leave his machine unprotected, his parents knew he had no interest in going off to be indoctrinated; they knew how schools were. They themselves had nurtured his belief that schools were factories for setting limitations. They'd kept him out of that yoke, and he was glad for it. So why the sudden change of heart? What was the hold Elderidge had over them?

He also worried about Lilly, because he knew she had sympathies for the old man, and he wondered if seeing him turn down this seeming opportunity was lowering his prospects in her eyes. Nevertheless, he felt cascades of supporting energy coming off her from somewhere behind him. He didn't have to see her to feel it. And bless her, she never said a word. He sat up taller in his seat, buoyed by her confidence in him. But it didn't last long.

"I don't think you understand," his father said. "Sergei Elderidge —*Doctor* Sergei Elderidge —has taken an interest in your work. He thinks you show promise, and he'd like to give you some benefit of his being your godfather."

Sunner's alarms flared even hotter. "What kind of doctor?"

Zip shrugged.

"He's got no business with my machine."

"Well, hell, son. Nobody has any business with it, do they? What good is it just sitting out there? It's hidden under a bushel, as they say. If you've done good work, you've got to show it around. Talk it up. Let the right people see it. Otherwise, what good is it?"

"It's not ready yet. It will be, soon. I'm at a critical juncture here and..."

"Bull-she-it," Zip said. "I've heard that going on two years now. How's taking up Sergei's offer going to hurt? It's a bird in the hand, son, and you'd be a damned fool to turn it down."

"Because I don't know him and I don't know what he wants. If he were so interested in me, why did he wait until now to show up? This has nothing to do with being his godson. Did he even know he had a godson? He was long gone before I was born. Jesus, this whole thing is off. Don't you smell it? Something's not right here, Dad."

"The only thing not right here is how stubborn you are. The deal was made, and you'll honor it."

"Dad, I'm not a kid anymore. I make my own decisions." He hoped the strain he felt didn't show in his voice. Why did Lilly have to be here for this? It was humiliating.

"I am grateful you are no longer a *kid*," his father said, standing up and taking the deed from the table. He folded it carefully and held it in his hands. He looked at it and not at Sunner as he said, "A *kid* only acts in his own selfish interest. A *kid* doesn't have to shoulder the responsibility of his family at his expense and inconvenience." He switched the force of his eyes to Sunner.

"Dad...I..."

"Thank you son. I know you'll do the right thing. Momma?"

Donna got to her feet looking both amazed and pleased. Hardball wasn't in Zip's repertoire, usually. She had the good sense to follow him out in silence and let his words hang undisturbed.

Sunner just sat there, maintaining the tension after they were gone. The back door slammed and a hollow silence filled the space where they had been.

"Wow," Lilly said. "They are a force to be reckoned with, aren't they?"

"Lilly, there's something I need to tell you."

She was startled by the gravity in his voice.

She sat down at the table and waited with serious attention, leaving the coffee to perk itself.

He cast about looking for a place to start and get a good toehold. He took the route he thought would offer the least resistance.

"Elderidge was here this morning. He knew too much. *About us*. I think he may have been... hanging around. Looking in windows or something. *Last night*."

"Oh. I see," she said, but she didn't blush. She just looked thoughtful.

"I can't very well tell my folks," he added, avoiding her

direct gaze. For her part, Lilly seemed to lack self-consciousness. She sat, taking weights and measures of the situation while he felt awkward and transparent under her gaze.

"Your parents think he walks on water," she agreed. "But hey, if he's an old perv, we'll just keep the curtains closed and the doors locked. It's not like he's a threat. I could knock him down with a feather and it'd probably break his hip."

"Yeah," he said morosely. He was unprepared for her aplomb, and remembering Hector made him squirmy with mixed feelings. Images of her with her 'decades older' husband trekked furiously between his ears, distracting him.

"I'm sure you can take care of yourself," he muttered, "although I'd kinda like the opportunity to take care of you myself."

"All right. Feel free to break his hip on my behalf," she said with a look. "You Tarzan. Me Jane."

That was a look he knew too well. His mother used them frequently on his father.

"No, me *sorry*," he conceded, and sighed. He chewed his lip and worked his fingers on the tabletop: evidently there was more he needed to say.

"Apology accepted. Now tell me what's really bugging you."

He didn't know if he should. He'd barely suggested the potential of his machine to her, making a joke of his paranoia. He'd laid awake many a night rehearsing all the ways it might go wrong, how *they* might come, and how he might thwart them if they did. But when it came down to it, his best defense was simply to remain off the radar, which he had until today – until Elderidge showed up and introduced a scenario he hadn't considered.

Now, in the space between sunsets, his secret was out. Not only did the old man have all night alone with it, Lilly knew a little about it, too. That had seemed a necessary risk, a necessity of the heart, but it loomed as carelessness now, and might even have put her in harm's way.

"Maybe you should go back to Fayetteville and let me commute," he said hopefully. "It's not that far."

"Nothing doing. I'm not going to be run off by a sad old

man with his hands in his pants, and neither are you, so quit screwing around and deal."

"Elderidge isn't what he seems," he said, and even as he said it, he hadn't yet made up his mind how much he should say, or if by saying it he was making her safer or putting her more at risk.

"He broke into the barn..."

Lilly's eyes narrowed in disbelief.

"Okay, technically, he didn't break in." He thought about how his lock had been undisturbed. "But, he got in there somehow. And he was talking about my machine like he knew too much about it. He said he was going to take it apart."

"So? Is that even possible? Just get a new lock."

"It's a *very delicate* piece of equipment. Building it was hard, but breaking it would be easy. Very easy. An engineer, on the other hand, could deconstruct it. He's a doctor of *something*. If he has strings at MIT, it's a pretty sure bet he's not a podiatrist."

"C'mon, Sunner, the poor old duffer can barely string sentences together."

"He was stringing them together just fine this morning, and *I'm not being paranoid*," he said the last with deliberate weight, even though he knew the degree of caution he was trying to convey would look exactly as if he were.

"I keep my machine locked tight for a reason. If I can do what I aim to with it..." he fidgeted in his seat. He was unused to talking to anyone about his work, and even Lilly's interest felt vaguely threatening.

"It's revolutionary." He said the word with apology, like it was a confession of a shameful thing. "I'm not saying that in the popular sense, and I'm not being an arrogant prick. Really. It is —it could be, literally revolutionary, as in 'revolutionary war'."

As a matter of fact, he didn't seem arrogant at all. He seemed unnerved, and he was; he had gone too far.

Lilly pursed her lips. She did it to hide her embarrassment for him. He had just stretched his credibility to the breaking point. She didn't look as if she believed him, but she could see he believed himself and that made her worry. What he wanted most was for her to believe *in* him. He wanted it very badly. He'd been alone in this too long. He hoped his credibility wasn't beyond recovery, but he had to pull her in after him.

"Unlimited water?" he reminded her. "Do you get what that could do to the world? When you have economic stability, social stability, you lose the leverages you need for government control. Balance of power depends upon unbalanced resources. All that shit they fight wars over."

"Because of water," she said. "Not oil?"

"There's nothing oil can do that water can't," he insisted. "And you can't drink oil."

Lilly looked off, but not at the same horizon. "I don't see it," she said. "Give me a downside to watering crops and bathing babies, flushing toilets and, hell, hydrogen, right? That's got to be a leg up. A literal rising tide to lift all boats."

"Think about it though. And forget about the hydrogen for a second. Screw free energy. How would power shift if everyone could meet their own basic needs?"

"I'm not a sociologist, Sunner. But maybe it would just be wonderful."

"Beg pardon? Are you new to planet Earth? Have you watched the news lately?"

Lilly was taken aback. She was beginning to suspect the depth of his paranoia.

"So what do you think? The men in black recruited Mr. McGoo to sabotage his godson?"

Sunner spread his hands out on the table and regarded them. She was getting warmer. He wanted her to see. He wanted her to believe in him, sure, but he also wanted her to know enough, to believe enough, to stay safe.

"It happens all the time," he told her. "All the time. People disappear. Labs burn down. Records are lost."

She remained absolutely silent.

"Take a good look at the technology curve: Everyone says, 'Oh, hey, isn't it great, we're making all these exponential leaps. Knowledge doubles every few months'. But take another look: Look at what's *not* changing. Look at what's leveled out. Not computing, toys, or entertainment. Not 'bread and circuses'. Look at the engines. Cars haven't changed in fundamental ways in 80 years. Think about that. We've gone from setting type by hand to supercomputers in our hip pockets in the same amount of time, but we're still dicking around with internal combustion engines. Ever heard of Stan Mayer? He was driving around in a water-powered car in the 1990s. Yeah, people were impressed: His last words soon after were 'I've been poisoned!'"

"Oh, come on," she said.

"Fill up your Honda with water lately? No? We're still burning coal, for Christ's sake. We have great swaths of humanity clinging to the edges of subsistence farming, or no farming at all, and dying for lack of clean water —and let me tell you: *The solution wasn't that hard.* If I could pull it off in my barn in two years with spare parts, then why the hell isn't everybody doing it? There is nothing out there that isn't standard tech in some form somewhere, and specs floating around on the internet. Why do you think that is? Status quo, that's why. Balance of power."

Lilly regarded him steadily.

"So Sergei Elderidge was sent here to sabotage your machine in service to the status quo? Why would he even care? As old as he is, he's not long for this world, Sunner. Seriously. Give me a motive here."

"Asymmetrical stability though subjugation. How's that for a motive? The world is run by evil-evil bastards, Lilly. And as long as everything stays the same, they profit by it. Who is this guy, really? The real Sergei Elderidge disappeared 30 years ago, and he was an old guy then. It just doesn't compute."

"All right, that's a nice field trip on the dark side, now flip it over and let's examine the other side of the coin."

Sunner barely managed to keep his indignation at bay. He was disappointed in her, but at least she wasn't rejecting it outright.

"All right. I'll play. Let's just see how close we can shave with Occam's razor: An old dude with phenomenal longevity takes a 30-year walkabout before returning to his hometown. Maybe he spent the last 30 years as an alternative student at MIT. You fill in the blanks. Good luck, there are a lot of them. At present he seems to be an escaped inmate of a nursing home and without full mental faculties. Yet, he is able to convince a lawyer *on a Sunday*, to draw up the transfer deed to his property. On that same Sunday, he's able to pull some strings at one of the most prestigious schools in the country to get them to admit an Arkansas farm-boy who doesn't even have a goddamned GED. And all these miracles he's performed are because he is impressed by a device he had no idea existed until yesterday, and couldn't possibly know the purpose of.

"At the very least he took a long close look at it last night and suspected what the machine might do. Maybe he does in fact have a whole cheesy omelet cooking in his brain-pan and wants to learn what I'm up to and exploit it somehow. And that's the best-case scenario."

Lilly looked genuinely concerned now. She was no longer trying to hide it. But not about Sergei, she was worried about Sunner. She had her own mild psychosis to deal with. Paranoia was a bit more than she bargained for. But the deal was done. The gavel was down and she was in, lock, stock and barrel. If he was willing to put up with her storm-fugues, she would make the necessary allowances for him.

"So why do you bother?" She asked him.

"What?"

"Why are you building a water-maker, and why are you throwing yourself under the bus? Take it down. Learn to shit guilt-free in potable water like the rest of us and live happily ever after."

He looked at her, astonished.

"Because I have to. If it can be done, and I can do it, I can't *not* do it."

"That's what I thought." She offered him a tentative smile. "So do what you have to do, Sunner. Control what you can control, and roll with the consequences, whatever they turn out to be. It's all any of us can do."

"I can get you out of here. Get you to somewhere safer."

"Sunner, if what you described is true, moving 40 miles down the road isn't going to provide much protection."

"It couldn't hurt," he said.

"Do you want me to go?"

He had to admit to himself that he didn't. "I haven't scared you off?" he asked.

"Not yet," she said.

He smiled weakly. "But what if I'm *trying* to scare you off?"

"Are you? You are doing a lousy job."

"Something is going on here, Lilly," he said seriously.

"Maybe. Time will tell. Look-it: I'll help you keep an eye on Mr. McGoo, and we'll both make sure he doesn't keep an eye on us. You just keep working. Your parents will come around. It'll be fine. And if it's not fine, we'll deal with it."

"Did you hear any of what I just said? You could be in some dark water here."

"We'll deal with it."

"You'll break his hip?" he gave her a half smile.

"He'll wish I stopped with his hip. Want some coffee?"

"Not right now. I need to do something first. I need to change the combination on my lock."

Yeah, that'll keep the forces of darkness at bay. Lilly's expression said.

He gave her a hapless shrug. "—And some other stuff. I can take some precautions. It will take a little tinkering."

"Married less than thirty minutes and I'm a garage-widow already."

"What?"

"You heard me." She stood and kissed him on the top of the head.

"Go play with your toys, Junior. Mamma's gotta run to town anyway."

"Yes'um," he said gamely, but it troubled him that Lilly just seemed to be playing along.

Sunner was unable to keep the urgency out of his step as he left the house to check on the shop. Besides changing his combination, he wished he could change his name. It was irksome that this was the godfather he was named after: *Sergei* Sunshine Tillman was on his birth certificate. As if Sunshine wasn't bad enough.

CHAPTER SEVENTEEN

"In the most eloquent sense, the infernal machine was a time bomb."
—*The Chairman*
The Wardenclyffe Foundation Archive

∞

In the year 2123

"The chronology... Here? That's what this is. A time stamp, see?" Chief Enge Nidhi Duganipali straightened up over the table display and rolled her aching shoulders with a grimace. The past few days had been an exercise in restraint and indulgence for both she and Lauder. The negotiations to get her there, with only one goon, weren't hard exactly. Lauder knew it was a lock from the moment he waved the redacted specs in front of her uplink. The tricky part was getting her to deal now that she was here, and to keep it on the down. Strictly offline. And her goon? She wasn't satisfied with a panic button. He had to be present the whole time.

Lauder didn't like that, and made it clear that an extra set of eyes indicated a witness —bio or no —and they were nowhere near that stage in the negotiations. So they settled for the goon to sit offline, phones on (loud enough for Lauder to hear), and eyes down, excepting peripherals. The goon was now flicking through a mag on his scroll, glancing up at intervals, but not in line-o-sight. He was validated not to be packing but he was three strides away from delivering bare-hand lethals. Of that, Lauder had no doubts at all.

For the meeting they'd rented a third-party security hatch with class A's. The kind with a con-table instead of a bed.

And of course they were all switched to private with third eyes dark.

And yet...

It was a wicked old world.

Lauder had only brought the memory. The specs were in his hidey-hole. He wanted the memory decoded first. He wanted to know what the missing Hadron cell was up to. That was the deali-o. After that, they'd have a look-see at the not-a-shunt. *In person.* High stakes, but every intervening moment gave the Murderer of the World that much more of a head start.

Okay, yeah. He was paying attention in class. He knew his primaries: You can't follow the slip-slide of a shunt. No way. No how. You just can't get there from here, because here isn't *here* for starters. It was a one-way ticket and no whining. Hence the waiting period. Hence the executor of the will. Hence the shrink and the screening, and, if need be, the honeymoon-double-bed shunt, the table-for-five family-shunt and the newly-cooly church-group shunt, where you could off your entire congregation in one go, dust off your hands and divvy up the spoils.

But you could not, absolutely could *not* follow in a separate unit, even one firing simultaneously. Not that anyone ever returned to report back. Not that anyone could even prove with any certainty that a shunt was anything more than a suicide slot machine, if forsooth it even counted as suicide if you entered it with absolute faith that you'd be exiting it a moment later all dandy-finey. Maybe here, maybe not here. But somewhere so *just like here* it didn't make a wit of difference. The salient point being that wherever you *no longer were* had one less mouth to feed and an extra resource allotment to spread amongst your next o'kin.

Lauder knew what it was. It wasn't suicide. It was murder, even if they did call it civic duty. The population problem, pollution problem, energy problem, the prison problem, natural resource problems, food shortages, teacher shortages, land shortages, endangered species habitat pressures...? Solved. The immortality paradox? No problem, mon. Bread and circuses for everyone, just be a nice bloke and lay down and die for us, yesy? There's a goody lad, for *no man hath greater love than he who lays down his life.* Or, so went the corporate-branding, the one stamped over the pearly gate of public service shunters everywhere. What a small price to pay for paradise.

Nidhi regarded Lauder and he bore it without flinching. The stakes were interesting, her expression read, but the path interminable. They'd holed up daily for fivers, and after a fortnight he still wore his dressies, still piped the corporate bee-esse with perfect elocution and never-no-never let down his guard. He was an actor in a play that just would not end and her hands were numb from the requisite clapping.

He knew by now he was pegged as a poser, but she matched him step for step. Nidhi Duginapali was not to be outdone. Not nevers. And certainly not by a dub. Lauder read her like a scroll. He knew right where he stood.

Just knowing that it bugged her was a nub he could get a bit of purchase on. There was always an angle waiting to be had, if you knew all your opts. Lauder didn't know shit from servos but he did have the knowhow to play the opts.

Take his affectation with the white gloves. The distaste in her regard showed she suspected his gloves hid meager bars that bespoke a contemptible caste: A shirker who was beneath her. This deplorable situation had her goon pulling double duty as a chaperone. But Lauder saw something else in her gaze: a grudging admiration. So points for discretion, at least. Points too for not once in real-time letting it slip that while unplugged he could barely negotiate his own specs. He managed his ineptitude with flawless panache. Yeah, she saw through it, and she saw that he saw that she saw through it. They were dancing the tango here.

She kept dancing because he had his goods laid out like a map to the cave of the 40 thieves. The time stamp was the big red X, apparently. It made her shiver. He had to tease out why.

He looked at her pleadingly. He gave her his most apologetic *'this is going to take forever'* look, his *'throw me a bone'* look, and his *'let's see how far we can play it'* look.

Fatigue was a useful tool. Her shoulders dropped, she waxed indulgent at him and said in the familiar vernacular,

"Mr. Lauder, this would go muchly more easy if you were to switch on your recall."

Lauder bowed deeply, *charmingly*, whilst executing the temple salute that complied. She saw his read switch on. The room simultaneously toned yellow, the Class A's indicating a receptor breech.

She smiled coldly, and gestured to the lower stool, where he was obliged now to sit in the inferior position.

Finally. Nidhi thought.

All-righty then. Thought Lauder.

"To begin with, Trans-dimensional Recourse Units are not equipped with chronometers," she said. "The TOD is an external measurement to facilitate various legalities for the transfer of properties. It has nil to do with the ops of the machine."

By TOD she meant 'Time Of Departure', not 'Time Of Death'. Thanks to shunts, the old euphemisms finally fit: The dearly departed 'passed on', 'passed away', 'passed over', or just 'passed'.

"Time is simultaneous at the point of divergence," she was saying. "So this is not a... shunt." She said it like someone would try out the word *intercourse* for the first time after a lifetime of primly saying *fuck*.

"As I've been saying," Lauder pointed out, "this is not a shunt."

"Obviously," she said. She'd seen the replays. They were edited, but only up to the point of the operator closing the unit, and Lauder opening the door an instant later to show it empty. A five-second 180 clip in three-dee. No body. No incinerator. No splicing of the data, except for the obligatory proprietorial blot. Her techs gave it a valid. That is to say, a valid as a highly-tampered-with, albeit authentic, clip.

Lauder had snipped the feed down to just the juicy bits. He hid the Geezers I-dee, although she could see through the treble-blur it was a withered hand belonging to an Elder wearing their age. He also redacted the panel where the count down was commencing. That he hid with a fat black bar. Proprietary info, those explosives. In his spares he re-rigged it entirely. Not dismantled, mind you. Just re-rigged where it wouldn't be seen. If the Murderer of the World hadn't the conceit of his big dramatic readout, Lauder himself would have *passed,* as it were.

He figured her techs were crunching the clip to squeeze out the juice of when/where it was made. Teasing out the hand, maybe, though he'd given it a blur in the semi-halo from all directions. He'd skiffed it through five manufactures of mods. They might dig it eventually, and by 'eventually' he meant 'too late'.

But in-all it was just a teaser artifact. The real money was in the memory, which she was poring over like an adolescent's first halo-view of porn. He'd laid it out. First take, raw and authentic.

Because he was reading it into his mem, Nidhi shifted into her native singsong Hindi-techno-babble. It was a tourist language to Lauder. One he could only order food in, or ask directions in without the help of his goog. He recorded patiently, catching the odd word. His goog would sort it out later. What needed no interpretation were her gestures. They became womanly and sensual and round and inviting. Tsk-tsk.

They both knew he'd be spending the night in distracted replay. Nidhi had her own fatigue tactics. He watched her in admiration, enjoying the slight grind of her hips, the lilt of her teeny voice, and appreciating her strategy. Discounting her goon, he'd take her to bed if she weren't a corpse already. It was pleasant to let his thoughts drift around her. He was beginning to see the appeal of a woman fixed at fourteen. Especially a tiny little Indiasian nymphet... usually girls didn't spike him at all, but she had the shape of some young men he had known, and that was something he could work with.

She stopped. "I need to see for certs," she said. "If it is what I think it is, then you have a deal. Full on," she said. "Witness!"

Her goon looked up and snapped on his mod and she did the same. The room went red. Lauder activated a tic later, barely able to contain his excitement.

The contingency contract was acted and archived. The sum was staggering, but of course it included the Hadron cell. He made a half-hearted parley at upping the price, and she made an indignant denial, so he settled for the merely astronomical sum, plus royalties, contingent on an open patent, which he'd already confirmed, and a working prototype, ditto. The Hadron had to prove legit, which it was. His own stipulations were a closed covenant: total sequester during her-eyes-only operations validations and himself the test pilot. After that she had full authorship in perpetuity across all verses. Absolute creds. If she smelled a rat, and she most certainly did, the payoff trumped it. He realized with sums like this he could buy his own damned moot-cred and never be compelled to shunt again. Not that it mattered. If the Murderer found a way to track, and if Nidhi would be so kind as to reset the box, he was as good as goners.

Oh, and she had to stay at-the-hip until it was sealed. Her and her goon, of course. She was surprised he offered that last bit, but Lauder insisted so she didn't have to. He didn't care about getting her alone. He just wasn't into Zombies.

CHAPTER EIGHTEEN

"Occam's Razor proposes that between competing hypotheses, the simplest explanation is the one most likely to be true. Of course when you introduce non-linear time and alternate universes, eventually everything is true."
—*The Artist*
A retrospective of 4D works from the Wardenclyffe Foundation

∞

In the year 2010

Lilly drove her Honda slowly through the streets of Decatur. That is, down one arm of the two main roads which intersected at the little farming community. Decatur wasn't big enough to have its own courthouse; but it did have a city hall. It stood back from the main road on its own side street at the highest point of the town. A squat one-story limestone structure, its only decoration was a mock archway facade that framed the entranceway. 1895 was carved beneath a fake keystone. Facing west, it was somewhat more weathered than it might have been, as that was the direction storm fronts blew in from Oklahoma before smashing into this western-most edge of the Ozark plateau.

Decatur was perpetually on hard times and you needed only to look at the municipal building to get the picture. Although constructed from chisel-faceted limestone, its charm was diminished by cheap cement steps with a bent pipe railing that led up to a mesh-wire and glass framed steel door that looked like it might have once been in a school where vandalism was a problem. The top banister post was freshly chipped from the concrete and the railing bent back to allow for a narrow wheelchair ramp slanting up from the right.

The ramp was lumber-yard yellow with earwax-colored sap oozing from the nail holes. Overly long, it sloped all the way to the far corner of the building. Without a sidewalk leading from the gravel parking lot, it set down directly on the weedy lawn and was waiting for its first customer. There was also a new planting of scraggly boxwood bushes in front of it, a fig leaf over the nakedness of the new wood. —The first civic improvement in years; so why did it have to be now? Nursery tags were still on the sorry little bushes. If their job was to impart discrete cover for the embarrassment of the ramp, they had their work cut out for them.

Lilly regarded the ramp with resignation. It had not been there on her last visit. The ramp complicated her plans considerably. Now Plan A —negotiations with the city —would mean the undoing of their first civic improvement in years, and she suspected small-town politics would make that a tough sell.

Now Plan B had a lot more appeal. It involved a shovel, a crowbar, a flashlight, a firm resolve and now, the merry companionship of Sunner to take his turn with the digging.

She took stock of her options. From here she had the tactical advantage of seeing the whole town, but conversely, she could be seen as easily from any point below. She felt foolish for having parked so brazenly at the scene of her upcoming crime.

The city hall shared borders with an unfenced cemetery belonging to the church on the other side of the hill. At this moment, most of the town's population was in the church, trying to fill the pews whose founders now inhabited the cemetery, and in greater numbers. The rest of the town looked abandoned. At the base of the hill was a low-roofed bank that shared an empty parking lot with a small steel warehouse that was the only grocery for ten miles around. Both establishments were dark. Next door, was a farm implement store of the same beige steel siding as the grocery, also closed. The old main street fronted single story brick buildings either derelict or occupied by struggling last-ditch efforts like "Neat Stuff Pawn". Across the street from those was the feed mill where the lightning had scared the daylights out of her just yesterday.

Everything was closed.

Decatur was one of the last towns in Arkansas to respect blue laws. Consequently, the only activity today was at the church. Up here, it was just Lilly, the sullen city hall, the residents of the cemetery, and a meadowlark trilling from the top of a tombstone. If it weren't for that damned ramp, she could practically dig in broad daylight.

Lilly walked to the southwest corner of the building and squatted to look again at the cornerstone. The ramp overshot the edge of the building by a couple of feet, nearly hiding the inscription 1893 along with its Mason's stamp, proving this was *the* cornerstone, laid with ceremony. With luck, it contained a cache.

It was the custom in those days to inter at the base of the first laid stone a commemoration that included artifacts. These so-called time capsules were never intended to be removed, but were a ritual pledge the founders sealed in perpetuity —or so they thought. Now as these old buildings come down, or restorations took place, the caches were opened. They usually contained a newspaper of the foundation day, along with documents containing prosy pledges of fidelity and patriotism. Occasionally, a more sentimental tribute was found. Maybe a little casket with a lock of hair or a photo of a lost loved one for whom the building is dedicated. Almost always a Bible was included, as founding an enterprise on the 'rock' of the Word of God was a powerful incantation for success. Lilly had a pretty good idea what was underneath this one: Pia Stiller's painting, *The Devil's Portrait.* Number one.

The new wheelchair ramp compounded the difficulty of getting the town council to agree to let her dig beneath their foundations. It was also going to make it harder to do her own unapproved exploratory digging first.

The University finally agreed that the painting as described could possibly be an early —if not the first —known work of Stiller. However, they had no jurisdiction over the property and no interest in engaging the city council in what was likely to be an unpopular and fruitless request. They certainly were not going to be liable for damages from the excavations. The required assurances that the painting was there, and insurance against the likelihood it was not.

Stiller might be an important artist, but she was still unknown, so her work had no monetary value with which to entice the city to let Lilly poke around. Early on, she thought she might find and convince collectors of Stiller's other paintings to pony up for the excavations, but she had only found the one.

Lilly wasn't going to steal it, mind you. She was just going to confirm it was there, replace it, and then pursue more legal options with the confidence the payoff existed. If it wasn't there, she could cross it off her list and quietly move her investigations elsewhere, without leaving a costly wake of failure behind.

Lilly knew Stiller wasn't everybody's cup of tea, but if someone without the context of art and history unearthed it, the painting would be subject to ridicule and other indignities. There were precious few women artists of that age, and none had broken the ground of aesthetic conventions like Stiller had. Her work was years before Marcel Dechamp did something similar in an enclave of like-minded individuals, defending their territory with manly intellectualism and the panache of the avant-garde. Stiller labored alone. Lilly meant for her to earn the recognition she deserved, even if that meant borrowing the painting from the city of Decatur for bit.

Today she had come both to pay her respects and test her resolve. Her priorities had unexpectedly shifted, but Stiller was a part of that, having brought her here. Whether or not the Devil's Portrait was actually her handiwork, it had led her to Sunner. How Sunner fit in her quest to liberate the artist from obscurity remained to be seen. Standing here, she was certain the two paths wouldn't diverge, as one had led to the other. But she was taken by surprise by the intensity of feeling she had for Sunner. In a stroke it had supplanted her mission with a new purpose. She understood the usurping power of love, but she hadn't expected that kind of lightning to strike twice, or for it to strike so differently. Hector had opened her like a flower to the rising sun, but Sunner had... well, plucked her suddenly and without warning.

She and Hector had prevailed against long odds in the time that was granted them. They had been splendid together and she tended the memory of his warm voice, of his steady dignity unruffled by the tongues that wagged at them wherever they went together. Mostly, they secluded themselves, living out his days in a golden haze of sorrowing love, away from her family who mourned the time as lost. But she felt, instead, made by those years. Refined and rarefied. But they also came at a great cost.

The age difference with Sunner was nothing by comparison. However, it was less socially acceptable, since she was the older one, and he so very... Well. Another ten years, and he'd grow into the role. He'd thicken, coarsen, and exchange that boyish tabula rasa for a legend of experience. They'd have a comparable patina of age in middle years, and in old age, their life expectancies would level out, wouldn't they?

She traced the *1893* chiseled in the cornerstone. It was so like a tombstone, and likely done by the same hand as many of the headstones that stood in ranks behind the building. It was a chilling setting in which to fantasize a lifetime with Sunner. Her premonitions were unnerved, and she sat doubting.

"Aloha," Sergei Elderidge said softly.

Lilly stumbled to her feet. Sergei was standing only a few feet away, regarding her. She didn't know how long he had been there, but apparently he'd slipped from around the corner of the building.

"You have a funny way of turning up," she said. "Are you following me?"

He turned and gazed at the cemetery. "Just visiting some old friends," he said. And he looked at her again in that compelling way he had yesterday. It was much akin to the way an artist stares at his model, fixing her in space and memorizing the contour of the shadows and the crests of light. His gaze was freighted with too much cargo. Too intimate. She took it for evidence that he had indeed been watching them last night, but instead of anger she felt sad for him, which was altogether different from feeling sorry for him. What she didn't feel at all was alarm. She decided in an instant that Sunner was wrong about Elderidge, insofar as he was some kind of threat.

"You are causing quite a stir down at the Tillman's'," she told him. "Why are you here? I mean, why did you come back, really?"

"I expect I haven't much time," he said. "—As comes to pass when a person has to mind their own accounts."

"Just what are you trying to do?" she prodded. She wasn't interested in an old man's regrets. Hector was never self-indulgent and she had no tolerance for it.

"Zip and Donna's boy," he said, shaking his head. "He's plumb off the rails. You know that, don't you?"

"Sunner is very passionate about his work." Lilly realized as she said it, that it was the very thing that she loved about him. She knew all about worn-out dreams and lost opportunities. She'd exchanged youthful enthusiasm for her years with Hector. In a way, her marriage had been a deathwatch, even before he was struck down. She'd not had her course of blind optimism and she was starving for it. Sunner was her second chance at her own unsampled possibilities. It was not the folly of youth. It was the splendor of it.

"He needs help, Lill, and I mean to give it to him."

"He doesn't want your help."

"I expect he doesn't want my interference. I wouldn't have, at his age. I used to be so damned single-minded. You think you are immortal, when you are young. Now there's a terrifying prospect. That, and being cut short." Elderidge scanned when he spoke, like he was harvesting the words from the landscape, but the phrases he chose presented themselves in random order. "I aim that this time, it goes right," he said.

"I expect you mean well, but this isn't really any of your business," Lilly told him.

"*The deed to the farm* —?" he ventured, and began mulling something over, as though he were exploring and idea for the first time. He did it by running his tongue over his teeth, like the idea had a faint taste he might suck out of the crevices.

"That's going to take some doing," he said when he had mouthed it long enough.

"You did right by his parents signing over the deed," Lilly allowed, "but Sunner is another story. He doesn't owe you anything. He's not going anywhere." Lilly wondered if she were being disloyal telling Elderidge this, but in the plain light of day, she could see he was harmless. Sunner was tilting at windmills.

If she could get the old man just to back off, Sunner would calm down.

"Sunner will do anything you ask," Sergei said. "How about you? Would you do whatever he asked? If Sunner asked you to go, would you go?" His intensity was a knife's edge that passed right through her.

"Why would he ask me to?" she wanted to know. Yet not an hour ago Sunner had done just that. He told her she should move back to Fayetteville, but she declined.

"We'll *need* you to..." Sergei shook his head and looked confused. "Déjà vu," he said. "Wrong tack."

Lilly watched him with narrowing eyes.

"Who is '*we*'?" she asked, hoping he could answer before his thoughts went down a different trail.

He didn't answer but took an abrupt step back and cast his eyes about, like he was trying to get his bearings. After a pause he jabbed a shaking finger at her. "You shouldn't be here. There's nothing here for you. It all comes to naught."

Lilly glanced worriedly at the cornerstone. "What are you talking about?" she asked.

"The Devil's Portrait," he said, and that changed everything.

"How do you know about the portrait?" Lilly was incredulous. Sunner's warnings about the old man suddenly seemed not so farfetched after all.

Sergei Elderidge looked distracted, but Lilly had no patience for his dithering.

"What do you know about The Devil's Portrait?" she demanded. He looked at the cornerstone, at the wheelchair ramp, and the freshly turned earth under the landscaping.

Understanding dawned and she was amazed.

"You're responsible for this." She tried out the thought.

"I will do whatever I have to." He said it earnestly.

"Why did you do this?" It didn't seem possible that this frail old man, this airy specter of Sunner's unreasonable fears, had the wherewithal to discover her objective and thwart it.

"Best you leave it alone," Elderidge said. "It's Schrödinger's Cat, and let me tell you, sustaining potentials is no walk in the park. I'd bring it to a full stop if I could, but I never had your talents."

Lilly was speechless.

"You look angry, Lill," he said, and then without any warning he pivoted backwards around the corner of the building.

Lilly stood, paralyzed with fury and astonishment for a moment before she lit out after him. She rounded the corner, full of biting rage, but he was already gone.

"What the hell?" she said and pounded around the next corner, and the next. She circumnavigated the entire building until she was back at the ramp where they had stood and faced the empty cemetery.

"What the hell?" she screamed at the empty landscape, but no one answered her back.

She glared at the ramp. If he thought having a wheelchair ramp constructed over the corner-stone cache of the building was going to slow her down, he had another think a'coming.

∞

"Occam's razor," Sunner said cheerfully as they retraced her steps around the Decatur City Hall, trying all the doors, jiggling all the knobs. It was nearly dark, but they kept the flashlight off. Watch the dog trotted ahead of them, her tail signaling her approval of the unscheduled outing. She secured the parameter, squatting to mark it off every few paces.

"You did check all the doors?" Sunner was careful to keep sarcasm out of his voice, as he tried the last one.

"I don't know. It didn't occur to me until the second trip around, and I was pretty freaked by that point."

"Tight as a drum," he declared. "But it may not have been then, or, more likely, he had a key."

"Occam's razor," she agreed glumly, feeling like a fool.

He knelt on the cellar door on the side of the building that faced the cemetery. He jiggled the rusty padlock and tested the hasp. The German Shepherd squeezedin and provided the assistance of her wet nose.

"Hand me the pack, would ya?"

Lilly dragged the duffel close, trying not to clatter the shovel, spade and pick inside.

"Outside pocket..." He instructed. She unzipped it and

rummaged through the tools there, coming out with an awl.

"What do you want me to do, pick the lock?" he laughed.

"How about that hammer and the big screwdriver?"

She handed those over instead and he went to work, not on the lock, but on the hinges.

Sunner took her story about as well as she expected. After her alarming encounter with Sergei, she had returned to the farm in a spray of gravel and shrieking brakes that summoned him running from the barn. The moment he sussed out where Lilly's story was going, he held up his hand to shush her and shoved her back into her car. He jogged around to the passenger side and motioned her to start it up and back down the driveway as he jabbed at the radio and twisted the knobs to full volume. They kept to the gravel roads, talking it over, under the blast of the radio and the soft roar of dirt and gravel scouring the undercarriage. Lilly realized Sunner's tactics were meant to discourage surveillance.

But despite his paranoia, Sunner took it well. He also took it very seriously, which underscored his belief that the game was afoot. That morning, Lilly would have thought the lengths they went to mask their conversation were a ridiculous precaution that would only feed into Sunner's delusions of being spied upon. Now she felt vulnerable and much more exposed than had the old man simply been a Peeping Tom. They talked long and covered miles, but came up empty. In the end, they decided speculations about the painting were unsubstantiated, and they had to be sure. They'd go back that very night.

The hardest thing was waiting for the long summer day to end, although they lubricated its passing with plenty of cold beer, and other preparations, not the least of which involved wrapping up every opportunity his parents might have to come around. Lilly tagged along as Sunner ticked through his farm chores, or 'paid his rent', as he called it.

She passed muster by not getting finicky about the manure, and by paying proper courtesy to the citizens of the barn. While Sunner milked, she gladly waded into the nursery pen and sat down among the riot of baby goats and provided them good entertainment until their bottles were ready. Sunner stepped over the low pen wall and instructed her on the art of holding four cola bottles fitted with nipples in two hands, with the added leverage of a chin when necessary. She was pretty sure that when finished she could have been wrung out to fill another bottle. Every inch of skin and lock of hair was milk-smudged and suckled.

A change of clothes was added to the list of things to do, but it was a happy mess: Babies of all species belonged to the same jolly fraternity. Or in this case, sorority, because this was a dairy, and the Tillmans only raised the doelings. Lilly decided not to ask the fate of the absent baby billy goats, as she might not approve of the answer.

The chores dictated another shower, which they took separately, both being subdued and businesslike and worried about the night ahead of them. Sunner sat at the kitchen table doing absolutely nothing beyond nursing one final beer while Lilly showered, and it felt to her like he was keeping watch.

Before they left, he backed his old pickup so the tailgate rested square against his shop door, and pocketed the keys. He gave his dog a sharp whistle, and the German Shepherd blasted through the doggy door to join them. After a moment's hesitation, Watch jumped into the backseat of the Honda, barely able to believe her luck and got busy making nose-graffiti on the passenger windows.

The town was as empty as they expected. The congregation of the evening worship service was long gone. They pulled behind the empty church, and parked behind the repurposed sky-blue school bus next to the cemetery. And then, for good measure, they killed a little more time chasing fireflies and swatting mosquitoes while the twilight lingered. Watch was filled with hilarity and tore through the graveyard in widening circles, ripping up the turf and dodging headstones. They let her run, until she was played out and flopped at their feet, tongue lolling and panting.

When it was finally time to pull the burglar tools from the trunk, Sunner gave Lilly a long reassuring kiss and together they sauntered, as nonchalantly as possible, through the graveyard and over the hill where City Hall sat brooding over its secrets.

"I can't believe we're doing this!" Lilly was bouncing on the balls of her feet, her arms hugging her middle, throwing off waves of nervous energy while Sunner worked at the hinges. The screws came out of the weathered wood with hardly any protest at all. Moving the cellar door was a bit trickier.

"You wanna give me a hand with this?" he asked her. "And try not to keel over. I can't run so fast if I have to carry you."

"I guess I'm not cut out for a life of crime."

"Well, lucky for you, I am," he grinned and they tugged the door back, revealing the cellar stairs, of which they could only see the top without the flashlight.

"Sunner, wait." She placed a hand on his shoulder. "Seriously, digging outside is vandalism at worst —at least until we find something. But this, *this* is breaking and entering. Are you sure you want to go through with it?"

"Well, technically it's just breaking, since we haven't entered anything yet. I can put the door back and you can dig all you like, but it seems to me, if a building has a cellar, that's a more direct access to your cache."

"The ground is already freshly dug," she argued.

"Maybe," he said. "Or it's a misdirection. —A nifty one, because it gave him access to the building. Hell, they probably gave him his own set of keys."

"Why do you think he'd go to all that trouble?"

"Because it's actually less trouble, and that's what I would have done." He winked. "Are we going in or not?"

Before she could answer, Watch darted past them, down the steps and disappeared.

"Oh. Look," Sunner said in loud deadpan, "now I have to go get my dog. *Bad girl.*"

"Okay. Fine. Get your dog, look around and then let's focus on the actual scene of the crime, okay?"

"Whatever you say, Natasha. After you?"

"Yeah," she muttered. "Age before beauty." He handed her the flashlight but she didn't turn it on until she was underground with Sunner close on her heels. She was about to complain about the mildew but interrupted herself with a walking-into-a-spider-web dance.

"Hey, watch the light!" Sunner barked to shut her down.

"Keep your beam low to the ground!"

"Here, you take it!" she squeaked, and shoved it into his hand so she could get back to the pressing problem of imaginary spiders.

He panned the beam around the empty cellar following Watch's progress as she cased the joint with her nose. The shepherd zagged once across the center of the room and then made straight to the southwest corner and flagged her tail, whining. Ordinarily, she was a good girl and kept her feet on the floor, but up she went, stretching with her front feet on the wall and vigorously snuffling as high as she could reach.

"What is it, girl? Timmy in the well?" Sunner asked and she barked once and wagged with the happy conclusion that Timmy was indeed in the well and he had a T-bone tied around his neck.

"I guess that's your corner," he said.

"I guess it is."

They approached and were quick to find a clean seam around the perimeter of a large square of stone. Even in the flashlight beam it wasn't hard to see white chisel marks freshly gouged around the edges. Sunner investigated the seam with his fingers. Bracing, he was able to wiggle the rock a little.

"Bingo."

"Do you need your crowbar?"

"No, I think actually..." The rock shifted. "Hey!" he cried as the weight tipped into his unprepared grip. He sank with it to the ground. It was just a facing stone, but it was heavy.

Behind it, was a neat dark hole.

"Wow. That's really it," Lilly whispered. "And it's really empty."

Sunner was back on his feet.

"Are you sure?" he reached into the recess. It was deep. He went in nearly to his armpit. Then he froze.

"What is it?" she asked. "Is there a box?"

"No..." he said pulling back slowly. "I think it's an ear."

"*Dude!*" she gasped.

Sunner laughed. "Not *that* kind of ear," and he pulled out a large curled triangle of cured rawhide pig's ear. Watch yipped happily, and very un-shepherd-like, walked on her hind legs.

"I guess this is for you," he said and tossed it to his dog. She caught it between her snapping jaws and bolted up the cellar steps before he could change his mind.

"We've been played," he said, and shone the light back into the recess. "Wait. There's something else."

"Good odds it's not The Devils' Portrait."

"More like the Devil's homework assignment," he said, and pulled out a crumpled sheet of notebook paper. It was wrapped around something, and he extracted it carefully and snorted, holding the beam on a plastic Bic shaver.

"*Son of a bitch*," he said. He held it up so she could see the masking tape wrapped handle where in careful block letters was written the name *Occam*.

"That's it?" Lilly demanded. "I'll kill him. I really will. Next time I see him? *Dead!*"

Sunner was smoothing out the paper and holding the flashlight close.

"What the heck?" he whispered. He looked oddly at Lilly and reached out and grabbed her arm, pulling it up to reveal Hector's wrist watch dangling loosely midway up her forearm. He read the time, and stepped back, letting her arm drop. He stood slack-jawed, leaning on the cellar wall.

"Hey..." Lilly said. She didn't like the way his eyes had gone funny. They were casting back and forth, like he was watching a pocket watch on a string. But he wasn't mesmerized, he was thinking. *Hard.*

She took the paper from his hand and retrieved the flashlight to read it herself. "Huh?" she said, and also looked at her watch. She whispered, "No way," and stood frozen a moment longer, and then she laughed.

"Oh very funny, Sunner! Very clever! You're a frickin comedian, you are."

"Lilly. That's my handwriting."

"Yeah, no kidding. I get it. Nice hoax. Well done. I suppose your dad is on the city council and has his own key too, right? Or did you just palm it and scratch in the time when you were 'feeling around' in there?"

He looked at her for a long moment and then said quietly, "We're leaving."

"Okay..."

He mounted the steps, his back ramrod straight.

"*Watch. C'mon.*" It was the only thing he said before he marched across the graveyard without a backwards glance. Watch did look back, struggling with her conscience before trotting after Sunner, tail low and unhappy.

Lilly was left to struggle with dragging the doors over the cellar entrance herself. She deliberated if she should try to fit the hinges back together, but without the flashlight there wasn't much she could do. Besides, Sunner was stretching out the distance between them.

When Lilly made it back, dragging the heavy duffel full of tools, Sunner was at the wheel of the car. The German Shepherd was sitting forlornly in the back seat, sulking with her pig ear as if certain it would soon be taken away from her. Lilly hefted the tools into the trunk and huffed into the passenger seat.

"You wanna enlighten me?" she snapped, clearly annoyed with being left behind.

"I don't know," he said. He turned on the ignition and in his haste to depart, gravel sprayed in a rooster tail behind the car.

"You don't know what?" she yelled over the din from the car's undercarriage.

"I don't know. And *I don't like it.*"

"You're telling me you didn't know about the note? About the message?"

"That's what I'm saying."

"But it's your handwriting. That's what you said."

"That's what I said."

"I don't get it. Are you saying you didn't write it?"

"I did not."

"So someone... Sergei... forged your handwriting? C'mon!"

"Yeah, Not likely."

"Then what?"

"I don't know."

"And what's the deal with Occam's razor?"

"I don't know!"

She pondered this as the yellow lines in the road flashed by.

"Why are you so freaked out?" she asked. "It's just a hoax. Right?"

He looked at her, scowling. "I. Don't. *Know.*"

"Okay," she murmured, and they both disengaged, finding it easier to stare out the windshield instead of at each other.

The temperature inside the car seemed to drop as a wall of ice was built block by block between them. Lilly hugged herself for consolation. She didn't know what had happened or why. Glancing his way, he seemed entirely preoccupied. His eyes moved more than necessary, as he was calculating more than just the road ahead of them. The term 'lost in thought' was literal. No more of him was present in the car than that marginal slice necessary for the safe operation of the vehicle. The rest of him was somewhere else entirely.

"Sunner?"

There was no answer, but he wasn't ignoring her. He was *not there*.

"Sunner, I need you." Lilly whispered.

His eyes snapped back into focus and he looked at her, measured her, summed her. Doing so seemed to pain him to the point of anguish. When she made no other requests, he retreated again inside his head. They drove the rest of the way home without speaking.

As they were parking, Sunner cleared his throat and said without looking at her, "I'm sorry but I have to ask: Did you put the note in there?"

"Me?"

He now fixed her with his gaze. She didn't like it. There was a manic intensity there that held no comfort.

"Are you playing me?" he asked.

Lilly's jaw dropped. "What, are you kidding me?"

"Just answer the question."

"Jesus, Sunner, that's the most paranoid load of..."

He jerked back like he'd been slapped, and fairly catapulted from the car, slamming the door behind him. Lilly sat dumbfounded as he stalked off. His clipped steps took him past his truck backed against the barn, to the goat-trail that led to his parent's house.

Watch whined in the back seat, bringing Lilly around. She got out of the car and opened the door for Watch, who bounded from the seat and shot after Sunner.

Hours later, Lilly was awakened from her troubled sleep by the sound of Sunner's pickup engine firing up. A few seconds more and it shut off. She realized he was moving it away from his shop door so he could enter.

But the next morning, both he and the truck were gone.

CHAPTER NINETEEN

"Is it even possible to consider eternity?"
—*The Chief Engineer*
The Wardenclyffe Foundation Archives

∞

In the year 2123

Quantum entanglement. That's what it was.

Lauder sat on the tush-cush. His legs were in a loose lotus as he replayed his goog for the nth time, drilling his recall and priming his brain to grasp the concept. On the other side of the den, Nidhi grazed in the Geezer's hydroponic bay, swaying to Ravi Shankar, a creative exempt. Lauder detested archaic music, but it was less grating than Bach, and the food didn't seem to mind. At least it wasn't catchy enough to get stuck in his head and distract him from his studies. Who was it who said plants preferred classics? —And if so, why not the B-52s or one of the other creative exempts worth listening to?

The ever-present goon was behind him, doing chin-ups hanging by his fingertips from the door casement. Lauder tried to ignore him.

They were a strange and guarded family now, squatting in the Murderer's abandoned keep. Lauder had made them take their locos offline until they arrived as a stipulation in the contract, to avoid complications and questions of ownership before the hook was set and they were committed. He knew he couldn't keep them in the dark forever, but it was a tense moment when he allowed them to geo-target. Nidhi never flinched, although she paused slightly at the read-in.

It was disappointing, really. He had timed it carefully and was banking on the Murderer's creds to up his ante, and he had the back-story all prepped and ready to roll, but she didn't even blink. Confused, Lauder tentatively engaged his own geo and was surprised to learn the estate had been co-opted by a corp with the grandiose name of The Wardenclyffe Foundation. The Murderer of the World had his affairs in order, apparently. His name was no longer affixed to the premises, and the corp held it as a set-aside, which was a relief. The last thing they needed was a Veep arriving for a bimbo vacay.

Lauder and Nidhi and the goon shared a moment of silence whilst they ran down the corp, but they all came up nil and eyed one another, as they tried to zone it up. The corp held some real estate, maintained an art collection and subsidized some garage labs, but was otherwise small potatoes. It sounded like a kitchen-table corp to Lauder. Some wealthy dabbler: maybe an old mistress the Geezer had, and by old, she'd sure have to be. Lauder shuddered. It was a ghastly thought. Worse than zombies.

Nidhi on the other hand, surmised the corp was Lauder's, and it fit to suits. Anyone with a Hadron cell was likely to cloak his assets in a front-corp. It looked paltry on the surface, but these digs decried it, and the board was double-blind with sophisticated crips her rank didn't make a dent in. She set her watchdogs and moved on. If anything cropped, she'd get an alert. She didn't waste any short-terms on it. The estate wasn't part of the deali-o, which was too bad. It was a nice little getaway. She liked rustic. And the retro-lab was like the basement at the Chicago Sci & Indie Museum. Except for that non-Shunt, and that was as good as hers already.

So eyeing one another with caution, they slid past it.

Lauder snapped his attention back to his here-now goog.

Quantum entanglement. That's how the Hadron cell was employed, and that's what made fireworks play in the night sky of Nidhi's eyes. The hole was binary, in a different capsule from its twin: the one that slid with its maker.

But 'missing' was relative, yeah? Because 'right here' and 'right now' was all a Hadron cell cared about. It was all here-now, as far as it was concerned. Look at one, you read the other.

Ditto memories. Ditto configs.

Nidhi's boat would have floated just fine if she could signal it. Talk to '*the other side*', to wherever the other cell was. Too bad it wasn't conned that way, but it wasn't. It was conned to a vibe. And that vibe was simultaneous: here-now and some-when-else, strobing in unison like twins conjoined at the heart.

Lauder didn't give a flip about morphic resonance. It was reconnaissance he was interested in. He just needed to go where it had gone.

Nidhi understood Lauder wanted to repeat the trip the first test pilot had taken, but that was a bigger 'ask' than he realized. By necessity, her strategy included careful redactions. Lauder would be informed only on a need-to-know basis and there wasn't much he really needed to know. She thoughtfully dipped her fresh green-stuff in the biotic sauce she held in a teacup, and munched whilst her servos reverse-engineered the schema and scenarios. Nidhi was obliged to be withholding, because there was an oddity in the destination data that perplexed her: When the twin Hadron fell, it hit like a pebble in a pond, radiating an echo in all directions like a 4-D ripple roughly calculated as an expanding sphere. What do you track within a displacement bubble where all points are possible? The circumference of the bubble nearly spanned one-and-a-quarter century. Pretty wide target zone, to be sure. Nidhi rightly divined this would not bring Lauder any comfort, so she didn't tell him. Instead, she simplified it for the simpleton. Although no trajectory in particular stood out, she threw a dart, so to speak, and picked one at random from the early side of the possibility matrix. She planned to send him to the backside of the equation and be done with it.

All that mattered to Lauder was she worked out a definitive destination. An actuality. A place-time that was as good as a map to the Murderer's hideout which honest-to-shits wasn't Trans-Dimensional; that is to say, one accessible without a shunt. Take the shunt out of the picture, and he was slappy-happy. As long as the Hadron cell was the compass that would lead him to the Murderer of the World, and he didn't have to kill or die to get there, everything was hunky-fine. Of course, once he got there, he might be obliged to do both.

Now all he had to do was wait, while Nidhi worked it out. To pass the hours, he amused himself by reading the book the Murderer left open on his breakfast table: "Tesla, Man out of Time".

CHAPTER TWENTY

"The distance between insanity and genius is measured in accordance with the majority view at any given time."
—*The Chief Engineer*
The Wardenclyffe Foundation Archives

∞

In the year 2010

Lilly was making her morning coffee in a fog of discontent. The air was already muggy and promised another day of oppressive heat. The cabin of course, was not air-conditioned but relied on the shade of old catalpa, walnut and pecan trees, and a breeze off the spring at the base of the bluff it was built on.

The Linoleum floor was clammy under her bare feet. It was practical flooring, yet she thought if this were her cabin, the first thing she'd do is get on her hands and knees and pry it up, because there had to be something prettier underneath. No, that would be the second thing. First thing, *air conditioning,* by God.

Coffee drove sweat from her pores and helped her cool down a little, but it didn't lift her mood. Sunner had been gone several days. Zip and Donna had stopped knocking at the barn door but she sometimes heard them doing a slow drive-by, in the hopes of seeing his truck parked askew in its usual place. Each day that passed deposited another coin in her bank of anxiety.

Gradually, Lilly realized she was being paged. Outside a now familiar and impatient bleating was signaling her to get a move on. It was Pi, the Tillman's errant goat. Every morning since the incident in the cellar, the goat cried at the barn door looking for Sunner at sunrise. Pi clearly had no respect for lazybones.

Every morning and evening, Pi led the way up the goat trail with a certain degree of dignity, now that Lilly knew to follow her obediently to the parlor. As it happened twice a day, Zip was finishing up with the herd as they arrived, and Pi acquiesced to let the common nannies take leave of the barn so she could get her special treatment of being hand-milked into a bucket, a chore Zip was only too happy to teach Lilly to do.

In return, Lilly took a daily allotment in a Mason jar to be chilled for her cereal and coffee. But as the days dragged on, Lilly began to feel an interloper, killing time walking Sunner's paths while sampling his abandoned life. Sunner had left. Just left. By rights she should push on to some other place; track down another painting.

That's what she should be doing. That is not what she did.

Lilly didn't bring up Sunner to his parents, as the mention of their son caused them to exchange loaded glances.

"It's all for the best, sweetheart," Donna said when she caught Lilly gazing at a picture of Sunner that was propped on the mantle. He'd been about 12 when it was taken. At that age his face was round and his mouth too full of teeth. But his eyes were keen and sharp and glinted with mischief.

"A boy like Sunner. Well... you know." Donna sighed.

But Lilly didn't know. She really didn't.

On the third day of his absence, Lilly started sliding a bowl of fresh water and chicken-scratch through Watch's doggy door in case the pigeon was trapped inside the barn. She lay awake that night, worried about it and feeling guilty that she hadn't remembered it sooner.

One week became two. Lilly hung on. Whatever Sunner's deal was, she could not extract herself. In retrospect they'd only been together —*really together*, a weird couple of days, if you figured it by clock or calendar. But by the calibration of the heart, time held no sway. If there was one thing she understood, it was commitment. *Faithful* was a word she had plumbed the depths of. Two weeks was nothing at all, unless the measurement was of uncertainty. In that, it felt too much like that endless last year with Hector. Sunner might leave her, too. —*Might already have left.* Her doubts yammered and barked little betrayals to her heart, gnawing on the outcome, fretting the timing and particulars. Her logical mind whispered that perhaps she didn't owe Sunner the kind of loyalty that kept the light on and the phone handy. But her light was on, and her phone was *right there.*

The second week he was gone, the sprung cellar doors at the municipal building were noticed and reported. Nothing was determined to be missing from the building, although the revealed cornerstone cache created a magical triangulation of speculation, intrigue and paranormal flights of fancy as only an empty hole can on an otherwise slow news day.

It didn't take too long for the curious to research the building and come up with the mysteriously named legend of The Devil's Portrait. Some wacko posted a diatribe on YouTube saying it was a sign of the end times. The video was so inept, it was massively entertaining, and it made its way to Digg. From there it went viral, though no one made allegations about who the artist was.

Lilly cursed herself for not covering their tracks. Now she couldn't publish her thesis because it connected the dots back to her. Is she did it would be too big a coincidence that she was living nearby at the time the portrait went missing.

Now that it was gone, all that remained was her motive for taking it, which of course, she didn't. What she couldn't figure out was why Sergei took it instead.

To escape the summer heat, Lilly retreated down the little hollow behind the cabin where a spring that ran along the bluff. It sluiced cheerily along the outer edge of an underground pond that exhaled a steady chill that suggested the spring was immensely deep.

Donna called it Fairy Holler, and she said it with such a fatally earnest expression the only safe response was to nod.

Lilly liked it here because it was cool and shaded by ancient trees. She carefully climbed down to where the powder-grey bluff formed a natural bench to dangle her toes in the water.

At the other end of this oasis stood a little stone spring house. Inside, it had a trough filled from the spring through an iron pipe driven deep into the hillside. A sluice under the door took the overflow down a mossy slip back to the spring.

The gurgling water and the buzz of insects eased her troubled mind. She listened to the grasshoppers take flight, sounding like the fanned pages of a new book. Down here in the hollow the pasture was above her, and she could see the top arcs of grasshopper trajectories as they sailed from one stalk of grass to the next on dry papery wings. Occasionally she'd catch a stray waft of hot air, but mostly the air was so still that dapples of sunlight lay as motionless as gold coins upon the ground.

Her contentment was dimly disconcerting, like she was falling under a spell from Donna's fairies. It dulled the inclination to leave and get on with her life, but so did her resolve to stay. Indecision was a gentle fog that encased her. The emptiness and hope she held in separate chambers of her heart became nebulous and indistinct, and sagged under delicious lethargy.

Lilly dimly noted a pebble on the path dislodged and rolled down to the bluff. She gradually returned to her senses and saw someone was coming down by way of the cabin footpath. The owner of the feet descended into her view and she was motionless with astonishment. It was Sunner. He was pulling off his T-shirt as he walked, surefooted on the familiar trail. He didn't miss a step with the white cotton shirt coming over his head, moving smoothly, whipping it from his head as he reached the door of the springhouse. He opened the door and leaned in, dipped his shirt in the trough, and pulled it out dripping. He mopped his face, his neck, his shoulders, and his chest, before wringing it out and giving it a shake to open it up so he could put it on again.

Lilly held her breath. He seemed an apparition. And she was pinned down by the longing that beat on her as she watched him. Perspiration oiled his skin and articulated every edge, curve and wall of his flesh, making the ache of her heart slide down through her belly and lodge deep in her pelvis. It throbbed there, a craven thing. The scent of him rode the cool air down to where she sat, and she drank it in, parched and dying of that particular thirst.

He had one arm fished through the armhole and was just

raising the wet shirt over his head when he saw her. He froze and stood looking at her, half in, half out of his shirt.

"Hi," she whispered.

He slowly resumed putting on his shirt and tugged it into place, where it clung to him.

"I didn't think you'd still be here," he said.

Lilly frowned. There was nothing in that statement she could hook on to. Did he want her to be here?

"I just got in," he continued. "Long drive." He looked awkwardly away. "No air conditioning in the truck," he added.

"Yeah," she said automatically. "You look hot." She realized her double entendre too late and blushed furiously. This was too trivial. She couldn't bear how vapid it sounded to her ears. It said nothing of her worry and longing and of keeping the light on for him at night.

He sniffed and looked down at his feet.

"I mean..." she retracted quickly, "It looks like you needed to cool off..."

This wasn't much better, so she just sighed and looked apologetic. There was profundity in her mouth but she couldn't find words with the heft she needed to express it.

"Well... look. I've got some stuff to do," Sunner said lamely and gestured up the trail. He looked at her as if equally appalled at his own words and turned away, hiking up the path in larger than necessary strides, and disappeared from sight.

Sunner hurried before she could catch up. His embarrassment was profound. Once his error became apparent, he thought he had fully calculated the damage he'd done — thought he knew what careful labors would be necessary to repair it if possible, and if not; what degree of self flagellation and regret would be expedient and necessary for the remainder of his life. But running into her without warning caught him flat-footed. It ticked over the first domino of his contrition, and all his calculations failed. In the full illogic of love, instead of running to her, he fled.

It took Lilly only a moment to re-align.

"Hey!" she called and launched off the bench and pelted

after him as fast as her flip-flops would carry her, toes gripping to keep them on her feet up the steep trail.

He was halfway across the yard by the time Lilly climbed out of the hollow, but Watch was nearby, catching up in the scent-network. Lilly startled her. The dog barked and raised her hackles.

"Hi there, Watch-dog," Lilly said absently.

The German Shepherd rippled with joy and bounded over to dance around her. Lilly afforded her a friendly cuff on the head, but she didn't have the time to entertain a doggy homecoming.

"Sunner!" she pleaded, trying to untangle from the German Shepherd. "Hold on a sec!"

Sunner stopped but didn't turn around.

"Why are you still here, Lilly?"

His words stopped her like a slap. Even Watch sat down abruptly and whined.

"I don't know," she said softly, not knowing if her voice would carry. He moved off again and rounded the back of the cabin, heading for the barn. Watch looked up at Lilly, full of question marks.

"Go for it," Lilly told her, and the dog trotted off after Sunner.

Lilly didn't follow, but entered the cabin, and after pacing from window to window to see his truck, to see the door of the barn closed from the inside, to see that he wasn't backing out again, she finally ran out of ways to fret and decided to take a shower instead, because the least she could do was freshen up. She checked herself in the mirror and despaired of the flushed face that stared back, looking crazed and desperate.

"Oh no you don't," she chided herself, and turned on the faucets and stripped out of her goaty clothes to stand under the cool stream that pulsed slightly with the cadence of the springhouse pump.

She failed to gain the confidence that usually came with a shower. Sunner's proximity jammed all her circuits, and she had no idea what to do about it.

Lilly redressed in a light summer shift. She left her hair wet to keep her cool, and braided it loosely over her right shoulder. After taking a full accounting of her appearance, and finding the total satisfactory, she ventured out across the yard to stand forlornly at his shop door. She raised her hand, balled it into a fist but found she was unable to knock. She feebly rapped the air once and let her hand fall, and then she retuned to the cabin in defeat.

Even the weather turned gloomy as the afternoon wore on. Dark clouds crept in and hung sullenly, trapping the heat and taking on that greenish tint meteorologists and old wives warn about. Lilly skulked around the house with nothing to do until evening, until Pi came down the hill to summon her to evening milking. When she heard the insistent bleat, Lilly got as far as the back screen door to see Sunner emerge, give his goat a scratch behind the ear, and follow her up the trail without even glancing back at the cabin. Pi asked no questions and just led him on, leaving Lilly with the conclusion her heart had lied. Her role here was temporary, and remaining any longer would definitely be overstaying her welcome.

While Sunner was milking and presumably giving explanations to his folks, Lilly began packing up her things.

The first thing she packed was her hurt. She tamped it down and out of sight in that fortified place that also held her memories of Hector. When she shut the door on that dark place, she knew it would hold, at least by light of day.

Lilly stuffed her backpack and her duffel and pillowcases with clothes, and tumbled toiletries into the laundry basket. She dumped her shoes into a garbage bag and stacked them next to the other parcels by the back door. From the attic studio she carried down her file-box of research on Pia Stiller, Mark Twain, and the missing paintings. She sat it down next to everything else that made list of immediate necessities that would fit in the Honda.

She planned to go back to Oklahoma; to the house she shared with Hector. It stood empty on a small lot, carved out from the land she was forced to sell to developers to pay his last expenses and debts. She would go, lick her wounds and brood until she hatched *Plan B*. It wasn't much of a goal, but it was something to do and she needed something to do very badly.

After the car was loaded, she made a final sweep. She was taking mental notes of what she was leaving behind, of what size of truck she would have to beg, borrow or steal to fetch the remainders, when the first rumbles of thunder intruded. She went back outside and frowned at the sky, twisting Hector's watch on her arm. The storm was blowing in –as usual– from the West, from the direction of Oklahoma. There'd be no outrunning it if she drove in that direction. That meant she was pinned down for the duration, because she'd not risk one of her fugues behind the wheel. Cursing floridly, she rummaged around in her car and took back her pillow and her favorite quilt. It was on that quilt that she and Sunner...

She stuffed it hurriedly back in the stack and pulled out her chenille spread instead.

Just one more night, she promised herself and darted back to the cabin as fat raindrops began to fall and made starburst splats on her summer dress.

By the time the lightning came in earnest, she was balled up in the corner of her couch with the coverlet pulled around her like a serape. She had her head down on her knees and was humming the tune of Clementine over and over, with the campfire lyrics of "Found a Peanut" running a perpetual loop through her head. It was a song from her childhood, from when the world was safe and calamity only occurred in books, on television and in the lyrics of songs. Every time the lightning flashed, she raised her eyes groggily to her watch and held her breath, counting along with the seconds, and then resumed "*I just now found a peanut, found a peanut just now...*"

The screen door rattled, not from the wind that had finally kicked up, but because Sunner was knocking.

"Lilly? You all right in there?" When he got no answer, he squeaked the door open a bit and announced, "Lilly, I'm coming in, okay?"

He entered the living room cautiously.

"Lilly?"

" *...died anyway, died anyway, died anyway just now...* " she softly sang.

He just stood starring at her, unsure what to do.

"Sunner, *I need you,*" she whispered.

"Oh Jeez," he sighed and sat down next to her on the couch. "C'mere," he said, and toppled her over into his arms and held her.

"I'm so sorry."

Lilly changed tunes and sang weakly with just touch of sarcasm: *"...a doctor, a lawyer, a fool or a witty, don't let her die an old maid, please take her out of pity..."* but neither of them laughed. They just held onto each other.

"I'm not doing this on purpose," she murmured some long while later. She hated her helplessness when the thunder started. She hated even more that it might seem she was using it to manipulate him somehow. She wanted to make it clear that was not the case.

"No, but *I am* doing this on purpose," he said, and he tightened his hold on her until it was clear that he was holding on to her for dear life.

"I'm sorry, Lill. I blew it. I didn't know what to say. By the time I realized you weren't... I thought it was too late. And then you were still here and..." He gave up when his voice choked off.

Sunner didn't know what to say. He didn't know how to confess how his faith in her had ripped away, how his heart and mind went to war. How he went searching for evidence and validation that his suspicions were right, and finding none, had to confront that he was wrong, *actually wrong.* And the awful realization it was he who broke faith with her.

"Sergei calls me that," she said.

"What?"

"Lill. Sergei calls me Lill."

"I don't care. Just let me keep on calling you something, okay?"

"Okay."

Sunner's relief allowed him to soften his hold on her.

"So, I guess I'm on probation."

"No. That's not how it works."

"No?"

"No. We can take turns freaking out, but the other one? The other one hangs in there. Keeps watch."

"Keeps watch. That's what you did?"

"That's how it's done. I have long practice there. You'll get the hang of it. I'm sure my freak-out day is coming. Then it's your turn. Deal?"

"Deal," he breathed.

"—But listen up. I packed the car. I was *that close.*"

His arms tightened around her again.

"Then we'll both have to do better."

"Yes, we will."

The storm wasn't a bad one. The lightning was content to play along the ridges and not dip into their valley. Sunner distracted her besides until the only thunder she heard was blood pounding in her ears and the only lightning was the crackle of electricity wherever they touched.

The next morning, before she got up, he unloaded her car without comment and then followed Pi up the hill for her morning milking.

A few minutes later Lilly heard a tentative knock at the door. It was Sunner's mother, Donna.

Lilly was wearing only her bathrobe, but let her in.

Coming across the threshold into her old home, Donna's eyes scoped the boxes piled near the back door, as well as the chenille bedspread and pillows on the living room rug. Her gaze also took in Lilly's disheveled appearance.

"You'll be leaving us, then?" she asked. There was a hopeful tone in her voice as she glanced back at the boxes.

"No. Not yet. Just... rearranging some things." Lilly had trouble meeting her eyes. "Coffee?"

"I haven't much time," Donna said and sat down at the table where she could keep an eye on the back door. "I just wanted to say... I mean, now that Sunner's back, I wanted to thank you for pitching in with the chores and all. You were a big help to Zip, and I know you kept him good company. But, now that Sunner's back..."

"You are asking me to leave."

"Yes," Donna breathed, looking guilty.

"Why?"

"You're not good for him, you see?"

Lilly sighed. This was feeling too familiar. What had Hector said when he sat across the table from *her* mother?

"Mrs. Tillman..."

"*Donna.*"

Lilly didn't feel like calling her Donna just now, but she

pushed past it.

"I didn't take a thing from Sunner that he didn't first want to give. I can see how our age difference would bother you. It bugs me too, but..."

Sunner's mother batted the words out of the air impatiently.

"I don't care about that. Zip and I figured it was about time. We thought it might settle him."

Settle him. That's what ranchers said about successfully breeding a mare in heat: It settled them.

"But it didn't," Donna continued. "He's worse, don't you see?"

"*Worse how?*"

Donna looked at her without comfort.

"I thought, you *of all people...*"

"*Worse how?*" This was clearly more than Donna fretting that her grown son went AWOL for a few days.

"Birds of a feather, right? You and your fugue states?"

When Lilly remained quiet, Donna plunged on:

"We thought it might be good for him, taking care of someone else's... well, you know. Taking on someone else's difficulties from the outside for a change?" She was struggling to be kind, but was losing.

"He was doing so well, don't you see. Tinkering away in his shop on his little projects. He was happy. He was safe. That's all that matters, right? Expecting him to go to school was a long shot, I guess. And maybe he would go if you weren't here holding him back, but I doubt it. He's just so..."

Donna stretched out her weathered hands on the table and regarded them.

"I blame myself. Drugs, you know. Me and Zip both. Children pay for the sins of their parents. Stupid wildlings we were. Like being feral was some kind of accomplishment... Trippin' around California, and I do mean *trippin'*. It was a mercy I lost the first baby."

Lilly didn't know what to do with that so she hastened to smooth it over.

"You're the most wholesome person I've ever..." Lilly was stopped by Donna's hand, which hovered trembling between them.

"I cleaned up my act." Donna had to spit the words out to gain control over them. "We both did. We both went straight. Sergei helped us. He saved us. He was wonderful. So kind. We were just a couple of strung-out hippie kids without a clue, but he cleaned us up and gave us purpose, here on the farm. When Sunner finally came along..." her voice caught again and she sighed so deeply she diminished in size.

"They warned us. A woman my age with a chemical past. God, what a risk, but we wanted him so-damn-bad. And it seemed like we'd won. We thought we'd hit the jackpot: He was *wunderkind*. He could read before he could walk! But by and by..."

Donna trained her pleading eyes on Lilly's face.

"The terrors started just about the time he was to start school. Gifted. Ha. Some gift: to see patterns and connections where other people can't? He connects the dots between everything. And I mean everything. Oh my god, *the news*. The world is such a dangerous place. All those calamities, and all the possibilities for disaster. He strings them together, all back to him. *Paranoid schizophrenia. Delusions of grandeur.*" Donna waved her hand, clearing the air of those terrible words.

Donna paused to level her gaze, but Lilly said nothing.

"You don't see it, do you?" Donna said.

Lilly shook her head.

"Oh for crysakes! Think hard. I'm sure you've seen it, if you just think about it." Donna was beseeching her to agree, to understand, and most of all, to leave.

"Is he seeing someone? A shrink or something? Is he taking anything?"

Donna's eyes turned hard as diamonds.

"Absolutely not! It was drugs what got him into this mess. Drugs I took, not him. Not so much as an aspirin has ever passed his lips!"

Try as she might, Lilly just could not disguise her thoughts of the little green baggie, and Donna read right through her.

"That's not the same!" Donna snatched absently at her own neckline and pulled her collar closed with a trembling hand, bunching the fabric together so tightly her fingers blanched.

"I didn't say he's not using natural herbal remedies. But

drugs? No ma'am-sir! No way! And no hard liquor!"

"So this is *your* diagnosis," Lilly said pointedly. "Look. Sunner seems fine to me. He's a little spooked about Sergei, is all."

"Where has he been the last couple of weeks?" Donna wanted to know. When Lilly couldn't answer, Donna leaned back in her chair and regarded her with a sorry triumph and a raised eyebrow.

"We had a little argument, that all. He's... young. He needed a breather. This has happened way too fast. I haven't even asked him where he's been, he just needed a little space, a little trust." Lilly didn't like where she was going and she noticed she was explaining too quickly, like building a hasty door of words she might be able to exit through.

She replayed the last moments with Sunner in the car, trying to figure out where it went wrong. After he fled the cellar under City Hall, Sunner had asked her if she had planted the note in the cache, and really, she was the one who'd be justified having a good mad-on over that. It hurt that he accused her. She said he was being paranoid...

Oh god. I told him he was being paranoid and he just bolted. That was it. I hit it right on the button.

Donna regarded her shrewdly.

"I knew you'd think of something," she said. "Step out of that pink haze of sex for a minute and see things like they really are, girly-girl. That's my advice to you. You're doing him harm and if you care about him at all..."

Lilly was in no mood for the rehearsed speech.

"Will you excuse me?" she said and rose from the table. On the dresser in the bedroom was the crumpled note that had been wrapped around the razor. Occam's Razor, so labeled. She went to it, smoothed it out, and read Sunner's handwriting.

All it said was: "Right now it is 10:13 pm, June 12th." — And it had been. They both saw it on Hector's watch. She figured he had written the time when she was poking around in the cellar, palmed the note and timed the reveal.

But he was more freaked out than she was. Way more. He even accused her of planting the note. And when she said that he was being paranoid, that was it. He vamoosed.

It *was* his handwriting. Occam's razor was staring her in the face, literally. The sarcastic prop gag pointed to the obvious: Sunner's favorite saying. Sunner's handwriting. Sunner's sense of humor. Had he been in some kind of fugue state and played a practical joke on himself?

Sunner was, putting it plainly, *nuts*.

Lilly carefully put the note away in the back of the dresser drawer, and stood there twisting the watch on her arm.

"What do you think, Hector? Am I up for this?"

She walked back to the kitchen and told Donna, "I think maybe I'll give Sunner the benefit of the doubt."

Donna rose from her seat.

"Do you know what an enabler is?"

"I have some idea."

"It does him no good at all to play along with his delusions. It just reinforces them. Sergei thinks the best thing is to..."

Lilly went on red alert.

"You've been talking about this with Elderidge?"

"I know Sunner is suspicious about Sergei, but you have to realize, he's suspicious about everybody. Probably even about you."

Lilly tried desperately not to flush.

"Sergei is an old friend, and he knows a thing or two, he does. He's never been anything but an angel to us."

"He told you to tell me to leave," Lilly realized. "You're following Sergei's advice when you know it is against what Sunner wants."

"Sunner wants a lot of things! He wants to save the freaking world with that collection of junk out in the barn. Do you know what it does? Do you? I'll tell you. Not a damn thing."

"Maybe what he wants most is someone to believe in him."

Donna jerked around the table toward her.

"Let's see how easily you believe in him when he tells you 'Men in Black' from a 'secret government agency' have him under surveillance from satellites through his cell phone even if he turns it off!"

"I think they actually can do that," Lilly said.

Donna nearly howled at this.

"Do you think that's going to help him? Help us help him!

Sergei is ready to take him under his wing. He's got resources. He can get him on the right track like he did us, but you... you are in the way."

Lilly took a deep breath, "Mrs. Tillman, out of respect for you and your property, I will move out and take up somewhere else. But seriously, my relationship with Sunner is my own business, and I'll thank you to stay out of it."

So help me, Hector, she added to herself.

Lilly delivered this to Donna with as much dignity as she could muster, given she was naked under a bathrobe and unshowered from the night before with her son.

Donna set her shoulders, took a deep breath but found there were no words left that needed saying, so she shut her jaw and pursed her lips instead. She stood, tugged her rumpled blouse back into order and gave a last glance around her old kitchen, looking for touch points, but not at liberty to go to them.

"Well," she said, as if the single hanging word summed up her point exactly, and having made it, she departed through the back door and pulled it to with a bang.

By the time Sunner returned, Lilly was fresh-dressed in blue jeans and a halter top and was sitting at the kitchen table deep into her third cup of coffee. The heel of her pink bare foot smacked the linoleum, making her knee bounce in a caffeine-driven blur.

Sunner himself was red-faced, but not from the morning heat. He pulled out a chair and sat down dejectedly.

"You too?" he asked.

"Ambushed," she said.

Sunner nodded and reached across to take her mug. She pushed it to him across the table, and he took a swig and sighed.

"Sergei was up at the house," he said.

"I thought as much."

"Do you know what he's saying?"

"Pretty much."

He nodded and avoided her eyes.

"And —?"

"Are you crazy, Sunner?"

His eyes crinkled up and he gave her a cockeyed smile.

"No crazier than you, peaches."

Lilly grinned back, feeling relief at his reaction sweep through her.

"Then I guess we're on the crazy train together."

"Are you up for that?" he wanted to know.

"I asked Hector the exact same thing. Just a few minutes ago, mind you."

"Did he answer?" His grin was big now.

Lilly took her coffee back and said, "He did not. So maybe I'm not ready for the straightjacket just yet. But... Sunner, tell me plainly. Are you dangerous?"

The degree and suddenness to which he sobered could be felt in the air. He locked his eyes on Lilly and said, "What do you know of paranoid schizophrenia?"

"Next to nothing. And it doesn't matter, because..." she was about to say his mother's diagnosis was, to say the least, unqualified, but he interrupted her.

"It's not the same as your garden-variety schizophrenia, with voices-in-your-head saying kill-kill-kill."

"That's a comfort, but look..."

"It's the belief that forces beyond your control are trying to get to you."

"Like your parents."

Sunner smirked. "It's more like a sense of *'They're out to get me'*. And no. I don't mean my parents, although, they've been a big disappointment here lately. I mean 'They' as in 'agencies out there, which might find me and what I can do, a threat'. Or just as worrisome, *'exploitable'.*" He redoubled the intensity of his gaze, waiting for her to ask the right question. She didn't disappoint him.

"*Are* they out to get you?"

"That's the problem, isn't it? I wish I could say, *'No, probably not''*. Especially in light of the fact I've been very careful. Even my parents believing I'm a harmless crackpot helps me in its way. It makes me unimportant. But what if they *are* on to me? What does watching out for that look like? What does that sound like? At what point does precaution turn onto paranoia?"

"When you disappear for two weeks doing background

checks on your girlfriend?" she answered quietly.

"Okay, *that*." He found that his eyes wanted to look away, but he wouldn't let them. He held his ground.

"So what did you learn on this so-called background check?"

"Plenty, actually: That you were a cute kid. That your mom worries about you. That you were a devastating tease as a teenager..."

"*Were?*"

"*Are*. And that folks around Enid, Oklahoma, figure you ... well... loved-up poor old Hector to death and are now in L.A. pursuing your dream of being a porn star..."

"They do not!"

"Gullible," he winked, "but they remember you. And not entirely kindly."

"Sounds about right."

He kept going: "Art school. B student. Not very impressive."

"Thanks a lot."

"A switch to art history. There's a professor there that's carrying a torch for you."

"Who?"

"Never you mind. And you aren't very civic-minded. Okay, except for signing a few anti-war petitions. You shouldn't sign petitions, by the way. Especially when they involve the federal government."

"You're drifting."

"All right. No organizations, no affiliations. No church. Not registered to vote. You've got a fitness center membership you've never used and a food co-op membership that's past due, and a public library card with nothing on it to worry Homeland Security. You've never had a speeding ticket, which I found so hard to believe, it nearly validated my loss of confidence in you, but you do have an impressive stack of campus parking violations. As a matter of fact, I would advise parking off campus from now on, because if they ever grab your car the impound is going to cost more than it's worth."

"Noted."

"You also have a shitty social life. Again, the fact that you barely exist raised all kinds of alarms, until I searched the internet. You never told me you were a virtual girl."

"It helped me pass the time, while Hector... you know. When I was just waiting."

"You don't have to make excuses. But I think maybe I do need to remind you that Facebook is public, and old AOL chat rooms are just a grade-school hack away. Oh look at that. Are you blushing?"

"Should I be?"

"Oh, yes," he breathed. "Yes."

Lilly cleared her throat.

"But the bottom line is: You are who you say you are. Although, I couldn't find anything about you getting treatment for your panic disorder."

"That's because I'm not."

"Hm. Why not?"

"Because it's nobody's business but my own."

"And mine," he said gently. "It's my business too."

"Okay," she said. "Tit for tat. You showed me yours and you've seen mine."

"Oh, I've seen yours," he rose, smiling, and took her hand. "But you've not begun to see mine. Let's go. I want to show you my machine."

"I've seen it."

"You've not seen the half of it."

She got to her feet and gave him a queer look.

"You never told me whether or not you are dangerous."

"I'm quite certain that I am," he said.

She hesitated, and he laughed.

"Don't worry, sweetheart. I won't kill you," and then he leaned in and whispered in her ear, in a way that made chills run up and down her spine, "*I will liberate you.*"

CHAPTER TWENTY-ÖNE

"You might think the trick is to wrap your head around cause and effect in no particular order. But if you're thinking of it that way, you are only considering a single event stream. The only question of importance is, 'where am I now?'"
—*The Artist*
A retrospective of 4D works from the Wardenclyffe Foundation

∞

In the year 2123

"You're telling me it's a time machine," Lauder said.

Nidhi rolled her eyes. Actually rolled her eyes. That was so unlike her, Lauder laughed.

"I don't know why I bother," Nidhi said. "But, okay, have it your way. A time machine. And the world is flat. And... Shiva Christ, haven't you been paying attention? It's *all* here-now. *You* are a time machine, so's my left shoe. We're all everything, everywhere, now-here, just experiencing one slice of time at a time."

"Except where we're not: the other 'verses."

Nidhi shrugged and scattered a handful of sunflower seeds across the floor of the loft. The pigeons squabbled at their feet, fussing over the feed.

"Forget Trans-D," she said. "Chronological-physi-shift. That's my say-so."

The pigeon loft was where they went for privacy. Nidhi was unaccountably fond of the birds, and the goon was unaccountably terrified of them, so it's where they went when Nidhi wanted to discuss the spooky specs – the ones that she didn't even want the goon to hear about.

The pigeons were the only livestock that the World Murderer didn't parse out. It was an open loft anyway and the birds came and went as they pleased. They foraged just fine without the Geezer. You couldn't dislodge a pigeon just if-you-please. They might fly around a bit, but they always come back. Even if you catch-and-release miles away, they'll come along home or die trying.

Lauder suspected the Murderer of the World ate them. He didn't suggest it to Nidhi, but with all the nests full and the loft overcrowded, it would be that or Humane Society Shunts for the lot of them, and he didn't think the Geezer had a HS service account or they'd have been around by now, thinning the flock.

Nidhi's hand darted out like a snake and she nabbed one. It thrashed and Lauder was surprised she kept a grip with her tiny hands, but she did. She quickly flipped it over on its back and captured its feet, wingtips and tail feathers all in one hand, subduing the struggling bird.

"Just like bio-tech in school," she said. "Some things are sticky."

Nidhi held it up, eye-to-eye. It blinked at her, lower lid raising to meet the upper one.

"Aren't you a pretty thing?" she cooed. The pigeon didn't coo back. It huffed, sounding like an asthmatic cough. Nidhi tipped it to show off its pink feet, the toenails were clotted with pigeon shit, but the rest of the bird was as clean and white as a snowdrift. Around one leg was an orange plastic band with the number 42 stamped on it. Nidhi thought that was funny.

"Remember that number, Lauder!" she said. "And remember this bird."

"Easy 'nuff. 'Tis the only one white withal."

"Look again. There are two," and she was right. A second all-white pigeon was at the drinking fountain. It dipped in its whole head and puffed its feathers and shook like a dog in a halo of dust and water droplets.

"Okay. Forty-two."

"You're about to take a little trip," she told it. "Here we go, a-shunting..." she crooned the old nursery rhyme.

Lauder broke protocol and clamped his hand on her shoulder with surprising forcefulness.

"No," he said. "That's not the deali-o."

She peeled out from under his grip and descended the stairs into the ark, and from there, to the living room. He was hot on her heels, one hand in his pocket, fingering the Fail.

"Don't be prickly," she said. "I'm like as not saving your sorry hide. Aside-wise, this pidge is prepped."

"How do you mean?" he demanded, looking around for the goon. He found him doing squat-thrusts in the media-room. He didn't even look up at their raised voices. He was getting sloppy.

"*Fixed,*" she flashed him a grin. "I expect this won't be his first trip. Or hers. Whatever."

"The pidge is *fixed?*" He'd heard of black-market pet fixes, but thought it unlikely. The church had no truck with it. It was taboo to tinker with the life span of animals. One just did not interfere with the spiritual imperative to contemplate the mortality of lesser creatures. They were left as they were that mankind might embrace their natural courses. It was one of the Forty-two Paths to Enlightenment.

Oh.

Forty-two.

"How do you figure it's fixed?" he asked her.

"The synapse age of this here pidge is 30-31 years old."

"Is that old for a pidge?" He asked, though he knew it must be. Her fondness for the birds was in a new light. She'd been up there scanning them.

"Goog it," she snapped. "Or take my word for it. This here bird is age-fixed, primed, tagged and I daresay experienced. You don't believe the Chief Elder Enge climbed in a untested time machine, do you?"

That knocked the wind from him, and she knew it. She stood now in the middle of the den, one hand on her hip, the other holding the pigeon as casually as a dishrag.

"Chief Elder Enge...?" he said weakly.

"C'mon, brother Lauder, do you think I'm estupido?"

That perked the goon. In one scary motion he was on his feet and towering over his charge.

I cleaned house. Lauder thought. *Total class-A purge. No memory. No rolls. PGP upside-down. Not a byte out of whack...* his jaw went slack.

"You knew him."

Nidhi hissed, kicked over a nearby stack of books and flipped open the cover of one with her toe. And then another. And another. Inside the cover of each, *'Ex Libris'* was stamped above a signature. The handwriting was too scrawled for him to read, but apparently she ciphered it just fine. It was the Geezer's signature. Sergei Elder Enge, the Chief himself.

"Read much?" she asked him. *"Think much?"*

It was too late to dust off that spiffy back-story. He'd been duplicitous too long.

Nidhi watched his expression harden.

"Naughty-naughty," she said.

"The patents are clear," he pointed out.

"Which means I don't need you," she pointed back.

Lauder fingered the Fail in his pocket.

"I go first," he reminded her.

Nidhi smirked. "Look sharp," she told him. "I'm trying to save your ass. Here's something to stick in your comp. If that were just a time machine, the Chief Elder Enge would be right here, right now, dig it?"

"Stipulating he's immune to unnatural causes," he challenged her. "Just because he's fixed doesn't mean he lives forever. It doesn't mean he can't pedal off a cliff."

Or be pushed, Lauder thought hopefully. He suddenly felt elated. The fact that the World Murderer wasn't back here right now making a squall-call was evidence Lauder succeeded. Or would succeed eventually. The only thing with a stronger homing instinct than a pigeon is a Homo sapiens. He wasn't here. Presto-ergo, the world was rid of him.

She treated Lauder to her second eye-roll.

"Time isn't a place you go, you dolt. If he managed to insert his physi into another event stream..."

"A *previous* event stream," he said.

"There is no previous!" she screamed. "No one goes anywhere in a time machine. You get in. You get out. Always only here. Because there is no *there*."

"He sure as shit ain't *here,* sister!"

"Exactly."

"Is this contract over?" the goon asked. He was holding his hands loose, ready to assume any tool the situation called for. He was obviously rooting for a termination of contract, and not the one Lauder had bargained for. He'd said it with the same sleepy baritone he used when asking for his morning coffee.

Lauder's thumb was firmly on the Fail now, and flexing.

"Stand down you two," Nidhi sighed. "It's a time-shunt, sure enough." There was a trace of kindness in her voice that surprised him. She leaned forward, saying in a stage whisper, "— And we all know how Wholly Rollers feel about shunts." She didn't even need to glance at his gloved hand that covered his tell-tale tats.

"You don't really want to get into a shunt, now do you?"

There it was. She pegged him as the fundamentalist he was. He imagined she may have already alerted Homeland Security. *Damn them and their 'War on Unitarians' too!* The muscles at his jaw began to rhythmically flex.

She watched his flexing, fascinated. It seemed irregular, but to a cadence, like he was clenching to the beat of an old familiar song.

"What's the proposition on the pidge?" he asked her through his teeth.

"Just a little test flight. A hop."

"The contract states no fooling with the Hadron."

"The resonance is fixed. Couldn't if I wanted to."

"You mean, you wanted to, but couldn't."

"What I *could* do was set a target, which I did a week ago."

"Explain."

"The cell is tuned to a frequency. I copped it and installed an emitter..."

"What emitter?" he demanded. "Did you also violate the sequester?"

"We are sequestered," she said. "Give it a think-through. That's a plum lab down the hall. More to do than ponder in there. I made it. I installed it in the loft and it's been on ping for a week now. The pidge is used to it. Pidges are hypersonic sensitive. It sets down through their peri-genes: they resonate to the memory cells, all on bio. They magnetize so, and it doesn't dim by distance. I daresay it doesn't dim by time-displacement no-how.

"If the Chief Elder Enge merely crossed a dime-stream, the pidge is lost: It can't backtrack a trans-dimensional branch. But, if he actually displaced in time, *well then.* The pidge follows and then does what it does best. It homes back to us."

"You expect a pidge to fly for over two centuries? There are a hell-of-a-lotta unnatural causes out there, sister, especially for pigeons."

"I'm only going to boot it for a week," she said. "I send it on its way, but it's going to hit the resonance mark; at that emitter I installed last week. X marks the spot," she grinned.

"Does it Trans-D?"

"How deep is your Trans-D?" she asked. It was a petty dig. She knew it was only rudimentary, and they both knew she wasn't going to bring him up-to-speed in the hallway. Before he could retort, she added,

"I know it works, brother Lauder, because it already has. We have duped pidges upstairs. This one and this one." She tic-tocked the bird in front of his face, and grinned at him again.

"The other white one, just now? The one I pointed out? It's this one. It arrived a week ago, where I'm about to send it. Now come witness me flush it so's you'll log it."

Lauder was confused.

"You've triggered the machine?" He'd have heard it, surely!

"No, not yet. *But I'm about to.* Ye gods, Lauder, sometimes you are just so dense."

He didn't see her bite her tongue before she said more.

CHAPTER TWENTY-TWÖ

"An inventor is a poet —a true poet—"
—*Mark Twain*
The Wardenclyffe Foundation Archives

∞

In the year 2010

Sergei had the hole at least. He carried it around with him in his wallet. It was heavy, this hole. It was a little universe of nothing, just a little tear with the edges worn smooth from passing to and fro. There were times when it was so heavy it made him limp and tugged his trousers so low he had to hitch them up and tighten his belt around his bony hips to keep from disgracing himself. A hole should weigh nothing. This one was heavy. But not always. When he thought about it, it made his imagination ache. Sometimes he'd take his wallet out and stare at it without opening it. The leather was polished where the hole was, like the wallet of a teenaged boy imprinted with the ring of its aspirational condom.

Sergei hung on to this weighty memento, even though he wasn't sure he needed it anymore. He seemed to skinny through the 'verses on his own now, like a ferret down a drainpipe in a God-child's game of chutes and ladders. With neither effort nor intention, he'd climb up, slide down, climb again to emerge somewhen else, craning his senses, sniffing to catch which way the wind blew. He always emerged blinking, not against the light, but like someone standing too near a hammer ringing down on nails. As one who knows a blow is coming.

Getting his bearings was tricky. Keeping his bearings was even harder, because he couldn't just dig in and watch, he had to keep moving, and move backwards, besides. It meant taking the stack he observed and then unstacking it in the proper order according to best-guess probabilities of how it might have happened. He had to compare *what was* against *what he suspected* and hold it up to *absolute dread.* Most of all, he had to be nimble enough to adjust for surprises, which came at every breath. This impossible equation would sometimes solve for n, where n was *what just happened,* and sometimes not. When it wasn't, he muddled through as best he could.

All the while he moved against the current. Always moving, because it took him if he paused. —Carried him right away, like a leaf on swift water and he'd emerge too far downstream and have to start again.

Keep moving and stay alert and figure out if what he was doing had made a damn bit of difference.

So far, it had not.

Sergei shambled down the hill; so glad to place his feet once more on the old goat trail there were tears in his eyes. He heard voices and he risked slowing, letting the moment drag long and taffy-like, because one of the voices was hers. She who both loved and hated him, and who he might have to make hate him more until hatred was all that was left.

He saw her down by the barn and a keening sigh escaped him at the sight.

So precious, that brief little flame that burned him through eternity.

So hungry was his gaze that he nearly didn't register that Sunner was with her. *Still.* They were together, in spite of all he planned to do to pull them apart. And worse, they were going together into that infernal barn.

"No," he said, raising his hand to prevent it.

His focus came to a full stop, and the tide took him.

Had Sunner and Lilly been looking his way, they would have seen him, and then not seen him. And if the breeze had been in just the right direction, drifting down the hill, they might have heard the faint echo of a cry, like a distant crow cawing for its mate.

CHAPTER TWENTY-THREE

"The practical success of an idea, irrespective of its inherent merit, is dependent on the attitude of the contemporaries."
—*Nikola Tesla*
The Wardenclyffe Foundation Archives

∞

In the year 2010

Sunner threw the switch that turned on the banks of lights that were in rows along the walls. It was super-bright when they were all on, and Lilly shielded her eyes and said, *"Ow."*

"You're not carrying a cell phone, are you?" he asked her.

"Nope. And not picking anything up on the fillings in my teeth either."

"All right, then!" Sunner said hurried ahead. "Just give me a sec to set up." He was so excited he was fairly skipping around the machinery into the center of the lighted space. Lilly wondered if she'd need to add *manic* to his list of peculiarities.

He whipped off the poly-sheeting that was draped as a precaution against pigeon droppings. There wasn't any. Everything was scrupulously clean. Sunner took time to carefully fold each tarpaulin before moving to the next one.

Obsessive compulsive. Lilly ticked off in her head. She followed him in with care not to touch anything or trip over the bundled electrical wires that snaked across the floor. She paused at a small frost-coated tank with a Plexiglas lid and peered in.

"Don't touch that!" he called. "Liquid nitrogen. It's

insulated, but still, you *do not* want to touch it."

She was pondering the three familiar black boxes inside. "Are those...?"

"Yeah. Playstations," he said with a grin. "You would not believe the processing power of a PS3 if you keep it cool enough."

Sunner approached a small aluminum platform that seemed the center focus of the odd collection of machinery. It was about the size of a dining table, but only a couple feet off the ground. Surrounding it were the three turbines that looked like scaled-down radio transmission towers. He was standing on the platform, on his toes, which made not a bit of difference, and fished the blue tarps off each turbine with a long fiberglass pole.

"Are we going to make rain?" she asked him, helping him fold the blue tarps.

"Not exactly," he grinned. "You'll see. Here. Let me take those and come stand right here." He took her by the shoulders and maneuvered her to the center of the platform to position her over a copper plate. It was warmer than the aluminum to her bare feet. He darted away on another mission.

"Is this safe for me without shoes?" she asked.

The room suddenly plunged into darkness.

"Sunner?"

"Don't move! I'm just diverting the current into the starter."

"Is it okay I'm barefoot? I'm not going to get a shock or anything?"

"No. Right. You're fine," he told her. "Just stay right there."

"You don't have Watch tied up on a similar plate behind the curtain, do you?"

"Not today."

"Pi then?"

"That was my last girlfriend. Why do you think she follows me everywhere? This is going to be neat. It might tickle a little at first..."

"Neat," Lilly murmured. She realized she was curling her toes. Then she heard a rustling above her and saw a vague white shape pass overhead.

"Hey, I think I just saw your pigeon!"

There was a tremendous clack and a whine and a deafening

clattering began. Lilly yelped a little and then stood holding her breath as a pale blue halo glowed out from the towers.

"Almost there," Sunner called out and she could imagine him flipping switches and turning dials, but actually when next she saw him he was carrying a laptop in the crook of his arm, illuminated only by the glow of the screen.

He walked toward her while keying with one hand, and stopped and regarded the towers for a moment while the halo pulsed more brightly. His eyes dropped to where she was standing right where he left her.

"Wow," he said. "You really do trust me."

She looked at him wistfully.

"Trust you? I love you."

He stared at her in awe for several heartbeats and then snapped his laptop shut which arrested the clattering of the machine at the same moment. There was now just a faint hum along with the glow.

"Check this out," he said in a kind of hushed reverence, and shut off the power switch. Nothing happened. That is to say, the turbines continued their glowing and humming with the power off.

"It just needed a jump-start," he said. "Sorry about the racket. I've got to work on that."

He set his laptop on a worktable, pulled one of the plastic sheets over it, and stepped up to the platform with Lilly.

"Let me stand here with you," he said, pulling her close. He looked down, making sure both of their feet were on the copper plate.

"Is it going to rain now?" she giggled into the crook of his neck, as he had to hold her that close for both of them to fit on the plate. "Or are we about to transport to Alpha Centauri?"

"I wish." He held her tighter, and not because he had to.

"I'm afraid what's about to happen is much more mundane."

"I get it. This just a ploy to feel me up."

"Do I need a ploy?"

"I was just going to point out you were going to unnecessary lengths when... hey!" She had indeed started to tingle.

"Wait for it," he smiled down at her.

Lilly felt a slight cooling chill, and then noticed a cloying moistness on her skin. She gasped and the air that filled her lungs was heavy and wet, like from a cool-vapor humidifier. Sunner ran his hands down her bare arms and the dew gathering there condensed into water droplets dripping everywhere he touched her. Lilly felt her hair start to frizz in an aura of fog, while Sunner's hair curled into black shiny tendrils, the end of each produced a fat water droplet. He shook his head to intentionally cause them to fall on her upturned face.

"There's your rain!" he said.

"Sunner, this is *amazing*." She traced her finger across his skin, feeling the water bleed under her touch. She was hypnotized by each tricklet and held her hand aloft to watch them course from her fingertips and run down her arm.

"How is it done? Is it some kind of condenser?"

"No. Something different." He kissed her fingers, as they were too close to his lips to resist. "Do you still think I'm nuts?" he asked.

"I think you're a freaking genius, Sunner," she whispered, and then did a little experiment to see how much moisture the contact of their lips could produce. She laughed, pulling away and licking the water from her lips. He was doing the same.

"This is amazing," she kept repeating. "Seriously, what's happening here?"

"Maybe I should turn it off first," he said, stepping off the platform. "Too much damp isn't good for the equipment. That's why I keep it under plastic. That, and that damned pigeon. The phenomenon is localized right there; the air gets really humid and then it condenses. But, this is not a condenser."

To Lilly's surprise, he didn't revive the laptop, but did in fact turn down a dial.

"Old school," he said, "now that the power is off." The towers changed their pitch, and the air changed subtlety around her. It didn't change the fact she was wet, so Sunner tossed her a shop towel and joined her patting and toweling dry hair and clothes as they sat on the low platform side-by-side.

"It's a resonance frequency generator," he told her. "Put simply, it vibrates."

"I'm suspecting it's not so simple." She gazed up at the towers that glowed eerily.

"Well, it has some very refined calibrations," he said. "But, really, it just pulses with the right energy signature."

"Of what?"

"Water."

"So you're just shaking water out of the air?"

"No. Not out of the air, and not shaking." He was quiet for a moment. "All mass is energy," he said. He was trying to be patient without being condescending. "Mass is energy behaving a certain way."

"With you so far."

"Its behavior is characterized by a certain frequency. When this energy oscillates in the precise frequency of water, then it behaves as two parts hydrogen and one part oxygen."

She just sat there.

"Yeah," he said after he saw a slight shift in her posture and decided the penny had dropped. "My harmonic resonator generates the frequency of water: It informs the energy —the energy that's all around us all the time —how to behave. The frequency is in fact information. I'm, let's say, programming energy to become water-like."

"What energy?"

"The free energy that's around us everywhere; and by free, I don't mean *doesn't cost anything*, I mean free as in *unoccupied*. Or unemployed, if you like. I like to think of it as lazy energy."

"Okay, but we were standing in the way and we're energy too, right? So why didn't we, like, melt or something?"

"That's actually a good question," he allowed. "Believe me, I didn't just jump on there the first day. I put things up there, and then some fertile chicken eggs, and waited for them to hatch. One day I even coaxed Pi up there."

He laughed at her horrified expression.

"She didn't stay up there for long," he said. "Goats really hate to get wet.

"See, energy has its own inertia, even in its non-material state. Energy that is busy being you and me and Pi and an egg, just ignores the information. It doesn't need to be water-like, because it's already Lilly-like. It holds to its own frequency cohesion. Just like you can sound more than one note on the piano at once and they don't cancel each other out. But, a piano string that is just sitting there, if it's tuned right, will begin to vibrate if one in the same key but a different octave is played. Likewise, there is a boatload of non-informed or untuned energy hanging about that has no intrinsic structure of its own. That energy is pretty easy to tune, or exploit, or employ, although not at first.

"It's like I had to coax it for months before I got my first results. I very nearly wrote it off as a fail." He looked at her with passionate conviction. "It's just that I was certain, you see." He tapped his temple with his forefinger. "It all fit together in my head, and I followed the idea precisely. I mean, the thought-experiment worked, so I knew it was only a matter of time and tweaking. Then once it worked, it worked. It's like I had to shoulder my way across a threshold, but once that door was open everything just started streaming through. Like the first success was a seed crystal, –you know what I mean?"

"And then, eureka. Water from nothing?"

"Something like that."

"Then you've done it. Sunner, you can make water! Just like you said. Clean drinking water! Sanitation! From nothing! No transport costs, and no electricity —except to start it up, I mean. Sunner, this is..."

"Hold on. Not quite."

He got up and pulled a white plastic unit from under his work table.

"This here is a de-humidifier. Picked it up at the hardware store. In eight hours it pulls a couple of gallons of naturally occurring moisture from the air and collects it here." He pulled out a receptacle from the back, and Lilly heard it slosh. "I'm not going to be saving any villagers by making them damp, I'm afraid. They'd be better off going to Sears. They ship anywhere, you know."

"Can't you just... I don't know... turn it up?"

"Well, yeah. Of course. But let me tell you, things got a little too exciting the last time I tried 'just turning it up'.

"Did you forget the bucket?" she laughed.

"No, that's not it. And what I need is a sealed tank. It's on my shopping list. This stuff," he gestured around the room, "all of this is cannibalized from this and that, but a tank is a tank and they don't come cheap."

"How is water going to pass through to the inside of a tank?"

"Water doesn't have to, and in the energetic state, the tank isn't even there. No, that's not a problem at all. What's needed is containment, and I don't mean just for the water. The energy just gets too excited. You can turn up the volume without changing the frequency. Think of your radio. Two buttons, right? But what happens here... well, it's like distortion. Like a bad speaker that can't handle too much juice without buzzing and popping. And buzzing and popping isn't good on the scale I'm dealing with here."

"Buzzing and popping... that sounds like... lightning," she looked at him long and hard.

"Yeah. I'm afraid so."

"Oh, Sunner."

"Yeah..."

She stood up and looked at the copper plate.

"I was standing there. Barefoot no less. And wet."

He rose with her and turned her so she could see the sincerity in his face.

"I told you, I'd never do anything to harm you. I love you Lilly."

"So you say! *Lightning,* Sunner. *Jesus Christ! What the hell?*"

He looked at her pleadingly.

"But I wanted you see, to *know.* You had to know. You had to feel that it's not dangerous. Not all the time. It's very, very important work."

"But that day at Neat's. *That was you?* You thought I was in Fayetteville, but I wasn't, and that lightning storm... *That was you?*"

He couldn't hide that it probably was.

"I only crank it up when there's stormy weather, so I don't draw attention. I have to cover the energy surges, and, you know." He reached out to her. "I wouldn't have risked it with you so close, but what you saw, it could have just been the storm."

"You could have killed me!" she cried. "You could have been killed!" But instead of pulling away from him she practically threw herself into his arms. It wasn't what he expected.

"I take precautions," he insisted. "Believe me. I want to be around for a long time. I want you around for a long time. Now that you know, we can work around it. I won't fire it up to that degree unless you are the hell out of the way."

"Like how far away?"

"Out of town, *like you were supposed to be. Like I thought you were.*" He didn't mean to make it sound like it was her fault for changing her plans, but he didn't take it back, either.

"But what about you?" she was shaking her head. "Good God, Sunner, I'm going to be scared to death for you all the time."

"No!" he said, "It's okay, really. Let me show you." He extracted himself from her clinging and sprinted to the ladder to the loft. She did not appreciate being left alone in the presence of the awful wonderful machine, but Sunner was down the ladder in no time, carrying a book.

"Look," he said, again switching on the too-bright lights. She blinked at the pages as he flipped through. There was a slight tang of mildew coming from the old book, and it had a glossy section in the middle just for photo-plates. He turned to one of them.

"Nikola Tesla," he said. It was a picture of a slender man in a dark suit standing casually in what could only be described as a cascade of lightning bolts. "A lot of the technology here is based on his work," Sunner gestured with a cock of his head, "and it's over 100 years old. But my point is, the electrical charges just flow over him. It's a demonstration of the skin effect: using his skin as a conductive path..."

"I don't get it."

"He's not grounded, you see. And the frequency is so high that..."

"You've done this?" she asked doubtfully.

"Sure. And so have you. Lots of times. Have you ever walked across the carpet in wool socks in the winter? That itty-bitty spark that snaps when you touch the doorknob is you discharging 12,000 volts of electrical energy. Lightning in your fingertips. Built up static charge, but harmless to you."

"Mostly harmless. Those things can hurt."

"Yes but my point is, here in this picture, he's not building up anything at all."

"And you've done this," she said again.

"Sure. Want to see?"

"No. I do not." She involuntarily took a step back away from him, like he might erupt in blue fire at any moment.

"You don't have to look at me like that."

"I'm downgrading you to 'nuts' again," she said.

He smiled and shrugged. "I could hardly call myself a mad scientist if I wasn't."

"Too much emphasis on the 'mad'."

"It's more fun that way," he put the book down and took her in his arms again.

She hugged him hard.

"Don't go killing yourself, okay?"

"Okay."

"And give me a chance to get the hell out of Dodge before you crank that thing up again."

"Okay."

"And give us a kiss?"

"Okay."

A few moments later and more stout-hearted, she asked him, "What else can you make with that thing? Gold, for instance?"

"In theory, I suppose," he said. "Pennies from heaven? But it's not exactly just a matter of dialing it up. Okay, it is, but it isn't.

"???"

"Hydrogen is simple. There's a reason it's the first element listed on the periodic table. I made loads of it. Of course, it just floated away. Fine-tuning it to co-materialize with oxygen, now, that was a real headache."

"But isn't gold a single element?" She remembered it was Au on the chart back in science class.

"Yeah, but it's not simple. And right now, gold vapor is

probably the best I could hope for."

"Gold vapor."

"About as useful to you as humidity is to a man dying of thirst. But there is something a little more interesting I can do." He walked back over to his dial panel. "Don't worry, this is way below the threshold of materializing anything." He pulled out a wrinkled sheet of notebook paper and consulted it for a moment.

"Everything has its frequency. Simple ones like hydrogen atoms... to really, really complex ones. Like living organisms. Remember that egg I told you about? Check this out... and don't worry. No lightning. I promise."

He adjusted his set of dials according to the notes on the paper. The aura of light the towers emitted intensified and turned a warmer violet hue. Lilly could feel, rather than hear, a calming hum.

"That's an egg," he said. "You are now experiencing egg-ness."

"You're putting me on."

"Feel it?"

"I do," she breathed. "It's... quiet. But, I don't know. Weird. Quiet, but like there's this outflow that curves around. Very... ah. Egg like. It's like I can feel the shape of the egg."

"Really?" He looked at her with interest. "I just thought it was soothing. Maybe I set you up with the suggestion. Let me try another one." He fiddled with the dials and double-checked his settings, and then straightened up and looked at her.

"What do you think?"

"It's safe, right?"

"Safe as houses."

She gingerly moved in a circle around the plate now, holding her hand out with her eyes closed, skimming the unseen cylinder of *somethingness* that radiated in the space before her.

"High-pitched," she reported. "Not so much a hum as a whine, but not unpleasant. Musical. Upbeat. Curious and..." She tapped her breastbone with the side of her hand. "It starts here," she said, "and just, *whoosh*, up and out with this spray of... of... Okay, this is really funny, but it feels like..." She opened her eyes to see Watch had come in through the doggy door and was standing at the edge of the platform, her tail wagging tentatively, her head cocked to one side, listening and watching intensely.

"Like her," Lilly said, pointing at the German Shepherd. "This is a dog frequency, right? Am I right, Sunner?"

Sunner switched off the mechanism and Watch barked once sharply and vamoosed out the doggy door, her tail and haunches low and not taking any chances. Lilly was laughing, but Sunner was stunned.

"Not just any dog frequency," he said. "But that dog in particular. I took that reading off of Watch."

"You can do that?"

"Oh yeah," he said. "I tried it on Mom's sheltie, Trigger, and it was a completely different vibration. It's not *dog-ness* per se, but *Watch-ness*. How the heck did you do that? How did you know it was Watch?"

"I don't know. Well, she was right there, and it just felt the same. Just a guess, really." She thought for a moment,

"Sunner..."

"Hm..." He was lost in thought, and she saw him do that odd back and forth panning with his eyes again, like you see behind someone's eyelids when they are in REM sleep.

"You know that saying, that two people who get along are on the same wavelength?"

His eyes stopped and he focused on her, waiting.

"I wonder if you could show that. Or maybe predict that."

"Damn," he said sarcastically.

"I'm serious. Aren't you curious if two people... like you and me for example, have the similar... as you say... *being-ness?*"

"Let's say I map you, and we see what correlates?" he said. "Then maybe you can show me what compatible being-ness looks like?"

"How do we do it?"

"Seriously?"

"Is it hard?"

"It just takes a moment." He looked askance at her hopeful face, "But you're tampering with the mysteries, you know."

"I thought tampering with mysteries would be right up your alley."

Sunner shrugged.

"Back on the plate, guinea pig."

Lilly took a deep breath and stepped on the plate and prepared to wait, suddenly not feeling as confident as a moment before.

"Okay," he said.

"Now what?"

"We're done."

"Really? Nothing happened."

He smiled indulgently.

"If you think you need more time to rev up your vibe or something, go right ahead, but it is what it is and it only takes a second to tap."

"So where are we?" she wanted to know.

"A second to tap, and about a month to read and a year to calibrate. You've got a lot of being-ness going on. And then after that, we have an unknown timeframe for finding correlations and who knows if we'll ever determine what they mean."

"Aw." Lilly shrugged and stepped back off the plate. "My instant gratification impulse isn't very satisfied right now."

"I'll try to do better to satisfy your impulses, ma'am. But right now, I'm much more interested in how you knew that last one was Watch. I want to try another. Here. Give it a go."

Sunner spun his dials to the settings on his cheat-sheet and the towers thrummed slightly and then went as silent as before.

Lilly stepped more eagerly back up to the dais and tickled her fingers in towards the space above the plate.

"Oh," she said. "That's... different. I'm not sure." She tried circling the area again, her eyes closed and concentrating, stepping gingerly, toe-heel, in careful balance, so she wobbled slightly at the ankles.

Sunner found this bewitching and very enjoyable to watch.

"Not getting it," she reported. "Not entirely pleasant. It's hard to describe, and maybe that's it. Like I don't have words for it. It's like an emotion and... a sense of entitlement? A resolution, a self-satisfaction..."

Lilly gestured up close in front of her face, crooking and splaying her hand, trying to describe a shape she was sensing.

"It's all right there. In front of my eyes." Finally she gave up and shook her head. "I don't recognize it."

Sunner's fascination switched to cerebral and he stepped up

to the table with her, wanting to take in her every movement in from close-by.

"Try stepping onto the plate," he told her. This time she didn't hesitate. She stepped on, but didn't pause, passed through and came out the other side, stumbling. She buckled at the knees and Sunner barely had time to catch her before she toppled off the low table.

"Lilly...?" He made a quick and fair exchange from fascination to fear.

"That was no good," she said, deciding to sit down on the edge of the dais. "I guess I have more unemployed energy in my head than you bargained for."

"In your head?" He was scanning every inch of her, looking for harm, touching her hair and face, looking into her eyes and checking her pupils to assure himself she was unhurt.

"Headache," she said. "Here, and here." She massaged two points at her hairline, above her eyes.

"Oh *that's* just not possible," Sunner said.

"Yeah, you try it," she snapped.

"I have. There's hardly more energy there than what passes through you when you use a cell phone. We are positively swimming in energy fields all the time; radio-frequencies, solar-radiation, magnetic fields, TV signals. This is *nothing*."

"Are you trying to convince yourself? Because I'm telling you, that was *something*."

His brow furrowed as he retrieved his laptop, flipped it open, typed furiously, double-checking against his settings. He kept shaking his head.

"Nothing out of the ordinary," he said. "The same as the others, just a different frequency, that's all."

"Was it you?" she asked, pretty sure she didn't want it to be.

"No. No," he shook his head absently, "it was Pi."

"Are you telling me I just shorted-out on the vibes of a nanny-goat?"

"Is that what it felt like?"

"I'd say so, yeah."

"Huh. Weird."

"Imagine how I feel about it," she muttered, vigorously rubbing her head. "What *is* that? Horns?"

"Don't screw with me," he begged.

"I'm just saying," she said. "It hurts."

"Still?"

"Well," she admitted. "Not as much. Can I go lie down for a minute?"

Sunner looked up from his laptop startled.

"It's that bad? Really?"

"Just crappy. Not horrible."

"Crappy trumps curiosity. Let me help you to the house."

"I'm not that bad. Stay here and play with your numbers. I'm just going to take an aspirin and check myself for little white hairs." She gave him a crooked smile. "Maybe this will make me even more horny."

"Now that's something I could patent," he tried to joke, but it didn't soften the worry. He went to her and eased her to her feet, clutching at her when she wobbled slightly, and let her lean on him. He carefully escorted her all the way to her bed and fed her the aspirin himself. Lilly laid down on her side and he spooned up next to her and pulled the soft chenille spread over them both. He tried to match her slow even breaths. His mind, however, was racing.

CHAPTER TWENTY-FÖUR

"The thing about pigeons is, they only use their remarkable talents to get back to where they started. If we knew what they knew and turned it outwards, where then might we go?"
—The Chief Engineer
The Wardenclyffe Foundation Archives

∞

In the year 2123

Nidhi would have preferred to send her goon first, but it became a game of rowboat. If he crossed first, that left the fox with the goose on the near shore. No sir. Lauder had to go first. Then the goon, for insurance. Lauder was in the dark on that one. Whilst he'd been pacing and fretting, the goon was cramming 19th century protocols. He knew the price of a cup of coffee. He knew where and how the money was kept, and how to get his hands on it. Lauder knew jack shit.

It was too bad the goon would not be there to greet him, but he would track him down and make double sure Lauder wouldn't be coming back. Nor the Chief Elder Enge, either. It was a safe wager because, well, they hadn't, had they?

Lauder and Nidhi were in accord on only one point: Prevent the Chief Elder Enge from returning. She had to protect her considerable investment.

The fact that they had gotten this far without interference made it a coin toss between their success or the Elder's ultimate failure to wend his way back the hard way. She could have instructed Lauder to lay a marker to be sure, but she didn't need to be sure. Not yet. She didn't want to risk that Lauder would finally *get it* and ask to see the results before the test was run. Paradox wasn't his forte, but no need to wave a red flag.

What Lauder's motive was she didn't know and didn't care. Wholly Rollers were an irksome lot, but harmless. The worst she could see happening is Lauder catching up with the Elder and handing him a tract or giving him a stern talking-to. He might be clever, but not nearly clever enough. Lauder didn't have it in him to cause any real trouble just so long as he wasn't around to testify. Getting him and her goon out of her way eliminated witnesses. If Lauder hadn't contracted for a class-A sequester for their meetings, she would have. Nothing made her happier than working in the dark. She'd be the only one there when the lights came on. Her and her new machine. She was in the sweet spot. Franchise, fortune and fame. It was in the baggy.

Whenever/wherever this joker ended up today made not a whiff of diff, although out of professional pride she'd given it a crank with her wrench, so to speak. Nidhi put some English on her calibrations and aimed like a pool shark, planning to bank him back to roughly 1890. Or so. Or not. He would land once. Probably. Maybe even alive and only in one place because she cleaned up Sergei's displacement bubble.

The beauty part of the machine was the chronometer. Otherwise, if it simply deployed a physi on the locale of a matching frequency, the universe would have drown in pigeons on their test run. An infinite lot of replicated birds at every pulse of the time-stream.

The chronometer narrowed the focus. The birds were, timeline speaking, nilly-infinite in number, but they happened one-at-a-time, spat out like bullets from an airplane's machine gun calibrated not to strafe the propeller. They were sequential, and in that sense, they were natural: This, then this, then this... and so on. Just like the real world worked. The Elder Engineer's art imitated nature to a degree measureless in distinction of the real thing, just like the difference between 'verses was academic when the experience was real. It mattered only to physicist engineers like Nidhi and crackpots like Lauder.

She only promised to get the crackpot in the general neighborhood of *before the Chief Elder Enge arrived.* But no telling exactly where or when he'd hit. Nidhi didn't burden him with her concerns, but when her goon jumped, she'd have *him* in a sky-glide suit with scuba gear on his back and an inflatable life raft. Mass cohesion might be enough to keep a traveler from manifesting inside an object, like a tree or building or mountain, but there were many more scenarios just as bad. She should do many more test runs, but frankly, she didn't give a damn. As far as she was concerned this *was* a test run.

∞

For all the bliss that ignorance should have afforded him, Lauder was not the least-wise comforted. He was not an engineer. He didn't know how the damndie thing worked. Trans-dimensional displacement was just too shunt-like. To get in, he had to dope to a point that compromised his clarity. Nidhi had to inject the juice, because the inhaler dose was governed too low. It hit him fast. She and the goon practically had to pour him into the machine.

He blearily sat in the cockpit of the Quantum Entanglement Tracer and tried not to wet himself. He wouldn't be flying by the seat of his pants, as they used to say, and that was too bad. It would have been easier if there was something for him to do other than just sit there. It was too much like sitting in the bore of a cannon waiting for it to fire. At least he was aiming at a pretty big target, and Nidhi assured him the numbers looked good.

And yet...

He wore a jackcoat, because when he was going, it might be winter. They had cold winters back then. He'd scanned it in the history clips and tried to imagine snow out-of-doors. In his roomy pocket, Lauder felt the beat of the pidge. The bird didn't struggle at all, but it vibrated there like a guitar string. He didn't know if it was because it knew what was coming and was nervous, or if it always did that. He did know that it had survived the first experiment, with the last-minute addition of Lauder's loopy 'L' of his signature added in ink to its plastic leg band. So, he had it now, as a kind of mascot. Nidhi was agreeable for him to take it on the long-shot it would home across 230 years. That was without the beacon, of course, because Lauder wasn't interested in landing on the roof last week.

It was a ruse, of course. They both knew the pigeon wouldn't make it, while they both pretended not to notice the bird with his signature on the band wasn't currently also in the loft. Ergo, the bird would not return here because it *had not.* Period. This was a doomed enterprise where the pidge was concerned, but only if success meant returning *here.* Lauder, for one, had no intention to returning to this 'verse. He took the MIA pidge as a good sign, just like he wasn't concerned that his own doppelganger wasn't present to see him off. He *wouldn't* make it back, not just because he *didn't,* but because this universe was a sham and a deceit, a dead end that would be cut off the moment he prevented the Murderer of the World from splitting the One True Universe.

And yet…

For Nidhi's benefit, he played the role of innocence. In his current state, that wasn't hard at all. He thought he might be drooling, even, but his hand couldn't locate his face to wipe it away, and he forgot how his lips worked. Nidhi loomed over him, unnaturally large in his distorted vision. She was saying something. Although he couldn't make out her words in his addled state, it was clear to him she was thinking, *Dude has no idea,* but she was wrong. Lauder knew very well all she cared about was getting shut of him so she could transport back to a proper lab with a crack team and do real specs and tests on the QET. She'd just been tinkering here, biding by her contract and ensuring nothing broke in the meanwhile.

But while she'd been tinkering, so had Lauder.

The Chief Elder Enge, the Murderer of the World, had once rigged this machine to blow. His mistake was making it so obvious. Lauder disabled it the first time, because it was right there, blinking in his goddamned face. He didn't make the same mistake as the Geezer. Although he didn't have the finesse nor the wherewithal to hide shenanigans in the hardware, it wasn't necessary. Instead, he had the Fail in his pocket patched to a simple timer packed in demolition putty beneath the floor of the lab. A *lot* of demolition putty.

Remembering it sobered him enough to close his thumb over the trigger of the Fail. Lauder took his fealty to the One

True Universe very seriously and timing was everything.

CHAPTER TWENTY-FIVE

"How does thinking you might be crazy prove that you aren't?"
—*The Chief Engineer*
The Wardenclyffe Foundation Archives

∞

In the year 2010

"Get up, you idiot."

Sunner jolted at the words. He was sure he hadn't slept while he meant to keep watch over Lilly, but they were suddenly not alone in the small bedroom that was barely big enough to contain the double bed. He and Lilly dished deeply into the middle of the sagging mattress, causing him to flail wildly, trying to work his way out from under the bedspread that was folded over them. It trapped his legs and he kicked, trying to get free and confront Sergei. He had no doubt Sergei was the intruder.

"If you want her to live, *listen to me...*"

Alarm gripped Sunner by the throat and thickened his tongue. Sergei was no longer his first priority. He threw himself across Lilly, and shook her hard.

"Hey, you alrigh...?" His words slurred with panic.

"Nuh!" Lilly complained, groggily. *"Whaz?"*

"You *okay?"*

"Get off or get on," she grumbled playfully.

He leaned down to her ear.

"Shhh, we have company..."

Her tone changed to annoyance.

"'S your mom?"

"No." He rolled back now to show her, but the room was empty.

"Is it morning yet?"

Sunner didn't answer at first. He was taking in the empty room. The space Sergei was not occupying took a big toll on him.

"Sunner?"

"Same day. Not even lunchtime," he said tightly. "You go back to sleep, I've got something to do."

"Wake me up for lunch," she muttered and rolled back onto her side with a contented sigh, completely oblivious of anything amiss.

He extracted himself from the coverlet and doubled it back over, tucking it around her shoulders. His scalp prickled and his skin crawled as if that disembodied voice could assail him again at any moment.

I'm okay.

It frightened him that he should feel compelled to convince himself that was true. He checked the whole cabin. They were alone.

Yesterday upon the stair, I met a man who wasn't there. He wasn't there again today. I wish I wish he'd go away.

Trying to get a grip, Sunner went for a glass of water but his hand stopped before reaching the tap. Through the window above the sink he saw Sergei gesturing to him impatiently from the open door of the barn.

Oh hell no!

He sprinted from the house, and was halfway across the yard before the screen door banged shut behind him. He leapt through the barn door and was about to let loose a torrent of outrage, but Elderidge was already revved up and shouting even before he crossed the threshold.

"What were you thinking?" The old man demanded. "Are you trying to kill her?"

"Lilly's fine," Sunner said, astonished in five different directions at once: Sergei was fully rabid, red-faced, gulping for air and retreating rapidly backwards around the jumbled piles of equipment, swerving blindly and narrowly missing everything in an ambling gait which seemed ever on the brink of toppling over.

"And then, you *left it on*," Sergei shouted. "Is that what you call safe? The door was wide open. And don't go telling me where I can and cannot go." He punched his finger at Sunner.

"This is my property, Sunshine."

"Not anymore, it's not!" Sunner remembered his rage and let it out. "—And if you come into my house or barn uninvited again, I'll see to it you're carried out on a stretcher. You have no business here. Maybe with my parents, but not with me."

Sergei looked fierce.

"You've got to stop this. I'm telling you; listen to me carefully: Every time this thing fires up, you're putting another nail in her coffin. And what do you do? You tuned her to the frequency of a goat? God Almighty! Have you got rocks for brains?" The old man fell stuttering in a fit of garbled nonsense and collapsed onto the shop stool.

The abruptness left Sunner to wonder if he'd had a stroke. If so, his sympathies were strictly budgeted. He was too busy adjusting to the realization that, once again, Sergei knew too much. Sunner did quick calculations on what to say that wouldn't add to what the old man might have sniffed out on his own.

"It's not that kind of machine," he said carefully. "It's perfectly safe. She'd get more wavelength exposure listening to a radio as she did *listening* to that goat."

"Indulge me," Sergei said. There was sharp sarcasm in his tone, but he was calming down, if obviously tired out. "Do it to me. Put me up there and take a reading like you did Lilly."

"Excuse me?" This just kept getting worse and worse. *What else did he know?*

"Take your reading," Elderidge said. "It'll take roughly 30 minutes for your program to run. Go make yourself a nice cup of coffee."

"It doesn't work like that. It takes hundreds of hours to run, which I suspect you already know."

"I took the liberty to reprogram," he waved absently at Sunner's computer. "Just a small change. It'll seem obvious when you see it, but it'll run like a son-of-a-bitch now."

"You couldn't have," Sunner said flatly. But he was already taking up his laptop, which was closed, and opened it to see the

ENTER PASSWORD field blinking benignly. He did a quick check of all the ports to confirm no juggernaut was plugged in. This 'top didn't even have net connections, so transmission wasn't a worry unless it had been tampered with. As far as he could tell, all ports were empty. However, some shenanigans may have been tinkered-in under the hood while he was in the house. He would examine it thoroughly later.

"Sorry, not playing," he said and put the laptop down again.

"Oh for Christ sakes." Elderidge was annoyed, and he recited Sunner's password for him. "3859998843"

The air in Sunner's lungs went stale before he remembered to exhale.

"Just shut your trap, enter your password, and do as I say. I have something to say and it's going to be hard to swallow, but it's critically important. It's life and death. *Lilly's* life."

"You're threatening Lilly."

"No, no, you idiot. I'm trying to save Lilly. The only one she's in danger from is you."

"Oh, you are *not* using Lilly against me..." Sunner's panic was rising. *Who the hell was this guy?*

"You will calm down, and you will listen. I'll prove what I'm saying. And this time you'll pay attention."

Sunner caught up with his odd manner of speech. Sergei was telling him what he would do with steady conviction. Was it some kind of hypnosis? Sunner felt slightly hysterical. Was this paranoia after all? Did he really think the old man was trying to hypnotize him?

Sergei was rubbing his eyes with intense fatigue. He didn't resemble a person in control; he seemed barely able to hold himself together.

"This time. You'll listen," the old man said wearily. "Read me, Sunner. That's all I'm asking right now. Afterward it will all make sense."

Sunner went through every scenario and couldn't find a reason not to. If it would make him happy, maybe he'd just leave and give him some time to sort this out.

I wish I wish he'd go away.

Sunner took up his laptop and entered the pass Sergei already knew. His program was live, the cursor ticking where new code had been entered. Sunner executed a Save As and killed it, and reopened a previous version. If he was going to play, it was going to be by his own rules.

Sergei Elderidge hefted himself up on the platform and took up a position on the dais, and shut his eyes. As Sunner adjusted the calibrations, the frequency shifted and caused enough shift in light that the old man seemed almost to flicker in the transition.

"There," Sunner said. "You're read. Now what?"

"You'll know what to do," Sergei replied with a sigh and backed off the platform and looked at Sunner apologetically.

"Sorry to have to do this to you, son," he said. "But I'm running out of options. I'm running out of time and out of patience, but most of all... I'm just so damned tired."

He leaned forward and whispered with grave importance, "It turns out you *can* kill your own grandpa if you have the balls to pull the trigger. But I can't. I don't. Isn't that a hell of a thing? I'm hoping all you really have to do is distract him." He made a weak gesture as though he might have put a steadying hand on Sunner's shoulder, but seemed to think better of it and let his hand drop. He stood there for a moment, sighed deeply, relaxed and whispered *"Aloha."*

Sunner stood for many minutes staring with unwavering eyes on the spot where Sergei Elderidge had simply and unequivocally vanished.

CHAPTER TWENTY-SIX

Into that darkness peering, long I stood there wondering, fearing, doubting dreaming dreams no mortal ever dared to dream before.
—*Edgar Allen Poe*

∞

In the year 2010

Lilly awoke. For the most part, she felt fine except for a vague disquiet. Her deep sleep had soothed away her headache from encountering the resonance of Pi in Sunner's machine, but the house didn't feel right. She knew without feeling next to her she was alone in the bed, although she felt Sunner should have been there.

Missing limb syndrome, she thought.

Sunlight was directly overhead and wasn't entering the room. She knew by the relative brightness it was midday, without having to consult Hector's watch. Her growling stomach informed her it was downhill from noon and she'd missed her lunch as well as her breakfast. Any lightheadedness she felt was only from that. Sunner had been right. She was perfectly fine. She wiggled her toes. *Not even any hoofies.* She noted. What had she expected? Some caprine version of the movie "The Fly"?

Lilly was tempted to squeak out a high-pitched *"Help meeee!"* to see if Sunner would come running, but thought better of it. That would just be mean. Instead, with a grin, she decided to go find him, assure him she was okay, and then at the very least take credit for not having goaded him with the line from the movie, but before her feet hit the floor, her grin faded.

She knew he was in the cabin. Quiet moving-about sounds had percolated into her sleep but there was an edge to them that had nudged her awake and she realized it was the feeling that something was wrong.

She entered the kitchen, and on the table was Sunner's laptop, as well as scattered pages torn from a yellow pad. Several sheets were crumpled into balls and lying on the floor. She glanced down at the pad on the table and saw equations that she could only read artistically. They had their own aesthetic symmetry, which appealed to her. She liked the way he made marks on a page. The press and the flair, the sweeping lines, the use of space. There was a completeness to them that made her think of Da Vinci's notebooks.

Genius looks like this, she thought.

In the living room, Sunner was pacing. His right hand was raking and raking through his hair until it stood up spiky and glossy and matched the deranged expression on his face. When he saw her looking at him with curiosity from the doorway he threw up both hands to keep her from entering the room.

"Sunner?"

"Lilly," he choked. "I never meant to hurt you." He said it as though over a freshly filled grave.

"You haven't. I'm fine," she protested. "Really. Fit as a fiddle..."

But he was shaking his head and distraught enough that Lilly felt soon he might be crying. She took a step back because all of his energy was in his hands, pushing the space between them, pushing her back by the weight of the air which had grown heavy with his intention, all the way back into the kitchen.

"You have to go." He was serious. "You have to pack up. Right now. *And leave.*"

"What are you talking about? I'm fine. What are you all worked up about?"

He made a frustrated cry and threw the weight of hysteria into it, making Lilly retreat another step.

"I'm not safe." The confession was made in the higher registers of his voice. "I don't know what I'm doing. I'm out of control. You need to get the hell out of here before I do something really stupid."

He could fairly see her grow roots into the floor as she stood there, holding her ground, hardening with resolve.

"Sunner," she said quietly, raising her chin like a prow to push through whatever storm was before them. "Let's just talk this through. Tell me what's wrong."

"I blamed you at first. You know that? I thought you were a... to make me doubt. To show me I'm crazy. And oh God, I wanted it to be you!" His words choked him. "It tore my heart and yet I wanted it to be you. It had to be you, because if you weren't screwing with me, then I put that note in the cache myself. And I knew... I thought I knew —*I knew* it wasn't me."

Lilly was dismayed that he was back on this again.

"We've been through that. We can deal with it." Then she bristled with a thought: "Oh jeez, what's Sergei up to now?"

"Sergei..." he looked at her pleadingly, begging for her understanding as he said, "I *am* Sergei."

"Bullshit." She slapped it down. Angry with the very idea.

"I've seen him. Old dude? Walks funny? Says 'aloha'? What's more, I've seen you together. So's your mom. So's lots of people. There's no way —*no way* this is some Jekyll and Hyde thing. I don't know what you've got going on in your head right now, but that is not it. You got me?"

Sunner pointed at the kitchen table.

"Sit down," he said. "Let me show you."

She sat, but fully armed, loaded and cocked should Sergei come up again. He took the chair opposite her and placed his palms flat on the table, on either side of the computer, gathering his thoughts. Lilly softened to drop her guard and reached across to take them but he pulled them back and put them in his lap, and leaned forward, closing off the gap between his chest and the table. He kept his head down, looking like a cyclist who'd just stripped his gears and couldn't pedal any further.

He told her everything that had happened beginning with hearing the voice in the bedroom. Now and again he glanced up at her from under his dark eyebrows, and her face was furious, yet none of it directed at him. When he got to the end, he couldn't look at her at all. He burned with shame as he told her Sergei had vanished into thin air.

There was a moment of silence where only the mechanical clock built into the old kitchen stove ticked off the seconds.

She finally delivered a stout explicative and let it hang there.

"The thing is," he whispered, "he was never there in the first place."

"Wait," she warned off.

"I'm not saying he's not real. That Sergei doesn't exist or some bullshit thing like that. I'm just saying today I'm delusional. Today I made him up."

Lilly didn't know what to say to that. She sagged with the possibility.

He reached out and brought the laptop out of its sleep and looked at it morosely.

"And then there's this. He... I... oh hell: *One of us* reprogrammed my machine."

"Okay. So it was reprogrammed," she repeated. "So what?"

"—To make it faster. Which it did," he conceded with a wave of his hand, "but that's not all."

He rotated the laptop and pushed it across the table toward her.

She glanced at it and said, "I don't read code."

"You can read this," he said, tapping the screen. "It's a text notation, in the code. It's bracketed off so it doesn't affect the program. Programmers use it to explain the sticky spots and to remind themselves..."

"Notes."

"Yeah, notes."

"Okay," she squinted at the screen to find the spot. It read:

PAY ATTENTION SUNSHINE. IT IS NOW 1:43 PM. AS YOU CAN CONFIRM THIS IS TRUE, YOU MUST ALSO CONSIDER THE FOLLOWING IS TRUE: IN ALL PROBABILITY LILLY WILL BE DEAD WITHIN FIVE DAYS. MORE THAN THIS, YOU WILL KILL HER WITH YOUR INFERNAL MACHINE.

Lilly tried to ignore the rash of goose bumps creeping over her scalp.

"Why would he put that in there? Why would you? It's

ridiculous." She looked at her watch, "and it's wrong."

"Well, *now* it is." He was exasperated. "It was right when I first read it. Dead on. But yeah. You're right: Why would I put that in there?" He looked at her pleadingly, wanted her to say it; so she'd hear herself and be more likely to accept it.

Lilly was stubborn.

"All I see is evidence that son-of-a-bitch is playing you. It's just a time-stamp, right? It just locked when you got to the page. I'm with your first theory, Sunner. He wants Manna, and he's playing you so he —or someone he's working for —can take it over. The rest is smoke and mirrors and your stressed-out über-imagination."

"No. No. No. You're not seeing the whole picture yet," he told her. "I scanned him. I couldn't imagine why, but he wanted me to and I humored him. It should have taken a month to crunch it, but..." He gestured weakly at the laptop, "it's done already."

"I'm skeptical," she said, making a huge understatement.

"Me too, but it looks kosher. The code, well, it's brilliant, yeah. I could have done it. Obviously, I *did* do it. I mean. Here's the kick: His scan is identical to mine. *Identical.*"

"So?"

"He's me."

"Bull. Shit." She stared him down, furiously. "I'm going with door number one: You've been hacked. Happens every day. He just made it look like they were the same, —like he fixed the text to read whatever time it was when the page executed. Jesus, Sunner, if he can program the reader, he can program the reading, right?"

"Oh no." He was shaking his head. "Not in a million years. No one could have done it but me."

"Because you're so smart."

"Yes, goddamn it, I am."

"Maybe you're not!" she bawled at him. "Maybe you've been conned. First of all, by yourself. Gawd, not everything is complicated, Sunshine. Just get pissed, don't go off the deep end."

"You think I didn't think it through? I've run three other scans. I even scanned that damn pigeon when it flew through the field, and it's working just as it always has. No, and he *left* right after the scan. What's more, I scanned him on a version of the program he didn't touch. He didn't tamper with it at all. Which means it's me: I'm dithering around out there talking to myself, scanning myself, believing all the while I'm with someone when I'm not. The only upside is my alter-ego seems to be looking out for me. It's trying to hold up the mirror so I can see just how bat-shit crazy I am, so... so I don't end up hurting you."

"I don't believe it."

"Hell, if I can do all that..." his voice cracked. "At least some piece of me is detached enough to leave a warning."

"I don't believe it."

"Lilly," he pleaded. "*Occam's razor.* It's the only thing that works. I wrote it out plainly, in that note I 'found' in the cache. I just wasn't prepared to listen. So I wrote it plainer here. If I'm capable of this, then I'm capable to carry that out." He pointed at the laptop. At the code. At the note in text.

"Screw it. Screw you and your, your... doppelganger too. C'mon, Sunner. Just listen to yourself. The only thing crazy here is what you're saying. Use that big brain of yours and let's sort this out. Flip it over. What's it say?"

Head-cocked, he heaved an indulgent sigh. Much like the old Sunner. "So my parents' old friend shows up with full knowledge of Manna, which he's never seen nor heard of before. He's able to hack my computer, reprogram it and —just for shits and giggles, put in threatening messages. Oh, and by the way, he's managed to wire the shop and the cabin to catch every detail of our conversations, including knowing the exact moment we planned our little heist. And the cherry on top? He knew right when I'd get to the right line in the code."

"Not likely," she allowed. "What else we got?"

"Let's just call them *men in black* as long as we're playing this game. So our men in black, they've been keeping an eye on me for years, yeah? Maybe I tipped my hand on the internet when I was, like, in junior high and didn't know any better, but it was enough for them to settle in and watch, just in case I might do something *smart*. Now, they figure Manna is a threat to homeland security because we can't just go around quenching people's thirst willy-nilly, now can we? And even though the hydrogen byproduct is a game-changer, so what? It's not like I'm in the public eye. They could just stroll in here and take the damn thing any time they wanted, and toss my body in the hollow. So why all the cloak-and-dagger 'let's screw with Sunner' stuff?"

"Because they *are* evil-evil bastards?" Lilly offered, using the description he supplied the other day. "Because they want you in a nice padded cell somewhere: A padded cell next to a laboratory so you can keep working for them, their own little drugged-up lab rat?"

Sunner smiled at her weakly.

"That was actually my first idea, only I thought it was you."

"I don't suppose you have a lie detector handy? I'll hook up to anything you like."

"I know you will, but, the guy vanished, Lilly. *Poof.* Right in front of me. You tell me what can do that, that doesn't have crazy written all over it."

They sat together in silence for a while, each sizing the other up.

"What are you still doing here?" he asked. "Are you humoring me? You should tiptoe out when I'm not looking, so I won't chop you up and store the pieces in the cellar."

"You don't have a cellar," she said. "And there are still some things we aren't considering. The painting, for one. What's the point in taking the painting?"

"There may not be a painting."

"Then he —not you: *he* —put a shitload of energy into pranking the cache. When I ran into him at City Hall, I assure you, he knew about the painting. He'd seen it. He said it wasn't what I was looking for: That it was just a picture of a cat."

"A cat."

"Yeah, some cat. Schroder's Cat."

Sunner looked at her steadily. "Schrödinger's Cat?"

"That could have been it."

"Why didn't you tell me this before?"

"I told you about the cat."

"No, no: Schrödinger's cat. That's something else entirely." His eyes were reading back and forth rapidly.

"I think we have another theory," he said, but he didn't look relieved at all. "Lilly, you really gotta go. Right now."

"Sunner, what the heck?"

He pushed back from the table, the fear in his face replaced by something bigger.

"Go. Now. Do it, Lill, or I'll call the sheriff to evict you."

She gave him an incredulous look. "This is me, hanging in here until you are done freaking out," she said. "Do you realize how erratic you were just now?"

He winced, but not at her accusation. This was no time for her to exercise her sense of duty.

"I'll call Donny and Roy: They'll box up your stuff and carry it down to Fayetteville for you, or if you like, back to Enid."

Lilly dug in. He could see it in every fiber of her being. There would be no talking her out of this. Not now. He carefully closed the laptop, stood and held it against his chest. He backed away from her, keeping his eyes downcast from the set of her face.

"Don't come back. Don't try to call and don't be a pest to my parents. They don't want you here, and neither do I." He turned his face away, "Thanks for the sex and all, but I don't need the distraction. I have to get back to work."

Lilly wasn't buying.

"Nice try, Sunshine." She rose to her feet and reached out to him, "What's really going on?"

He finally looked at her, stared at her hard, taking all of her in: He saw her resolve. Her love. Her endlessly forgiving nature. Her belief in him, first, last, and always. *Undaunted.* That's what she was.

He ran the numbers and they failed him. Rapid-fire, he re-calculated, discarded and approached again. Paring down and down. The option he was left with made his face as dark as his eyes.

"What's going on?" He could barely whisper the words. "I'll show you what's going on." He transferred the laptop to his left hand and with his right extracted a paring knife from the wooden block on the counter.

"You like old movies. Ever see the movie Psycho?" with a flip, he palmed it so the blade was facing down and he advanced on her, stabbing the air, like a pantomime of a bad horror movie.

She wasn't laughing. Real shock shone in her face and she

shielded herself with her hands.

"It says you'll be dead within five days," he said. "Maybe that's how long it will take you to bleed out," and he stabbed the heel of her hand, slashing downwards and back up with snakebite speed.

"Hey!" she cried and jumped back.

He was breathing through his teeth, poised with the knife held up and ready for another go.

But Lilly was on the move. She flew around the other side of the table and out the back door.

Watch burst into wild barking at her flight, and a few heartbeats later her car revved to life and she was gone in a rain of gravel.

Sunner sank back into his chair and hugging the laptop, he let himself cry. He felt desperately alone and he wished, just once, his math had failed.

CHAPTER TWENTY-SEVEN

"Beginnings and endings are messy."
—The Chief Engineer
The Wardenclyffe Foundation Archives

∞

In the year 2123

From the cockpit of the *not-a-shunt*, Lauder offered Nidhi a bleary smile which was the best he could do since his dopes kicked in. She'd promised him at least two years lead time to Sergei's insertion point. That would give him time to acclimate and position himself and make whatever preps he needed to intercept the elderly Murderer of the World and do him in. Then all he had to do was keep breathing until he could suss out the original: the Murderer's first pass, as it were. To succeed, Lauder had to track him down also and off him in his youth before he first split the world.

That was the beauty part. The verses branched with every shunt, but they shared a past. They all sprang from the same trunk of history. Ergo-ipso, he could save the world, he really could.

He gave Nidhi a boozy bye-bye wave, but his hand was shaking violently.

This is not a shunt. This is not a shunt. That is what he told the panic that seeped around the narcotics and raced his heart anyway. His last look at Nidhi was one of desperate remorse.

"God forgive me!" he begged.

She closed the hatch before he could change his mind. The controls had been moved to the outside, like a conventional shunt. All Lauder had to do was sit there. He only had one button to push: the Fail in his pocket, which he just had the presence of mind to remember as the door ticked shut. Unseen and unheard and certainly without a readout display, the timer would begin its countdown to the moment when the Murderer's keep would be nothing but a smoking crater with no trace left of this accursed machine nor of anyone who knew of it.

He'd have jubilee'd but he was too busy throwing up and pissing himself.

CHAPTER TWENTY-EIGHT

"Be good and you will be lonesome."
—*Mark Twain*
The Wardenclyffe Foundation Archives

∞

In the year 2010

In her Spanish-style stucco ranch house just outside Enid, Oklahoma, Lilly was laying low. New construction chewed up the once-pleasant horse pastures around it. The white board fence was in a heap of bulldozer rubble in the paddock where Lilly's gelding John-boy once grazed. The skeletons of three oversized frame houses were already standing along an unfinished street where the arena used to be. Each oversized home stood about an arm's length from the next one, keeping nature and countryside at bay. Loads of bricks stood in jumbled columns where they had been unloaded along the front road. A barracks wall was going up and work had started on the entryway to this new pseudo-gated community.

Hector's home, which seemed palatial to Lilly once upon a time, was hunkered down and humbled by its new neighbors. The developers were trying to buy it, to 'doze it down because it wasn't in keeping with the style and size of the new houses. Lilly realized with regret they were right. It was only a matter of time before she'd leave. Selling the land had been a betrayal of necessity. Now the house was bereft without its stables and horses and open spaces, and far from a refuge, it was now just a sad memory. She'd have to let go of it, just as she'd let go of the rest, beginning with Hector.

He hadn't died sweetly with a sigh and a gentle closing of his eyes. There wasn't any softening of that memory. He'd been driven through death's door with a spasm of pain so intense, he seemed to want to turn inside-out with it. Lilly watched as he choked and clawed and arched and then went rigid in a petrified grotesque, a silent contortion. She had rubbed and stroked and pleaded with him to relax, relax, to let go before she realized that he had indeed let go and was gone, although his body remained torqued and the air so knocked out of him, no death rattle marked his passing.

Her bandaged hand ached and throbbed as she futzed with the key in the lock and wrestled open the front door. A musty heat wave enveloped her along with the stale soundlessness of a house offline. No appliances hummed, no clocks ticked, no cooling air breathed from the ducts. She went about opening windows, first of all, to let in some air.

Except for a few pieces of large furniture, the house was empty. Neutered. She had made the purge soon after the funeral because she realized if she didn't move fast, she'd be in danger of never leaving at all. The crumbs and scraps of their life together would find crevasses to take root in and grow. On them she'd feed, weaving herself into a cocoon of mourning, sewing up her own death shroud from the inside.

Making her escape, she'd struck out to art school, and threw herself into it with full focus so as not to notice the shadows behind her. And it had worked, for a time. But the truth was, she had no art in her. She wanted to be an artist, but she had nothing to say. Her charcoal, graphite, oils and ink were mute. She dithered with the styles of others. Copied work she admired and was good at it. Her teachers cautioned her against being too eclectic, but one stalwart professor confided to her the truth. She was a craftsman. A very good craftsman, a very clever one, but not an artist. He was right and she was grateful after she'd had a good cry.

She transferred to the art history department, won a post-grad appointment, and spent the next two years wallowing and reveling in what was to her the history of the human heart:

comical, eccentric, over-wrought, and glorious. And then she'd seen that Architectural Digest magazine article with the Stiller painting in it, and it cast its spell. The fact that next to nothing was known about the artist was a budding historian's dream come true. And it also re-awoke the artist in her.

The scent of that painter had put her on the trail to Decatur, Arkansas, and Sunner.

And now back again. Full circle and empty handed. Well, one hand was empty; the other was wound with a bandage to keep the dressing from slipping off. The stab had been fairly superficial. In and out, no tendons slashed, no damage done other than to the tender flesh that throbbed. —Say nothing of the wound in her heart. She kept it firmly in check with long practice.

After the windows were wrestled open, Lilly went and stood at the door of Hector's old room. As his wife, she occupied a different bedroom. A genteel custom, which gave her an oasis away from his suffering, but also locked her in with her own guilt. Looking now at the bare mattress below the elaborately carved headboard, she tried to remember it as her marriage bed, but all that came to her were images of her and Sunner.

Her own room was also stripped bare. A small modest bedroom which opened out to a veranda where she'd set up her easel and paint the horses when Hector was too ill for her to leave him alone and go riding. The only personal belonging left in this room was a small framed photograph on the highboy dresser, which she had neither the heart to take with her nor the heart to pack away. It was her husband, astride his Criollo stallion, and instead of his usual sober grace, he was glancing sideways at her behind the camera, a big laughing smile on his face. It was this image of him she embroidered over her heart to suture over the more recent memories of suffering.

She took the photo down, and lay down with it on the bed, hugging it to her chest. Too bewildered to cry, she commiserated with Hector over Sunner, and let the long hot evening turn into a sleepless night.

The next morning, a pickup arrived stacked high with her

belongings from the Arkansas farm. Sunner made good on his promise. Two red-faced boys unloaded it for her, stacking the boxes into the garage and made as hasty a retreat as they could. No further messages, not even from Donna and Zip.

Fine. She thought. And shoved one of the boxes with her foot.

Not even a message from Sergei! She didn't laugh at her own joke, especially where the mocking sound might echo back at her.

The box was over-heavy; moving it scuffed grit tracks on the floor. She recognized it as the one with her Stiller files. She stood staring at it in the gray glare bouncing off the concrete. She wanted to pull down the garage door, and go back to the bare mattress of her room and sulk. But she knew she had to keep moving, or self-pity would take over. For the first time in a long while there was nothing *next*. She needed to find that next thing to do, and the box was the opportunity that presented itself.

Dragging it to the living room, she excavated the files and laid them out across the hardwood floor in a kind of geographical map. A gallery flier mentioning two small Stillers was at the top of the room, near the north wall, in the position she thought of as 'Chicago'. To the left, or west, and lower was her auction bill from Colorado Springs.

Below the magazine, three feet south, were her own prints of the Devil's Portrait IV in Kansas City. She tossed the closed Architectural Digest far to the right. Connecticut. And for Serbia, she propped the manila folder neatly against the east wall.

She dropped the "Ozark Folklore and Tall Tales" book in the center of the room, where she first read of the painting.

Decatur. The Devils' Portrait I. In theory, at least.

She stood over the spot, scowling. She wasn't accepting that it simply wasn't there. Someone had it. Maybe that someone was Sunner. Probably. Maybe. She wasn't going to leave it indefinitely, but a cooling-off period was needed.

She let the Folklore book lie, and turned east to go through the manila folder. There was a small museum in Belgrade, Serbia, that cataloged a curiously defaced photograph, signed Pia Stiller: it was also listed as destroyed by Nazis as deviant art. Well, it was in good company there. She imagined her correspondence lying untranslated in a box. No one had bothered to respond. She wanted there to be more; Even if destroyed, there may be a picture of it somewhere. A description? Someone still alive who recalled it? Not enough reason to put a pin in her map, but it nagged her that the stone needed turning.

Lilly left it and schooched over to the magazine, the one with the Day-Glo orange Post-it flagging the page she needed. The three-quarter page photograph showed the library at Stormfield, with the wingback chairs facing the fireplace, over which the Stiller was hanging in an oval frame with curved glass. The photo was intended to show the room, not the picture, and there was a slight glare off the glass. Along with the angled perspective and diminished size, it was hard to make a detailed observation of the portrait. Months before, she'd spent some time with a magnifying glass before having the bright idea of scanning it into the computer and working on her own enlarged enhancements, vectoring it and eliminating pixels. It was from this work she was lead to Decatur. Besides the overworked photograph, the portrait was further defaced with devil's horns and bore the legend. "Devil's Portrait II". It seemed an act of mischief, which fit in perfectly with everything she'd learned about Samuel Langhorne Clemens. It was possible he'd added that rakish flourish of horns himself.

But in the title, there was the underlined notion that there was a painting number one somewhere to be found.

Well maybe. Or maybe just a wild goose chase. She was pretty certain number one was in Decatur. But if so, why had someone —Sunner or not —gone to the trouble to heist it? At least for now, they had very little value. You could do as well at a pawnshop.

Lilly lay on her stomach on the floor and propped on her elbows. She paged back through to the opening pages of the article. Something she hadn't done since the first time she found this old edition was read the copy. The story was about the house, and how it had been lost in a fire during renovations in 1928. The opening page was an exterior photograph of a nice two-story stucco-and-stone villa built for the author in his twilight years. Having lost his wife and youngest daughter, he wouldn't return to the memories of his more celebrated house in

Hartford. Lilly found it odd that a man associated with the Mississippi and Missouri should live in a house that looked as if it might sit on the Italian Riviera. But Mark Twain was always confounding his own stereotype. He spent much of his life traveling the globe, and was even the first travel writer to tour Hawaii, of all places, back when it was called the Sandwich Isles. At the time he was a young man in his twenties. Barely older than Sunner.

Lilly flipped the page and did a brief eyeball side tour of the other rooms. The pictures were black and white, of course. It cast the interiors with a cool stillness that seemed to encase the furniture in a vacuum. The furniture was wickedly ornate with deeply carved scrolls and flourishes that included fat cherubs, clusters of grapes and braces of rabbits dangling by the feet. It was queenly furniture marooned in time and looking ready to lift skirts and make a break for it should anyone leave a door open and leak in some atmosphere.

The rooms looked dressed, or rather undressed by a decorator before the photo shoot. If someone were indeed living here, they lived in monastic simplicity, provisioned with only a few belongings in grave and solemn arrangements. It was a tomb of a house. A house which might have an unseen room where its most famous occupant's corpse lay cooling on a wicker death cot.

The Library, with the much stared-at page, was the focal point of the article. It was an interesting aberration of the home as a whole. A touch of warm mahogany elegance ensconced in the cool masonry of the rest of the house. It felt like a shrine or an inner temple. The holy-of-holies.

Lilly's observation, not the Digest's.

Full and satisfied with looking, she commenced reading the rest of the text. It was as she remembered it. No new revelations. She was finished, but she realized she was not done. She sat staring morosely at the last photo, the one of Stormfield after the fire and wondered for the hundredth time which hearth on which floor her painting had hung over. It nagged her that there had to be more to it than ashes in a foundation; more than the empty tomb under the municipal building in Decatur, and more than all of the other dead-end-artifacts stacked around her. The sense that it wasn't over, —or that there was something obvious that she was missing, —just wouldn't go away.

Lilly's phone chirped once to signal she had an incoming text. She sighed, crawled over to where it was and read the display. Probably from her mother, she thought. There wasn't anyone else in the world right now who might need or want to speak with her.

But it wasn't from her mother. It was a Google alert; telling her that one of her subscribed searches was showing a hit. Keyword: "Pia Stiller". She hit the URL in the same second her hand started shaking and waited for the electrons to leak down the phone network and pool onto her little phone browser. And then there it was. A Craigslist garage sale listing from Redding, Connecticut.

Redding. The very same town Stormfield was in. She was nearly nauseous with the coincidence, but it didn't feel wrong to her. It felt right. It was way past due in fact. She may as well have been all dressed up wearing a corsage and sitting on a suitcase.

She re-read the words crammed on the screen 100 times, scrolling and squeezing and pinching and dragging them into submission and comprehension:

Garage sale: tons of brand new still in packages items. Flashlights, lanterns, some tools, tool boxes, remote control hummer. Never out of box, etc. Aquariums, one with stand. Recliner, window air conditioner, extra large wooden dog cage. Very nice and hardly used. Bought for $100! Great deal if you need a nice dog kennel. Encyclopedia set. Other old books. Old Picture with Pia Stiller on it. Size 16 women's clothes. Not my fat clothes, nice barely worn skinny clothes. LOL. Saturday only. 8 am to ?

The name Pia Stiller was helpfully underlined and highlighted. Belt and suspenders helpfulness. The ad didn't have a phone number, but it had an address and Saturday was the day after tomorrow.

There was just enough juice left in her phone battery to get a complicated call through to a travel agent who found her a seat on the next flight out of Tulsa, which made a connection in Atlanta with a different flight to Connecticut. Lilly tried not to think of her dwindling bank balance.

On the way out of town she stopped by Book Trees & Etc., and in the tiny classic section debated over a couple of Signature Classic paperbacks: "A Connecticut Yankee in King Arthur's Court" (the back cover said that it was the first American time-travel novel) and "Huckleberry Finn." She opted for the latter because it came back to her that Hector once remarked that every child should read Tom Sawyer, but no one should read Huckleberry Finn until they had the perspective of well-seasoned adulthood; for it was only then one could appreciate the depth and breadth, the nuance and pathos of what he thought was the greatest American novel.

Having sat through a forced reading of Tom Sawyer in fourth grade and having been spoon-fed the pabulum of several weak and grainy teleplay versions on a rollaway TV in class-period increments, she had withheld her skepticism from her husband, but neither had she picked up his well-worn volume.

Unlike "Connecticut Yankee," "Huckleberry Finn" looked to be about the right size for a long flight but a short trip. So she bought it and then she tore off the cover because, hey, she remembered vaguely it was removed from the school library for racist undertones, and she didn't want to spare the energy mustering up a defensive argument if she got 'the look', especially over a book she was pretty certain she would be suffering through. She had dipped into Twain's later works, the irreverent ones, like "Eve's Diary," and had laughed over his short story "1601" (about farting), but until now, she'd never read the novels he was most famous for.

Lilly was resolved; if she was going to go to the last hometown of Samuel Clemens, she would do him the courtesy of reading his most celebrated work.

Five hours and seven hundred miles later, she found herself not canned at 30,000 feet, but deep in the mud of the Mississippi and dreading each turn of the page because it drew her closer to the end. And she disagreed with the back cover of "A Connecticut Yankee". *This* was obviously the first time-travel novel, except it was the reader who traveled.

CHAPTER TWENTY-NINE

"That is the trouble with many inventors; they lack patience. They lack the willingness to work a thing out slowly and clearly and sharply in their mind, so that they can actually 'feel it work.' We all make mistakes, and it is better to make them before we begin."
—*Nikola Tesla*
The Wardenclyffe Foundation Archives

∞

In the year 2010

Sunner had a T-shirt that read, "Schrödinger's Cat is Dead." On the back it read, "Schrödinger's Cat is Alive." The shirt was guaranteed to draw puzzled stares whenever he wore it to town, but it was worth the feeling of camaraderie he got on those rare occasions when he was rewarded with a geeky squee of delight, usually accompanied by a double thumbs-up. But the truth was, Sunner only knew of Schrödinger's Cat anecdotally, and what he knew wasn't enough to hang his hat on. What he did know made him vaguely uncomfortable in a nagging 'this doesn't feel quite right' sort of way. But not enough that he ever bothered to suss it out on his own and pin down why, exactly.

The infamous cat was imaginary. A thought experiment. It began with an argument between Erwin Schrödinger and Albert Einstein over the nature of Quantum Entanglement. Schrödinger used it as an absurd analogy. A proof that Einstein must be wrong, but the cat itself took on a life of its own, and is now famously used to illustrate the Heisenberg Uncertainty principle.

It goes something like this:

A cat is placed into what Schrödinger himself calls a *diabolical mechanism*: a box in which a Geiger counter is trained on a particular subatomic particle. See? Already it's nonsense. It goes on to say that should the particle remain stable, nothing happened inside the box, other than the boredom of the cat. Should the particle decay, the diabolical mechanism would deploy and shatter a vial containing hydrocyanic acid, thereby killing the cat. In the realm of quantum physics, it was pretty much a coin toss. When it came to the Heisenberg Uncertainty Principle, the point of the experiment wasn't just that you could never know if the cat was alive or dead until you opened the box to see, but that until you opened the box, the cat would be both alive and dead, because matter existed as both waves and particles until observed as one or the other. It wasn't the nature of the particle that was in question, but the nature of the observation.

Tell that to the cat.

Every science schoolbook in the country gave it at least a brief paragraph, usually accompanied by an unfunny depiction of the hapless cat sitting in a box. This was generally in an early chapter. It was a sexy wink and showed a little leg to the scientifically inclined. But more often it served as the defining moment for students; it told them to abandon hope and see the school counselor straight away to change their major, thus filtering the sheep from the goats. But at least the illustration was concrete enough to fill a 45-minute period with actual classroom discussion instead of the usual mix of dumbfounded incomprehension and slack-jawed disinterest.

Sunner, having never attended public school except as a brief tourist, nevertheless had his own shelf of books that gave their own cursory nod to the cat. Einstein had no truck with the cat or the uncertainty principle either, but Richard Feynman happily waved the cat like a banner with the jovial warning that nobody understands quantum mechanics, but only accepts it up to the point that their brain goes *tilt*. Sunner had no quarrels with the cat being either alive or dead or both, while in the box. What really twigged him was that he when he thought about it; he was inclined to believe that the cat was both alive and dead *after* the box was opened.

And the first time he thought about it —really thought about it —was when Lilly told him Sergei told her the Devil's Portrait was a Schrödinger's Cat. If thoughts had weight, she might have then heard a big thud coming dead center from between his ears. Just before he deftly, precisely and oh-so-carefully stabbed the heel of her hand in such a way it was more insult than injury. It took a tremendous amount of concentration, as his mind was simultaneously going *tilt,* just as Feynman predicted.

The universe wasn't supposed to play you like that. Grasping that it had was a drop-lift of sickening horror and wild elation at the revelation that he wasn't mad. He wasn't insane before, because *this* is what insanity felt like, and he hadn't been that up until now. No matter how surreal, uncertain and disorienting his conclusions were; they felt like nothing compared to having his reality compass spin as he grasped the impossible and accepted it as so. Merely seeing Sergei go poof was nothing compared to this. That was merely a not-real mind-fuck.

This was... wow. *No.*

He had been relieved and heartbroken to confirm that Lilly was in the sorority of women who had as a bylaw to never give a man the opportunity to assault them a second time. But despair crowded out pride as she abruptly left with neither a word nor a backward glance.

That's my girl, he thought desolately. And then amended: *Was.* And then he sat down and cried with his hands over his eyes to hide his face from the knife lying on the table in front of him.

Schrödinger's cat is dead.

Schrödinger's cat is alive.

Schrödinger's cat is both.

Sunner sucked a big lungful of air and rocked back in the chair to expel it, letting his hands fall where he could observe them and steady his breathing. He had to compose himself. Sergei would be returning soon, he was sure of that. Just as he was sure that the warnings about Lilly were genuine.

Lilly would live.

Lilly would die.

Lilly would do both.

Well, not on his watch. He was determined to stay in the universe of positive outcome. He speculated his doppelganger hadn't been so lucky, and marveled that he had —he would —he *did* —figure out a way to travel a different fork in the road.

Mission accomplished, he thought bitterly, and set his intentions to disembark from the crushing heartache and catch the next wave of scientific wonder instead. He was marginally successful; at least between the beats of his heart.

CHAPTER THIRTY

"Beware the Lazy Eight."
—*The Artist*
A retrospective of 4D works from the Wardenclyffe Foundation

∞

In the year 2010

Even though they were early, Lilly was worried about the time as the cab wended through an old neighborhood on the outskirts of Redding. Its heyday had been on the sunny side of the 20th century with homes built to fulfill housing grants from the 1940s GI bill, but not much sought after since. A few of the homeowners were gamely working to restore their down-at-the-heels houses, but most of the houses looked as though they had externalized teenaged-room-syndrome with piles of random junk and stacks from unfinished projects banked against walls and scattered over weedy lawns. It's the kind of neighborhood Lilly's mom would have clucked her tongue at before declaring it 'tacky'. If it survived another 20 years, it might mature into 'distressed' and either be rescued or demolished, but right now it could go either way.

It was 7:30 when the cab pulled up to the address, a full half hour before the garage sale was set to open. Lilly didn't want to cut it too fine. The morning was bright, the sun just easing over the neighborhood to clear out the blue shadows on the dewy grass. The curb was painted with the number Lilly had given the driver at the motel. She'd said it like an incantation, like it was the secret password that must be uttered with the right inflections before the mouth of the treasure cave would reveal itself. From the curb, the driveway led to a west-facing house that seemed to dim as the houses across the street brightened, as though reluctant for the day to begin. The advertised garage sale was actually in the garage, not out on the lawn, so there was nothing yet to be seen. The rollaway door was down, but lights were on inside. Somebody was busy in there, making last-minute masking-tape price tags and counting the coins in the shoebox, making sure there were enough to make change.

The cab wasn't the only car waiting. Other early-bird garage-salers were sitting in their front seats, idling, sipping coffee from paper cups and circling the adverts in newspapers of other sales they wanted to hit today. Lilly felt conspicuous in the cab, but she didn't plan to stay there long. As soon as that door was up, she was grabbing the painting and getting out of there. She had $300 in her pocket. Enough to ensure that any obstacle that might complicate the transaction went her way. It was unlikely that any of the other people waiting were after her painting, but if they were, she was going to get there first, cash in hand.

Lilly couldn't contain herself for long. At 7:40, she stood outside and leaned on the cab. At 7:44, she started to pace up and down the driveway, stepping off her territory and casting looks at the other car-sitters, hoping her message was clear. A couple from a Toyota pickup accepted the challenge, and emerged to stand at their tailgate, arms folded and meaning business.

The door creaked. It was 10 'till. Someone was struggling inside to get the door open. Lilly tugged on the handle on her own side just to be helpful and gave the startled middle-aged woman a big smile when it rolled up between them.

"I've come for the painting!" she blurted. "The picture, I mean. The one signed Pia Stiller!"

Behind her, car doors were slamming and the other bargain hunters strolled up, faces held in studied boredom to preserve their bargaining advantage. Lilly had none of that.

"The picture," the woman repeated. "Oh, I say."

Lilly didn't like the way she said that, and felt the first cramp of worry compress her chest.

"The picture that looks like an old photograph drawn over." Lilly said helpfully, but the hope was leaking out of her voice at the woman's expression.

"They came and got it last night," she said. "That and a load of other stuff..."

"Who? Who came and got it?" Lilly tried to keep the childlike wail out of her voice, but it was hard.

"Oh you know. *Pickers*. They just can't wait for you to open. I know I should've run them off, but. You know," she shrugged. "A dollar is a dollar." She was looking at Lilly now a little vexed. "That picture wasn't worth much, was it?"

"It was," Lilly said. "Who took it? These pickers... Do you know them? Do you have a name or number or something?"

This was a garage sale. It was too much to hope for a receipt, but it didn't stop her from asking about that too. To each of these inquiries, the woman just kept shaking her head. Not only to say '*no*' to each of Lilly's questions, but with a seller's remorse. She could clearly see she should have held out and got something more for that painting. Maybe even a lot.

"What was it worth?" She wanted to know, saying it low and with resignation already poised to receive the answer.

"I'd have given you three hundred dollars," Lilly said, selfishly wanting to inflict as much pain as possible. "I still would, if you could get it back," she added. There was no use in dickering. She was already thinking she could find an ATM and release the last of her funds if she had to. But not much more. After that, she'd be dry.

The woman loudly sucked her teeth before declaring, "Dangit! If I'd only known!" then she laughed a little dispiritedly, "There was two or three slugs of those pickers. Don't expect I can remember which got what. Pickers come from all over, you know. Redding is good garage sale'n. Kind-of famous for it. People come down from the city all the time. I'll be darned if that picture was worth anything though. I'll be gol-darned." Denial was more palatable to her than feeling the fool.

"The city?" Lilly was stuck on the idea that the painting could be beyond retrieval.

"Boston," she was told.

"But they might be from around here?" Lilly held out hope.

"You've got some flea markets around here, don't you? Antique shops?"

"They didn't get no antiques from me!" The woman said, then she turned to say, "No, I won't take less for the dog crate." The woman she told it to frowned and sighed.

"But where did you get it?" Lilly drew her back in.

"That old picture? I don't know. It was just in a pile of stuff. You know."

But Lilly didn't know. That didn't help at all.

"I don't suppose you have a photograph of it somewhere? Did you ever take a picture of it?"

"Why would I take a picture of a picture I already had?" That was too much for the woman. She made a chuff and dismissed the very idea with her hand and turned to accept two dollars cash for an old Tickle Me Elmo doll, and then she said, "I expect it isn't what you were looking for. Didn't even look like an Indian. I mean, Native American," she said it with an apologetic little smile.

"Indian?" Lilly asked.

"'Supposed to have been some Ind... Native... oh heck. An Indian chief, anyway. Or maybe some medicine man or tribal elder, or something."

"What makes you say that?" Lilly asked. This was an odd turn.

"Well, the title, I suppose. Couldn't tell by any other way, that's for sure."

"The title wasn't 'The Devils' Portrait'?"

"That would have been a better one!" the woman said with a companionable grin. "Ugliest darn thing. Really."

"How do you know the title?" Lilly pressed.

"Written right across it, wasn't it?" she said. "'Chief some-such'. 'Elder something.' Something like 'Engay', like pig Latin. Ring any bells?"

It didn't. Lilly was powerfully dissatisfied. She stood silently, gazing into the garage with the flotsam of the household laid out on card tables and doors laid across sawhorses, and couldn't reconcile in her imagination that a Pia Stiller painting had recently been among them. She could also see there wasn't anything else for her here. The woman was now caught up in haggling over a stack of LPs, so Lilly just walked back to the cab and climbed in and sat basting in the awful truth while the cab driver waited, content with the meter running. The painting was just gone. Missed by less than a day.

After a few fruitless minutes, Lilly asked him to take her to the nearest pawnshop, and she pulled out her phone to locate other pawnshops, flea markets, thrift shops and used furniture stores. Red pegs filled the screen. There were more in Redding than she imagined, and she only had a day before her flight left.

Lilly was blankly watching the town glide by the windows when she spotted the sign reading: "Mark Twain Library", and under that it said, "The Public Library of Redding, Connecticut".

"Stop here!" she cried, and the cab pulled over.

Lilly got out and went to the doors. On them were stenciled the hours: It opened at 10 on Saturdays. Lilly groaned. She walked back and slid into the back seat again, telling the driver they would come back here later.

She didn't make it back to her hotel room until after the last flea market closed at 7 pm, and she surrendered nearly all of her cash to the cab driver. She'd have done much better if she had rented a car, but from the first she kept telling herself her search wouldn't take long. She was wrong, the day wore on, and that was that. The only thing her search did produce was a list of possible antique pickers in the area, which she would follow through with, every one, but not tonight. With her feet up on pillows on the turned-down bed, and her laptop balanced on her stomach, she Googled Mark Twain to see what else was in this neck of the woods. She was considering canceling her return flight. It would be costly, but 'in for a penny, in for a pound' as they say.

The library had been interesting, but fruitless like everything else. She'd even made the cab driver go out and do a drive-by of the old Stormfield property, but it was a different house now, and had nothing more to offer posterity or Lilly's curiosity. It was a private residence; a metal sign hanging on a drooping chain across the driveway said so. Up the road was a small gallery, and she'd stopped in there too. It was also a rebuild on yet another foundation that had burned from the time of Samuel Clemens. Back then, his personal secretary had lived there. It was called the Lobster Pot when it had been a house. Now, it was the Lobster Pot Gallery. Lilly thought it funny and a bit pretentious that the Clemens named all of their properties, like they were pets or something, but maybe it was a habit of the times. She didn't know and didn't ask. The Gallery didn't have the one painting Lilly was interested in, so she went on, but not before giving them her phone number in case it showed up.

Google Maps told her Elmira, New York, was a four-hour drive, and there she could tour Quarry Farm with an English department grad student of Elmira College, but not until classes began again. Quarry Farm is where Sam Clemens and his family spent 20 summers and where he did much of his writing. It was too bad they didn't do summer tours. She might have rented a car after all. Elmira College was now a repository of Twain archives, in friendly competition with the other Twain archives in California. Hannibal, Missouri, where it all began, just had a touristy main street and the requisite Mark Twain summer festival and parade where boys dressed as Tom Sawyer and Huck Finn and girls had to be content with merely being versions of Becky. In Missouri, Tom and Huck eclipsed their maker, except after dark when Hal Holbrook's one-man show "Mark Twain" was shown on a sheet hung up in the square. If you wanted to see it, you were advised to bring your own lawn chair.

Online, Lilly was able to do a virtual tour of Mark Twain's little stand-alone writing study from a web cam that looked in windows, which was all anyone could do in person anyway. It was less a gazebo and more an oblong ship's bridge with tall windows that would have given him a grand view overlooking Quarry Farm but now only looked out at the Elmira College campus, because it had been moved to the Quad. It had its own fireplace, and above it was hanging a portrait of the writer. Not of the Devil, unless you considered the two interchangeable, which some people did. Once he was ostracized for being too liberal. Now, his books were taken from libraries for the opposite reason. Because he was a throwback and used the N-word in the speech of people who actually would have.

A mouse-over told her it was here in the little study that "Huckleberry Finn" was written. She didn't think they should have moved it.

She then Googled Chief Elder Engee, or Enge, or Engay, and also Gen, if the unworthy former owner of the painting was right and it was pig Latin. She came up empty. Tiring, Lilly resorted to random searches, plugging in just about anything that popped in her head. She wondered down bunny trails and hit dead ends. There weren't even any references at all to the Architectural Digest magazine she already had, which dimmed her faith in the internet and made it easy to decide this was a complete waste of time and it was time she let it go. Pretty much the opposite feeling she had when she began her internet search and was considering extending her stay. The internet could be dispiriting that way.

She shoved the laptop off and located her shoes. She was hungry. She fancied she even could use a drink, even though 'needing a drink' wasn't the way she usually rolled but she felt particularly inclined to make an exception.

Inquiring at the front desk, she was directed to the hotel lounge, which she glanced into and hastily passed by, went out the door and down the street. It was a balmy summer evening and for the first time in a while, she just went with it. Here she was in Redding. Right here, right now, it no longer mattered that her search had come up empty. She had reached a natural end point and it was time to choose a new path. That was pretty okay with her. Her fascination with Pia and Sunner had become intertwined for a while and she'd let her passions for both get out of proportion. Her feelings for Sunner —for both Sunner and Pia, would recede in time. She just needed to keep moving and keep looking forward. She was going to be okay.

Her feet and the growling of her stomach led her south down toward what looked like an interesting and old part of town, of brick row houses which were now occupied by microbreweries, bistros, galleries and book shops.

This was more like it.

One stood out. A corner pub. The sign read "The Old Pilot's House' and 'est. 1889'. A chalkboard at the entrance promised unassuming brews, burgers and a signature mutton stew.

All righty then.

Lilly obeyed the sign and waited to be seated. It was the kind of place that had walls bristling with memorabilia, but none of it, as far as she could tell had anything to do with aviation. To her delight, old pictures were tucked in with tin kitchen tools and bicycles and mysterious farm implements. Yay! Yeah, she was itching to get back to work, and tapping in to old photographs was just the thing to get her juices flowing.

She ordered the house beer, took a gamble on the stew and began her Easter-egg hunt, starting with the photographs that shingled the wall above her own booth.

She loved, simply *loved* old photographs. It was the convergence of past intentions and intuitive vision that dipped her inner divining rod: Some photos were weighty and hard to maintain eye contact with. Some were airy and distant and misted with ambiguity. Some had figures that seemed to haunt the frame, rather than occupy the photo. Photographs were an artifact of light. A moment trapped by photosensitive dyes. Captured souls. A fossil record whose energy went on and on and persisted its action against the neurons that flashed in the brainpans of those that looked at them, all these years later. It was light turned to particles, turned again to light, and held on the brink of its own event horizon forever after.

What was it that made a photo a candidate for her rework? It was the mute portrait. The one that had lost its voice; the one that struggled like a prisoner against the silence of silver and glass. It needed her help. Lilly was a narrator in search of a story. She issued a medium's invitation that folded time and rescued the lost. Never-mind if the picture itself was disfigured in the process.

When she worked, she felt urgent with a sticky embryonic obsession, and afterward, there was a stillness and a sense of relief. It put spirits to rest, this work. To be sure, it put *her* spirit to rest. That's the only way she could describe it.

The server interrupted her trance by setting a large stein of beer in front of her. Etched in the side was a mustachio'd face with madman's hair. The portrait was unmistakable. Beneath it the legend: 'Old Pilot's House.'

"Mark Twain?" Lilly asked.

"Yup. Came here a lot, back in the day," she answered. "S'why it's called Pilot's House."

"I don't follow. What does Mark Twain have to do with

airplanes?"

Lilly was given a long-suffering look. "Mark Twain was a river boat pilot. Pilot, not captain. I dare say he never rode in an airplane."

"Are you saying Mark Twain lived here once?"

"The *Pilot House* was where the wheel was, see? On the river boat. I dunno where he lived, but this is where he hung out."

Lilly got it.

"It's a 'George Washington slept here' thing," she sighed, sorry that she'd almost gotten caught up in the fever again.

"We got pictures. Go look by the front door."

So Lilly did. She grabbed her beer and held it out in front of her like a magnet pulling her along. At the entranceway she found a good standing spot out of the swing zone of the door. There were several old photos of Samuel Clemens here. In most he was striking his pose in various locations around town, usually with his thumbs in his lapels. His eyes seemed always to be twinkling out from under his bushy brows, exuding a rakish tolerance of having his picture taken, even at a time when doing so was an ordeal of holding still for long seconds of exposure.

There were even a couple of candid shots taken here in this very establishment. One showed him standing at the bar, glass of ale in hand, caught in blurry mid-turn and in spite of the motion distortion, managing to look distinctly annoyed at the photographer. Lilly liked that one. A lot.

The next photo was captioned across the bottom half with an inscription in silver ink: *Lazy Eight*, it read. But there were only three sitting at the table, not counting the blurred edge of a fourth standing in the foreground. Mark Twain was in the center, the table and drinks laid out before him, his hands outspread in parody of Christ at the last supper. Probably not by accident either, as his amusement at the joke fairly leapt out of his mischievous eyes. Seated with him, two male companions. One, tall, string-bean-lanky, with dark hair and trim mustache. His black suit was formal and in opposition to Sam's rumpled white linen. He was at the right side of the table, legs crossed, and totally absorbed in a small book he held in his lap. Not a pose, but a genuine disinterest in anything beyond the page he was reading. The stillness and expectation of his posture gave him the tension of a high-tensile-wire, and guilelessly, he somehow completely upstaged the hamming Twain. Across the table from him, on Sam's other side, was another man, in workman's clothes without vest or jacket, bare-faced and earnestly looking at the camera with a mixed expression of curious surprise and hopefulness and... Something else.

Lilly knew that look. She knew that face.

She was unaware that she'd let her beer-hand sag and was pouring the drink in a puddle on the floor.

"I think you've had enough!" a waiter said, catching her arm and leveling her drink. He gently took it from her hand when she turned her wide and amazed eyes away from the picture and looked at him blankly.

"It's my first," she murmured, but let him take it from her with no further protest, and hardly noticed the bar rag he dropped at her feet and mushed around to sop up the beer on the floor.

"Do you want to sit down?" he asked her hopefully. She ignored him and went back to staring at the photo.

"That looks like Sunner," she murmured. *Looks like. Let's be serious.*

She meant to catalog the ways it wasn't Sunner. The date was at the top of her list and hardly needed any other points to follow it, except, damn-it, it looked just like him.

The hair was off, but why wouldn't it be? The hands... she looked hard at the hands. The right one rested on his thigh, the left on the table, fingers curled around a tall glass that was half empty. He was wearing a watch.

Lilly's knees went weak: It was Hector's watch with the gaudy turquoise and silver band; The one she wore right now, pushed up high on her forearm because it was too big. This watch here and that one there. It was more tell-tale and certain than Sunner's own face looking hopeful and expectant and curiously out at her from a century ago.

Lilly fumbled in her purse for her camera-phone. With numb and tingling fingers she managed to find the right combination of buttons to snap several copies of the photo on the wall, and then she stumbled out the door and made her way to a bench. She sat under a halogen street lamp and managed to keep breathing while the planet spun so fast she felt she must hang on to the wrought-iron arms of the bench or be slung off into space. When she started to laugh she had to stop because it sounded too hysterical; so she cried instead. Not great gulping boo-hoos, but quietly, the way one does after witnessing a miracle. Tears of wonder and grace.

CHAPTER THIRTY-ÖNE

"Even dreams may occupy their own plane of existence. There is a dimension to dreams that no one yet has proved not to exist."
—*The Chief Engineer*
The Wardenclyffe Foundation Archives

∞

In no year at all

To say a trans-dimensional shift happens instantaneously, is not entirely accurate. Nothing happens at all within the perspective of the subject. There is no time to think, no time to dream. As far as you are concerned, you simply continue to be. But this was not a shunt. Trans-dimensional shift wasn't happening. So, Lauder dreamed, but it is impossible to say from where.

In his dream the Lord said to Satan, "From whence hast thou come?"

But it was the Murderer of the World, and not Satan who answered the Lord and said, "From going to and fro between the worlds, seeking whom I may devour."

Lauder believed himself to be in the exact spot where all the to-ing and fro-ing took place, because he felt utterly devoured. He was consumed by displacement; he was at the center of a cacophony of chaos, as though the whole inventory of his mind was chaff on the winds of a zephyr, and he stood bereft and empty-headed at its center. In this state, he had nothing to call his own, not even himself. He was an observer who watched the chaos and the workings of his mind as though it were the same thing, without any aspirations or reiterations.

Lauder was annihilated, and in that state of nothingness, with all of his defenses shattered, a single thought arose to capture his attention. It was a little scrap of white paper caught up in that dark hurricane. It grabbed him like the sudden cessation of a terrible noise, like the flash of a white dove's wings, like a too-long pause between the beats of his heart. He turned his attention to it and there it was. The thought he'd not thought in years, the pain he'd buried too deep to remember. Yet this was it, the kernel of all of his purpose. There it was, exposed.

Arlee.

The scrap of paper that had caught his attention was Arlee's note to Lauder that he'd found in his shaving kit that morning long ago.

Folded once, Lauder knew what it was before he picked it up. It was just like Arlee to write a note on paper instead of texting. Lauder opened it, standing alone in the bathroom with his kit balanced on the edge of the sink.

Arlee's handwriting.

Lauder could see at a glance Arlee's anger hadn't abated. The script was furiously put down, and Lauder eased into it, his own irritation springing up and ready to stand in defense from this surprise attack. So unfair, this note. So one-sided. A lover's quarrel by proxy. Lauder's anger bloomed, and he had nowhere to channel it. His head began to throb again, the remnants of the hangover of the argument fueled by too many beers.

"*Heed up, spiker*," it began. Nice.

It had not surprised Lauder to awake in an empty bed. Arlee's temper was easily roused, and he was prone to jog it off when it got the better of him, which was often, and at all hours. It had been four in the morning when the door slammed. It was now pressing in on 10 a.m. and Arlee still hadn't returned with his customary bag of bagels and hang-dog apology. After jogging and rambling and whatever it was he did to blow off steam, he'd need a shower, and that was good. They always made up in the shower.

Except there was no shower, no bagels, no Arlee. Just this note.

Starting to read the note, Lauder was struggling to remember what the argument had been about this time. Nothing new, really. Same old, same old. Arlee wanted them to get their own place. Wanted to 'up' for an allotment in the country. A nice little freehold with its own ark and garden spot.

The trouble was, upping for an allotment required mucho dinero or adequate shunt creds. Arlee and Lauder were scraping the barrel in the dinero department, and Lauder didn't shunt. Lauder had reached 45 with no shunts whatsoever. He wasn't a fanatic about it. Not yet. He just exercised his right not to. He never saw the need, he said; although deep down he nursed an unease that would someday grow into fanatical outrage. Not yet, but much sooner than he anticipated.

It was all well and good until Arlee came along. Arlee, who opted into a partnership with Lauder almost right away. It was Lauder's first contractual arrangement, and he jumped in with enthusiastic glee. They'd taken studio digs in the service dorms where private quarters were costly, especially for those who labored for their keep, as Lauder did. Arlee had been attached to a prosperous family, ensconced in a group marriage before he met Lauder. He was accustomed to more.

At first it hadn't been a problem. Arlee even enjoyed the Spartan life, as long as it was with Lauder. They were terrific together the first few months. Sacrifice added to the romance — at first. But the hard labor exchanged for studio rent was galling to them both. Lauder was used to living light and heaving-to only enough to fill his belly, pay his goog fees and park his bedroll. Arlee was not, but neither was he used to working hard for his living. Arlee was an actor, and in this age, like every age preceding, it wasn't enough to meet the bills. What's more, Arlee was a *temperamental* actor.

When the honeymoon was over, Arlee started dropping hints. He left images of micro-estates on the channel they shared. He tagged partner-shunt vacay packages with all the amenities.

Lauder shrugged them off.

And that's when the arguments began. They could shunt together, Arlee said, in the same unit. Togetherness guaranteed. But Lauder wasn't about to ride the suicide express to earn the creds they needed. They'd get their freehold the old fashioned way: by the sweat of their brow. It would take a long time, but what did they have if not time?

The harder Arlee pushed, the more resolved Lauder got. He began googing for reasons not to shunt, and he found them. Lots of them, in little back-alley info nuthouses on the net. The more he googed, the more alarmed he became. It was like fertilizer to the doubts he nurtured down there in the dark.

Arlee couldn't understand this. He begged, he jeered, he cajoled and he threw the few belongings they had out the window. Lauder was firm. He would never shunt, he told the love of his life, not even with him.

Lauder knew he shouldn't have said that. He was angry. He was a little drunk, and his feelings were hurt because Arlee demanded more than he could provide. It loosened his tongue with words that served only the demands of the argument, but weren't true.

In the conviction that comes with hindsight, he'd have shunted with Arlee a thousand times rather than let what happened happen.

He first read about it standing naked in his bathroom on that once folded scrap of paper: Arlee was going to shunt. Alone. Without him.

He signed it, perhaps a little sarcastically, perhaps a little bit forlorn: Love, Arlee.

Enraged and terrified, Lauder grabbed a pair of cargos and a tee and dressed on the run. He didn't bother with shoes.

"50/50." Lauder chanted over and over again as he leaped into the car and peddled like mad toward the municipal shunt, boosting the solar and breaking speed limits to get there.

He was almost on time.

It was an economy shunt. Nothing fancy. No organist, let alone a band, and no one in attendance except the required shrink, clergyman and an appointed lawyer to award creds either to Arlee or to his next of kin. The three were standing in attendance over the chamber where Arlee was, where he might emerge in a moment, or might not. As Lauder hit the door he felt the displacement wave and heard the crack, but he didn't slow down. As he threw himself atop the chamber and wrenched open the lid, the three attendants just stood there, open-mouthed and in shock that anyone would do such a thing.

It was at that moment the jets ignited and Arlee's corpse was consumed. Lauder dove screaming into the flame, tried to pull him out, and was nearly immolated before the jets shut down.

He had no memory of them dragging him out. He didn't recall that he'd held some of the charred remains of Arlee to his chest and sobbed over them until the paramedics got there and he tried to climb into the box again, but he was too weak and overwrought. He read about it later. He read how he'd begged them to shunt him to where Arlee had gone, but of course they couldn't. That ship had sailed, my friend. Arlee had gone to... well, not a better place; He was gone to a place exactly like this one where he would pop out of the chamber with no harm done and would laugh at Lauder and tell him, "*See, spiker? Ain't no big!*" and they'd return home together to argue some more or perhaps make up.

But not in this universe.

Arlee did the shittiest thing possible: He'd rolled odds that Lauder would suffer, while he himself would return most assuredly to a love only somewhat chagrinned, and live to fight another day. Arlee found the ultimate way to blow off steam, to get it out of his system, with no dire consequences to himself.

Yeah, shitty. But Lauder only blamed himself. He loved Arlee. Occasional fits of shittiness were par for the course, and in this case, Arlee had been goaded by Lauder's careless remark.

After his burns were healed, his skin restored and his goog adjusted to administer regular doses of tranquil thoughts, Lauder was charged with desecration. Arlee's shunt cred was applied to the fine.

When Lauder left the hospital, he didn't even return home. He went straight to the municipal shunter, filled out the paperwork and then waited in line.

Emerging into maybe a different universe, maybe the same one, he'd gone home, confirmed what physicists said was true, that Arlee wasn't there, and drove back to the shunt, and filled out the paperwork again. He was caught this time. He was denied and given a 30-day cooling-off period.

He spent those thirty days in a stupor, and returned on day

31 and tried again. It goes without saying; he had the same result. For the next thirty days, he roamed the streets, searching every face he saw, looking for Arlee and looking for anything else that had changed: any sign at all that something was different, that he'd spun off a new world, and maybe found one where Arlee was. But that's not how it worked. Even infants could tell you that.

His third shunt was different. The lid opened and he sat up slowly. He turned his head as though intoxicated and stared at the three attendants, who were smiling benignly down at him. He didn't even blink as they scored the back of his hand with his third tat. He climbed out and made his way out of the building on wooden limbs.

Something had changed. Nothing was different, nothing at all, but something had changed.

Stumbling down the sidewalk toward home, a figure moved out of the shadows and put a hand on his shoulder. "Brother, have you heard the word of the Lord?" he asked Lauder. "Have you come from the One True Universe?"

CHAPTER THIRTY-TWÖ

"The artistry of time takes persistence and the willingness to start over when things go awry, just like any other human endeavor."
—*The Artist*
A retrospective of 4D works from the Wardenclyffe Foundation

∞

In the year 2010

Lilly swam through the dark, swift water of her own thoughts back to the hotel where she packed her backpack and lay on the bed fully dressed and unsleeping until morning. She felt the whole time like she floated an inch or two above the mattress, because now all the laws of the universe had changed and she was no longer certain of anything except how fragile was the tether which bound her to an earth she really didn't know at all. It seemed likely to break at any moment and set her drifting.

Only three things seemed certain.

One: Sunner's conclusion that he and Sergei were one and the same was now a distinct possibility. If Sunner had —was going to —would and did —time travel, conceivably he could, would, and did visit himself. How could he not? Wouldn't anyone? Unless thinking he was insane had made it so during the past few days, Sunner was not mad. Far from it. He had dared to believe his own evidence even at the cost of the awful conclusions they left him with. That sounded pretty rational to her.

Two: She knew by the look on his face, the one she stared at in the photo gallery on her phone with the cord plugged in so the battery wouldn't run down and zoomed to the max, that Sunner was posing for her. He had that look: The '*I get you*' look, the '*do you see what I see? Do you feel this too?*' look. That startled look of love and wonder and daring to believe.

The look that everyone has but only their lover sees.

That was the look he gave the camera. It was surprised, but it was also in the transition to a realization that *this is it*. He knew what the photo meant. It was her future. It connected them, and he knew it. And what she knew from it was that he loved her. Then, now, and ever more.

And *three:* Lilly was frantic to get back to him. To tell him he wasn't crazy. To tell him he was a freakin' genius. To tell him she loved him, too.

So, why wouldn't he answer his phone?

The next morning when the taxi deposited her in front of the airport and she blearily navigated through security and to the terminal where she found her flight delayed. Although skies were blue here, there was heavy weather across the Southwest and planes were stacking up over the major hubs of Atlanta and Dallas/Fort Worth.

So she waited in a delirium, planning to catch some z's on the plane, once they were allowed to board. Meanwhile, she prowled up and down the concourse, dragging her carry-on and feeling dazed and crazed as she looked into the faces of those who passed her while she thought, *They don't know. They have no idea.*

When queerness amped up too much, Lilly looked at her phone, thumbing up the photo. She did this often. Every few dozen steps. There was a lot of confirming and reconfirming required before her mind would bend in that direction without threatening to snap, but she was gaining on it. She only felt like she was going to lose it and freak out about twice a minute. Better. Much better.

After each photo recheck, she punched in Sunner's speed-dial number. Still no answer. But he was all right. She knew he'd be all right. He'd be sitting down for a beer someday with Mark Twain for crysakes. So why was she so worried?

That *was* him with Mark Twain, *right?*

She checked the photo again.

When the boarding call finally came two hours later, she collapsed in her window seat above the wing and without tilting it back, laid her head against the fuselage and was instantly asleep.

CHAPTER THIRTY-THREE

"We've all been there... If you haven't yet, rest assured you will be."
—*The Chairman*
The Wardenclyffe Foundation Archives

∞

In the year 1888

"Brother, can you hear me?"

The insides of Lauder's eyelids felt full of grit. He could only heave them open in tiny painful stages to see the face of a woman swim above him.

"Neetheee?" he slurred.

"He is returning to his senses," a man stated.

"By the grace of God," the woman added.

Their voices were dim behind a waterfall of static. Lauder fumbled his hand to his temple and raked at his mod.

"Turnid down" he muttered. He slapped the side of his head, his coordination gone. "Mod-damned. Offline! Killit! Reboot!"

The static continued unabated and he tossed his head on the pillow to be rid of it, not moaning as much as barking in distress and dismay. He beat at his ears and his wrists were grasped and wrapped with bands of sheeting and tied to the iron bed-rails, as were his ankles. His aching muscles informed him this wasn't the first time.

Lauder thrashed and begged his keepers for mercy and drugs, but all they did was pray and lay useless wet cloths on his forehead until he succumbed and let the howling white noise of

an offline goog take him back down into unconsciousness, where
he dreamed again of Arlee.

CHAPTER THIRTY-FÖUR

"We share a lot of characteristics with pigeons: They live in tight-knit communities, both parents share in sitting on the nest and caring for the young, they mate for life, they fly just for the joy of it, they have their little family arguments, and they grieve. Like us, they have a powerful drive to go home again. They will go back, or they will die trying."
—*The Chairman's Notes*
The Wardenclyffe foundation Archives

∞

In the year 2010

Lilly's connection to Tulsa out of Dallas was also delayed. She spent the layover time watching the Weather Channel in a narrow dark bar on the concourse just a few paces from her gate. She was crammed in and lucky to get a stool just under the wall-mounted flat-screen, at the far end of the bar. You can be certain the weather is dicey when it's riveting to patrons in a bar, and it was. People pressed in around her, pantomiming exaggerated listening positions, frozen postures with cocked ears and index fingers held to lips, brows furrowed, eyes wide and gazes locked, meant to permit only the TV sound to find them and block out all other noise, with maximum dramatic effect. It wasn't working, and some had to resort to outright shushing. No one was between her and the screen, which would be okay if she were a few feet further away. As it was, it was directly above her head and she had to crane her neck back and strain to adjust to the too-near focal point with slightly crossed eyes.

Storm masses were advancing across Kansas, bumping up against a second mass swelling up across the Texas and Oklahoma panhandles. This was shown in an animated Doppler 3-D cutaway that demonstrated wind sheers, rotations and wall clouds in a celestial mix-master recipe for tornadoes. It was headed, as usual, southeast across Colorado and Kansas, east across Oklahoma, northeast from Texas. The boundaries of Arkansas defined where it all come together. The hairy stuff would be somewhere between Tulsa and Fort Smith this late afternoon. Sunner's farm would be ground zero tonight. Lilly watched this unfold with an uncharacteristic calm. She had the photo. The future was secure in the past.

She had a window seat on destiny, and it didn't include her dying in a plane crash or being electrocuted by lightning, regardless of how breathless the weather anchor was relaying grainy videos from ecstatic storm chasers showing rainy windshields illuminated by stupendous flashes of light.

"We've lost you again, Kevin!" the weather girl said. "Can you hear me, Kevin? Well, hopefully, Kevin is all right, (nervous laughter), and we'll get his live feedback online again soon. Be careful out there, Kevin!" High drama on the Weather Channel.

They don't know. Lilly thought, and sipped her first martini, because, what the hell? The world just wasn't the same anymore. In this world, people traveled in time, had beer with dead authors and Lilly drank martinis. Lilly realized she rather liked martinis, and had another. It was all good until she heard her flight call and tried to stand up.

During the next leg of her journey, adrenaline burned the alcohol out of her blood –adrenaline from excitement rather than fear, which is saying something, considering the weather they flew through. The little 737 dipped and leapt and ran the rapids of the sky over Tulsa for over an hour before a hole opened up and it was able to dart down through the rain to the runway. The passengers gave a weary cheer when it touched down, and the clouds slammed shut over them again and the smattering of applause was drowned out by the sound of hail on a tin roof. The plane shuddered and flapped its wings as they rolled to the gate and waited for the accordion walkway to rescue them. It was driven by a cheerful fat man in a yellow slicker which, true to its name, slicked down, plastered wetly to his clothing and cheered him only the more. He greeted everyone stepping off the plane with big booming laughs. Lilly was aware some people got high on the ozone of thunderstorms, but this was the first time she'd seen it.

Except for her mounting anticipation, Lilly had remained steady throughout the flight, even though the stewardess had required her to turn off her cell phone and stop looking at the photo. She held the dark phone in her left hand. Her right hand laced into Hector's watch on her left wrist. The very watch that Sunner wore in the Pilot's House where he had a drink (would have a drink) with Mark Twain and that other guy. The watch that was *safe*, and therefore, so was she, as long as she remained with the watch.

She cradled it like a baby all the way to where the crew was stacking up the carry-on bags too big for the overhead. She had to let go so she could grab her backpack and put the phone in her pocket. Tulsa airport didn't have a covered parking garage, just like she didn't have an umbrella. So she squared her shoulders and muscled her way into the wind and rain and found her car. Mercifully the lightning ignored her suicidal walk and she was back in her own seat in her own car before the next one bolted down and blew out a street light about 50 yards away, which had been on in the gloom even though it was only three in the afternoon.

Lilly held steady, but she was hyper-aware of her breathing. In. Out. A bit whistling and tight, but no fugue descended to loosen her grip on reality, let alone the grip on her phone. It also did not tear the watch from her arm. So far, so good. But she was afraid to turn on the phone again. Afraid some stray filament of electromagnetism might seek it out and erase its memory. So, she tucked it in her bra over her left breast. Over her heart, oh yes.

She knew from the TVs in the terminal that the bulk of the storm was ahead of them, and she didn't fancy hunkering down in Tulsa for the night to ride it out. Not when she was only a couple of hours from Decatur. Maybe only an hour and a half if she pushed it. So she peeled out of the parking lot after paying her ticket and hit 412 going east, just like the storm, but just ahead of the worst of it.

The radio popped and buzzed and sounded a klaxon alarm before issuing warnings from the national weather services for Tulsa, Delaware and Adair county: "Severe weather," the mechanical voice said.

No kidding.

"Chance of dime-to-golf-ball-sized hail."

Check.

"Tornado watch in effect."

Watching, thank you very much.

When the radio's 'take cover' siren sounded, and the tornado watch recording was replaced with a tornado warning, she floored it on the Cherokee Turnpike and shut off the radio because it was just making her more nervous. She drove, waked by zephyrs of rain in a halo of lightning. Absurdly, giddily, she tried to sing an approximation 'Ride of the Valkyries'. She yodeled it shrilly, and at the top of her voice, like it was meant to be sung. It was marvelously awful and she dissolved into laughter that was only slightly maniacal, but relieved some of her tension, nonetheless.

"Wish you were here, Sunshine!" she yelled past the windshield wipers, and laughed harder until she had to wipe tears from her eyes. She kept her foot to the floor.

Around Chouteau, Oklahoma, the rain was much lighter, and by the time she hit the rolling Ozark hills, it stopped altogether and she pulled ahead of the leading edge of the cloud wall. She prudently slowed going through Siloam Springs, but gunned it again when she turned north and had only 18 miles to go, but at a right angle to the storm which loomed out of her driver-side window. The afternoon sun was behind the storm but cast a weird yellow green light beneath its belly. The two-lane highway was nearly empty and shone like a mercury spill across the luminously golden-green of the pastures and hanging oaks.

Still. It was all so *still.* Even the cows she passed were hunkered down, lying together in baleful congregations. It seemed to her they were kneeling together in prayer. A surreal landscape in an increasingly surreal world.

When she churned through Decatur it was with a glad heart. When her tires met the dirt road of the lane that wound down to the farm, she was gladder still. She went down the hill, past the bluff and across the low-water bridge, which would likely be underwater before long.

And then she saw it. In the middle of the valley, atop the knoll under which the spring kept faith with the family: Sunner's cabin, the barn behind, sitting quietly, tucked safely under the canopy of walnut and catalpa trees. It was like seeing the jewel in the lotus.

As she approached she scanned anxiously for his truck, and by the time she pulled in she was adjusting her high to a much lower octave. His truck wasn't there. But she was. She made it, and she would wait for him. She removed the phone from her bra, hit power, hit 1, but still no answer. As she rolled to a stop, she tossed the useless phone in the passenger seat.

All good things come to those who wait, she told herself.

Before going to the house, she confirmed that the door to the barn was locked from the outside. It also occurred to her that Watch wasn't currently planting doggy footprints on her blouse. So: *Nobody home.*

She then went to the cabin and had to remind herself not to just let herself in. She rapped loudly on the door.

"Sunner?" she called. "Anybody?"

A rumble of distant thunder encouraged her hand to reach for the doorknob and it turned. She pushed the door open and stood dallying in the doorway, uncertain.

"Sunner? You home? It's me..."

"*Lill.*"

The voice didn't come from the cabin, but from behind her. She turned in surprise and elation and, and, and... Standing there was Sergei, who was not Sergei to her anymore. All her thoughts and crazy ideas cascaded as she looked at him with new eyes.

He stood with that same imploring, curious, wonderstruck expression that she had on her phone. That look was burned in her brain from countless recent memories. It was tattooed across her heart.

"Oh, Sunner!" she said and ran to him and his arms opened out to receive her.

"*You must go, you must go, you must go...*" he kept repeating, even as he clutched her desperately to him. And then he was kissing her, and any lingering doubts she may have had evaporated. She kissed him back, and hard. Lilly cooed and awed over the wear of time. He was Sunner, shining and perfect and himself, though carrying an enormous weight of knowledge in every cell of his skin. He eyes stayed locked on hers, and she knew the soul of him blazing out at her.

She knew in total that they were old lovers together; that all of creation was theirs and this was only a point of awareness on the wheel of time.

She knew that here was a man who had returned to her across time and space, after a lifetime of effort and intention. It was all in his eyes, in his breath and in his touch. He touched her like she was a miracle, he sighed like he was dying and willing now to die. He trembled as all the energy of his life's work converged here now and grounded into her like lightning.

"*Lill!*" he said as though begging, and then he fell through a hole in the universe and was gone.

CHAPTER THIRTY-FIVE

"Temporal relativism cannot be demonstrated without external comparisons. The same can be said for moral relativism."
—*The Chief Engineer*
The Wardenclyffe Foundation Archives

∞

In the year 2010

Grief undid him. When Sergei saw her at last, there in that first moment, in her final moment, coming and going, existing, and about to die, it was too much. He as the outside observer, engaged in the act of fixing the event by the awful act of seeing and collapsing potentials. Bearing witness to all his future efforts, here and now in this event stream: FAILED.

He discorporated at the sight. He vacated the universe. Wrong stream. Wrong path. Pointless life. His and then lost. Lilly dead.

Again.

And when he next came to himself, it was further along, and he was amazed to find himself in her living embrace. Lilly locked tight to him. Alive, alive, alive!

"Lill!" he cried in astonishment and wonder, and then just let go, let her unmake him, let it just be. No barreling into the past, no futures left behind. Just *no* replaced by *yes*.

Alive. Them. Together and now. If only for these few brief seconds.

As he held her and she held him, he knew he had to try

again, had to keep trying, had to keep seeking the event where the box was opened and the cat was alive.

So he told her: *"You must go, you must go, you must go..."*

He kept repeating it, even as he clutched her desperately and even though she didn't understand that he was trying to divert her from the threshold of her death.

But already, she was pulling out of his arms, reaching to meet him, calling his name and lighting up with a big smile: But pulling away, and the moment was lost as the receding tides of time took him again.

CHAPTER THIRTY-SIX

"... the one whom he loves above all is a marvelous work of art of indescribable beauty and mystery beyond human conception, and so delicate that a word, a breath, a look, nay, a thought may injure it."
—*Nikola Tesla*
The Wardenclyffe Foundation Archives

∞

In the year 2010

Sunner was trying. He really was. By his own insistence: his own, which is to say, Sergei advising him —his first order of business was to harness his mind, calm it down, discipline his focus.

"Your mind is like a drunken monkey, swinging from thought to thought," Sergei told him.

Well, he would know.

Sunner was on the back-side of the property, in a little clearing across the dry creek bed and up the hill. He was hidden away in a cove of old oaks and hoary cedars. This place had that special vibe, and even better, a coffin-sized slab of limestone lying flat as a table and covered in a deep soft turf of moss. It was on this he sat, in unaccustomed lotus position, spine straight, eyes closed, breathing in through his nose, out through his mouth.

He'd seen his mother do it a thousand times.

"Smell the flowers, blow out the candles," she said. But only his body was quiet. His mind was wobbly from too much use of his brain-pump. The last couple of days had been a marathon of furious thinking and incredulity. He felt he might need to take off the top of his head to make room for this new reality, but he was a great believer in empirical evidence, so adjust he must. *Alternate universes. Infinite worlds.* Physicists disagreed, but what the hell did they know? He'd just discussed it with himself.

Empty your mind.

If only he could stop thinking about Lilly. Stop seeing her face as he had last seen it. Shock and hurt and love in free fall.

Empty your mind.

If only he could stop thinking about Sergei. Himself. His alternate. His doppelganger. His future. Maybe. Sunner kept running the numbers, but one plus one kept coming up three.

Empty your mind.

Sergei had not congratulated him at all when he told him how he had driven Lilly away. He seemed instead just as distracted as ever, so haggard and tired Sunner wondered if he were seeing the end of himself.

"We'll see," was all Sergei told him. Scant payment for what he had done.

"If you are able to control yourself, maybe she will live," Sergei warned. It was all about self-control. Self-discipline. Stoicism. This thing Sergei had done. A lifetime of it, to get here. To get back here.

To save Lilly, he said, *empty your mind.*

Well, mission accomplished. Sunner thought as he slumped out of position and stretched his legs. What the hell was he supposed to do now?

His German Shepherd was immediately alert, sitting up and looking at him curiously until she was assured all was well. She stretched and broke into a panting grin at his foolishness. He swung his feet over the slab of rock and gave her an affectionate scruff behind the ears.

"What are we doing here, girl?" he asked her. Watch didn't know either.

The atmosphere had changed while he wrestled with meditation. The leaves above him were suspended in a pewter sky. But the light that filtered through was eerily luminescent.

Lime-inescent, he thought. Like viewing the world through the bottom of a glass 7UP bottle.

He had made an oath to Sergei he would remain here for at least two hours. Literally raised his hand and made his promise. Sergei had made him swear he would. Sit here, and clear his mind. Two hours. Minimum. No exceptions.

"Two hours in dog years?" He asked Watch and she wagged in confirmation. That sounded about right to her.

"Let's go," he told her. If Sergei wanted him to discipline his mind, there was only one way he knew, without fail; the tool to get back into the flow of focused thought was in his barn. Besides, if he stayed out here much longer, he was going to get wet.

He came down the steep hill in a shambling walk, with one weather eye on the sky. When he broke out of the trees to cross the pasture, he could see the storm was brooding right overhead. It looked like a good one. He grinned to himself.

"Let's fire her up!" he told Watch, feeling some of that old enthusiasm nudge at the weight in his chest. By the time he crossed the pasture and made it to the farmyard, the wind had kicked up, the clouds churning overhead.

"Oh yeah," he said, his pulse kicking up with it. This was just right. Thunder peeled above him.

He raced to the barn, head down and not seeing Lilly's car as heavy drops fell around him. Only a few actually struck him, but they left cold quarter-sized marks like bullet holes wherever they hit. He pulled the key from his jean's watch-fob pocket and undid the new lock. No more combinations for him. One lock. One key. In his possession only. It was a small rebellion to fate. A little control of his own destiny. Sergei might have been him, but he'd be damned if he'd become Sergei.

Let's all root for Heisenberg's Uncertainty Principle.

Sunner hastened through the door, Watch pressed against his knees until they were through and she shook vigorously. He dodged the rain she flung from her coat and hurried to the power bank. He threw the switches that brought the room into stark brightness. It was piercing after the gloom outside. Blinking in the glare, he rolled the dial on his old weather-band radio, and canted its antennae until the station came through the clicks and pops of the storm. The severe weather warnings were like music to him, making him dance as he fetched his laptop. This focused his mind better than meditation.

He brought his machine online.

"I got your bliss right here, pal!" Sunner grinned as the engines started to whine, and he cranked it all the way up.

The rain let loose and he heard the barn door bang open. He was startled to see Pi explode into the barn, aghast at being wet. The goat barged through the room, bull-in-china-shop fashion. Sunner didn't know how she managed to get the door open. He just needed to get her out before she busted up the place. As he moved to ward her off, he was utterly dumbfounded to see Lilly bolting in after the goat, trying to catch her, trying to catch up, laughing and wet and perfect and...

Here. Now. Oh no. *Not now.*

On the fringe of his awareness, he saw another figure in the room: Sergei, with a look of abject horror on his face. His mouth was open, but no sound escaped, just a thin and horrible whistle of anguish.

"Lilly, get back!" Sunner yelled and turned away, back to his laptop, furiously stabbing at ESCAPE, ESCAPE, ESCAPE, but the machine was already running on its own.

Pi jumped up on the aluminum platform, right over the copper plate, humping her back and tucking her tail to brace herself against capture. Lilly was one step behind her, *barefoot and beautiful,* and her hand closed around Pi's collar.

"Got you!" she cried out in triumph and looked at Sunner with a huge love-filled grin. She wiggled her bare toes with happiness.

Sunner could neither move nor breathe nor speak because time had stopped.

Lightning only appears to strike down from the sky. In fact, an electron corridor opens up from the ground and tunnels upward through the atmosphere seeking savage union with the energy there. This conduit is the sheath down which the lightning explodes, with such force the electrons separate from their atomic orbits and become pure plasma.

But that's not how it looked to Sunner.

Blue fire danced from one tower to the next, gathering strength against the desperate willpower of Sunner's horror. He could only watch as the tempest was summoned and forked lightning shot down through the roof of the barn in a shower of shingles and rafters. But all Sunner cared about was Lilly. She burned whitely into his retinas as one quick convulsion, —one jerk, —one hideous caricature of ecstasy took her and the goat together.

Lilly and Pi were gone.

CHAPTER THIRTY-SEVEN

*"Every beginning is an ending. Every ending, a beginning.
And so it is with every measureless article of time."*
—*The Chief Engineer*
The Wardenclyffe Foundation Archives

∞

In the year 2010

"Help me out here, Sunshine. I expect she's nearly here."

Sunner stirred where he lay in a pile of rubble.

"Here now, give me a hand," Sergei said. "I never got the hang of un-moving things."

Sunner bolted to alertness and heaved his way through the roofing, insulation and shingles.

"Lilly!" he cried and shoved his way past the old man and stumbled through the ruined barn, searching.

"There's no use in that," Sergei called out after him.

"What are you talking about? What are you saying?" Sunner's voice was slurred, like he was drunk. He dared to look at the spot where he last saw her, full of dread and terror.

"She's gone. For you, she's gone."

"She's been hit by lightning! She's here! I just saw her. Where is she?" Sunner was going wild now, smashing aside his equipment, and overturning tables.

"Lilly!"

"She's gone."

"What have you done with her? We need to call an ambulance!"

"Lill is *not here*. She's..."

"Don't you say *'dead'*. Don't you say it!" Sunner bellowed and he kicked and dug and spun around like a man in a pond looking for a drowned child.

"Sunner, you need to listen to me now."

But Sunner would not hear him, so Sergei backed away.

It was some minutes before Sunner wound down, with nothing left unturned and unable to hold aloft his hope any longer. He collapsed and sat in the middle of the room on the aluminum deck and wept, holding his arms over his head underneath a column of rain pouring in through the rent in the roof. He gasped and sobbed and screamed and roared until his voice was hoarse and wheezing, until all he had left was ragged breathing. His shoulders and chest heaved in silence, barely contained in the thin white placenta of his torn shirt that was plastered to him in the rain.

Sergei waited, taking everything in with lively eyes.

At last he said, "You may as well move. Lightning isn't going to strike twice."

That brought Sunner around. He looked up through his hands with a ruined face and stared at Sergei with shock and hatred. By his accounting, the old man didn't show near enough remorse.

"Ah. This is what you call self-loathing," Sergei observed and rage painted over Sunner's grief.

"You knew this would happen," Sunner seethed and gasped. "How could you let this happen?"

"Say again?" Sergei asked, his eyes tracking like he misplaced something.

Sunner roared to his feet, finding his voice again.

"You as well as killed her!"

"Listen to me now," Sergei insisted. "This is where you sit down and listen."

"I'm through listening to you." Sunner took another drunken step towards him.

"Take it easy. This won't do Lilly any good. What is done is done."

As he said this, Sunner's strength evaporated. His legs failed and he sank again to the ground. The grief-tide went out and sucked his soul with it, and now nothing mattered anymore but Lilly, and Lilly gone. In that at least Sergei was right. There was no more to be done for her. He lost focus, waiting for the next wave to crash down and finish him off. In the far distance a tornado siren sounded, but neither of them cared, even as the wind picked up and caused sections of hanging roof above their heads to flap and threaten to fall. The barn moaned like a tall ship's rigging.

"I'm going to do some talking for a while I and I need you to keep quiet and just listen. Long passages are hard enough to back through without you interrupting all the time."

Sunner turned empty eyes to him.

"See if you can keep up," Sergei said sharply. "Do you know what just happened? Do you know what that is?" he pointed up to the three towers that stood undamaged.

"I saw... *Oh God.*"

"Stay with me and just listen. *And remember.* That machine of yours: It's a Schrödinger's box and Lilly is the cat. But more than that, Sunshine, what we have here is a *Quantum Suicide Machine.*"

"*It's a water-maker,*" he whispered in empty defense. "She just —the machine, it —the lightning and —she just turned to nothing. Right there."

"The cat is both dead and alive."

Sunner just looked at him.

"Say it with me. That's right."

"The cat is both alive and dead," he croaked.

"The cat is both alive and dead. In the box... and *after.*"

"But I saw Lilly die." There. He said it, but bile rose in his throat, to purge those words from his mouth.

"Think!" Sergei commanded him. "What that is," Sergei pointed at the machine again, like an impatient teacher, "—what that is, is pure potential."

"I saw Lilly die! So did you!" Sunner struggled to his feet again. He felt like murder was possible. Only in this case it would be suicide, wouldn't it?

"In Schrödinger's box, the potential exists for a living cat or a dead one. As long as that potential exists, the cat is both alive and dead."

"We *observed* her," Sunner choked. He knew what that meant. It was awful. It was done. It was finished.

"You did. I did not."

"How can you say that? You were right there. You saw it. You were as... as..." Sunner couldn't continue, the awful moment took him again as he remembered the old man's face, the mirror image of his own, as struck dumb with horror as he was now, but that was as Lilly ascended the platform. But now, *after,* only Sunner was grieving. Sunner's eyes narrowed and he tried to clear his head, cast his eyes back and forth, peering through the doubt that fogged his brain. It was a gesture both of them shared.

"I have not seen it yet, Sunshine," Sergei said in a voice hardly louder than the rain. "For me, it is pure potential. For me, right now, right here in this space-time, anything could happen."

"What *the hell* are you talking about?"

"I have not seen Lilly for over, well... many years. Although," his voice shook a little, "I know I am about to, and for that I am hopeful." But he didn't sound very hopeful, to be honest.

"What. *The hell.* Are you talking about?"

"We have her coming and going. Haven't I explained this to you yet? We have her bracketed. She's safe: quantum-locked between us in *perpetual potential.* I'm wading through time backward: you, forward. As far as I'm concerned, Lilly is about to arrive. And this time, maybe we get it right."

"Will you look at this place? Does this look all right to you?"

Multiple universes.

Clear your mind.

Sunner floundered as his hope tried to kick-start, sputtered and died again.

"*Potential,*" Sergei said. "*Pure infinite possibility, and Lilly perpetually between us.* Do you copy? I lost her too. A long, long time ago. But I lost her alone. And maybe she died. I don't know. But here we are again, and this time, and for all time, we are on both sides of the event: You are on one side looking forward, and I am on the other looking back. We must hold to the unknown potential. It is possible —*possible!* —that she did not die. You have to keep looking forward! For me now, there is the possibility that as I move back something will be different. Another universe forks off, and maybe, just maybe, a few moments from now I will *not* see what you just saw, nevermore or ever again." His words were hopeful, but his voice betrayed him.

Like Sunner, he was also hanging on by threads.

"*Oh yes,*" Sergei breathed, like a benediction, like an 'amen'.

"You're still moving *backwards* through time," Sunner realized and with that knowledge, numbness tingled all his fingers and face, completely juxtaposed to his grief. Was this the resurrection of hope?

"Say again and I say yes."

"You're moving backwards through time."

"People play out the same patterns over and over. They barely listen, they ask predictable questions, and then don't pay much attention to the answers. The rest is best-guess and BS. It helps when you repeat yourself. It gives me a handle on it."

"You are talking... backwards... right now?" And then Sunner caught on that he'd already answered that question, before he asked it.

"When did I start swearing so much?" Sergei asked with annoyance.

"Oh shit. Oh hell no. *Fuck. Fuck. Fuck.*"

And then Sunner hiccupped into hysteria. It was nothing at all like laughter, except to the already demented. But in the midst of that little breakdown he registered Sergei staring at him curiously and expectantly; having not yet had the conversation just concluded, and behind him was everything that was coming. The old man looked more rattled and less resolved then he had a few moments before.

Holy shit.

This was, apparently, the moment Sunner took up swearing in earnest.

The cat is both alive and dead. He was pinning Lilly on a thought experiment, like a butterfly to a collector's board. He looked at Sergei looking at him, and knew himself, looking back. He believed it. He would believe it enough to find his way back and ...

Sergei abruptly backed away a few feet, his steps unsteady, his expression melting into awe. And Sunner got it. He was usually quick on the uptake.

"Sergei, you're going to have to give me a hand here," Sunner told him, comprehending now, finally.

The old man surveyed the damage with troubled eyes.

"The cat..." he said absently.

"Sergei," Sunner said sharply. "*Get a grip.* I'm going to need your help here. I don't take this very well." His voice choked up with the confession, and then he resolved to say it again, and added, "tell me about the cat."

"Just how do I do that?" Sergei asked, anxious and grasping that Lilly was just ahead, and that he had come to it at last.

"I'm going to need your help, and you're going to make me believe in the cat. We're going to help Lilly, but I need you to keep it together for me." Sunner felt disoriented. Branches of potential have no problem with paradox, but he did. He was queasy with the effort.

Note to self, he thought, and another fit of hysteria tested his perimeter, but it held.

How many universes were spinning off of each word he said? He was fate: He turned the spindle, he spun the thread. He snipped it with his shears. He was Shiva dreaming: batting his eyes and making worlds. He was Kali the destroyer, with a hundred hands and in each a sword. He was Oroborus, swallowing his own tail.

"Jesus, what a mess," Sergei murmured, "It didn't go well, did it?" and Sunner had to look away when he next asked, with a voice high and hopeful, "Where's Lilly? Is she here yet?"

CHAPTER THIRTY-EIGHT

"For the majority of us, the past is a regret, the future an experiment."
—*Mark Twain*
The Wardenclyffe Foundation Archives

∞

In the year 1888

"I thirst," Lauder rasped.

"There, now. The words of our Lord are on your lips," the woman said. He could barely hear her.

"Jus gimme fuggin' drink."

"I dare-say you've had enough of drink, brother. This will put you to rights. Here..."

His head was tipped and a glass of tepid water was pressed to his lips. It tasted dank, but he swallowed until he sputtered and choked. He tried to raise his hands to his mouth, but found they were tied. He let his arms go slack in resignation. His nurse blotted his lips with a linen towel and laid his head back down.

He looked at her dolefully. She had a sturdy face with a kind of bluntness unsoftened by makeup, and more, she was a Geezer. Not decrepit, not nearly, but her skin was creped with age and her eyes lay in a nest of creases. Her hair was tied back severely, under a black bonnet, and she'd let it go grey at the temples. She was pushing a natural 40.

Her third eye was dark.

"Madame Elder, I require a tech. My mod is toast." His

throat was raw, like he'd been screaming. Nevertheless he said it loudly, to be heard over the feedback squall and hiss in his head.

"Oh dear, oh dear. Just rest now," she tutted and patted his shoulder with wistful comfort, and turned away to refill his water glass from a tin pitcher.

He looked past her and saw he was at the end of a row of occupied beds in a room utterly chalk white, as were the rails of the beds, the sheets, the ceiling, the painted wood floor, the straight-backed chairs, the casement window-frames and even the sky outside was a filmy grey-white.

He tried to goog his loco, but regretted turning his attention to the squall of his broken implant. His brain had managed filters over the last hours or days or however long it had been that he'd been in this constant roar of static. It held it at bay as long as he didn't give it his attention. But he slipped and now it rushed to the forefront of his awareness, and blotted up every other sensation. He collapsed back and rode it, checked out and found the place where he could let the snowstorm rage and detach, where he could float above it and back to compartmentalized awareness. It was not unlike walking and downloading at the same time. He just had to press it to the back of his mind and go about the business of peering through the blizzard and dealing with his immediate surroundings. He was used to doing that. But this was different. This *hurt.*

He looked at his fellow inmates, to have something to focus on. Geezers, every one, to varying degrees. Some were lapsed into shocking decrepitude. They either slept or lay in a desultory funk. Some were strapped to their beds as he was. White faces, white hair, mostly. Only his nurse stood out, in a crisp navy-blue uniform that robed her to the floor.

"What ashram is this?" He asked her.

"Just rest, brother. God will bear you up."

"You are a nun, check?"

She winced and smirked, and tapped her shoulder, where a stripe was embroidered.

"Certainly not, brother. I am Major Edna of the Salvation Army."

"Army?" He futzed with the word, which was tricky biz, as his synapses fired crosswise across deep grooves that wanted to route his thoughts toward retrieving info from his goog. He wavered in and out of his blizzard, trying to get purchase on the word without prodding the angry hornets in his head, keeping his iffy-whatty's to bio only.

"This is a military installation?" He was incredulous. He didn't know of any militia since...

His mem took hold; Rough going without access to his short-term, but it started to dawn.

"When am I?" he croaked. The water he'd just swallowed rose to his throat, and panic with it.

"There is nothing for it but time," she scolded him. "You will have to persevere until the demon rum has run its course. Temperance is the only cure for your tremens, brother. Now let us sing a hymn to fortify your spirits."

"What?"

She stood erect at his bedside and clasped her two hands together and sang "Upon Golgotha Was Rent the Veil" and followed that with three verses of "Onward Christian Soldiers," upon which the man in the next bed began weeping and she turned to comfort him with stalwart prayers.

Lauder was weeping too. Silent tears slid down the side of his face and pooled in his ear. He realized he'd made it. It was terrifying, yes, but he did it. He took a deep shaky breath. The room was ripe with vomit and urine and shit, but carrying all that was rich unstretched atmosphere. The world was whole. It was weighty and present in a way he'd only dreamt of, in a way he'd only tasted as hints in his earliest childhood when the shunts were new and only used to thin out the prison population.

But this was it. *Wholeness.* This is what living felt like.

He was sorry for the roar in his head, that he couldn't drink in the full ripe stillness of his world restored, but the static from the offline receiver was a reminder of his sacrifice and his mission. This was where, eventually, Arlee would be. He had only to intercept the Murderer of the World, the assassin of his lover, the maker of shunts, and stop him. Then Arlee would be safe forevermore in a whole and singular world.

The sound his goog made was like the holy and terrible choir of angels. Yes, if he listened, he could hear them. The heavenly host in a frenzied crescendo, cheering wildly over his success. His own heart leapt up with hope.

"Sister Edna," he sobbed. "Untie my hands that I may pray. The Wholly Ghost is upon me."

CHAPTER THIRTY-NINE

"Shift happens."
—*The Artist*
A retrospective of 4D works from the Wardenclyffe Foundation

∞

In the year 2010

Sunner was on his own. Sergei had left, or failed to arrive, or whatever one did backtracking through time. One moment he was there, full of wonder and horror and surprise and hope, then he was gone. Sunner made the necessary adjustments to his psyche and locomoted out into the rain the old-fashioned way; on his own two feet, into the future at the usual rate and in the direction he was accustomed to.

The ruined barn barely stood, illuminated by decreasing degrees of lightning as the storm went on East to chew across north-central Arkansas, and ultimately to spin off multiple tornadoes over Harrison, Yellville and Mt. Judea. Here, the only thing spinning off was universes, with much less fanfare and no warning sirens.

Sunner and Watch took up vigil in Lilly's car. Watch sat panting in the passenger seat, while Sunner sat with his hands on the wheel, where her hands had recently been, and watched the barn just in case Lilly should re-materialize and come picking her way out of it, like a refugee from the Twilight Zone.

Watch could only sustain interest for so long before she tested the inadequate dimensions of the seat and gingerly lowered herself into it. With one leg sprung off the seat to the floor, she put her nose on Sunner's lap. A clunk followed, which she only registered with a flick of her ear, but a steady glow caught Sunner's attention. He picked up the phone the dog had knocked from the seat.

His throat thickened as he saw his own name and number on the display. *No answer,* it read. He thought of his phone laying on the dash in his own truck. He heard its ring in his imagination and fresh tears blurred his vision. He hated carrying a phone. How would the world now be different if he had? Did she leave him a message? Thinking she had was almost too much to bear.

He thumbed off the display and a photo replaced it. Sepia. Poor quality. One she had snapped, rather than downloaded. He squeezed the tears from his eyes and looked again. He didn't remember taking this, but there he was, a mushy headshot in cheesy antiqued effects. He fumbled with the phone, found the zoom and reversed it.

He didn't think himself capable of sustaining any more breaches of reality today, but he was wrong.

Heart pounding, he sprung from the car and ran back to the barn, with a startled dog on his heels. He found his laptop with a little trouble, and was impressed when the screen resolved after a reboot.

Well, he was *due.*

He emailed the photo from her phone to his Google account, and then tucked the phone in his front pocket to keep it safe. He switched back to his laptop to pull the image up; optimized it, raised the contrast for good measure and then, and only then, he jacked open his brain enough to take in what he was seeing.

The pic was a photograph of himself seated at a table and having a beer with Mark Twain and Nikola Tesla. The caption 'Lazy Eight' was scrawled across the bottom, which made Sunner expel his breath in a single *Pah!*

Infinity looked like that: A numeral eight laying on its side. But that wasn't all. It was, —just like the note in the cache beneath the Decatur Municipal Building, —in his own handwriting.

Time travel. He already had a reedy grip on that. Mark

Twain was clearly already in the equation, but *Nikola Tesla*? Clamping the laptop under his arm, Sunner gingerly climbed up to the loft and found his copy of "Tesla, Man Out of Time". He had to pause for a moment to come to grips with the title. Perspective was everything.

It was the same copy he'd shown Lilly, the one with the photo of the inventor standing unharmed in cascades of lightning. In spite of his nearly eidetic memory, Sunner wanted to compare the pictures side-by-side. When he did, mapping every contour, practically every hair, he found nothing to dispute his first conclusion, and he had to sit down.

This was Nicola Tesla.

He did the same with Mark Twain, pulling up his image from Wikipedia. Same crazy-assed hair. Same soup-strainer mustache. The details of his hands? Dead-on, down to the ring he wore and the crook of his pinky.

Sunner wasn't ready to buy it. He took the image to 400% and evaluated every pixel, looking for a smear, a bent line, or an unnatural edge that would expose the image as a Photoshop fake. He found nothing. He even carefully examined the out-of-focus form in the foreground of someone who had stood next to the camera and a little out front, so all that could be seen was a shadow of a shoulder and an enlarged hand hanging at the edge of the foreground. The hand, oddly, had on its back a tattoo of three parallel bars.

But the most arresting thing in the photograph was himself. Not just that he was there; Sergei was moving in that direction, after all. —It was that on his wrist, he wore Lilly's watch.

The same watch she'd been wearing when she was taken by the lightning.

Sunner gave a little laugh, stopped as though self-conscious or afraid, and then laughed again. Then he took a great gulping breath and let out a rebel yell. He kept going until he'd wrung all of the despair out of his heart and replaced it with a buzz of hope.

He would find Lilly. He had found Lilly. He and Lilly would be together again, and if that were true, nothing else mattered.

END BOOK 1

∞

Preview of
THE DEVIL'S PORTRAIT
And The Art of Time Travel

FROM PART ÖNE OF BÖÖK II

∞

*"In our dreams – I know it! – we do make the journeys we
seem to make: we do see the things we seem to see."*
—*Mark Twain*
The Wardenclyffe Foundation Archives

∞

In the year 1893

Company didn't usually arrive at Granny Idee's by way of
her privy, but that's how it happened this time. She wasn't
expecting callers, not even by the usual route, and certainly not
callers from beyond the grave.

Truth be told, Granny Idee was in the privy and doing her
business when the goat rose up. The old woman was seated atop
the hole and letting her water go when all of a sudden, she felt so
queer and peeved she stumbled out the door with her drawers
unhitched down to her knees. She was so addled she felt she
might spew her breakfast, and so she staggered to the bushes to
be sick, but as soon as she moved off some, the queasiness
passed and her attention was drawn back to the commotion she

left behind.

Lord help her if a great white beast didn't suddenly hurl itself from the tiny space she'd just come from. With her eyes gone bad she thought maybe it was a deer or a sheep but then she heard the alarmed tenor "Wah-ah-ah!" she knew it to be a goat, because it hadn't the baritone "Maw" of a sheep, nor the brittle bleat of a deer.

The first thought that came to her was that maybe it was Lucifer's riding-goat, escaped from the nether-world through the hole of her outhouse. Before the notion could take hold, it was chased away by the flapping and chortling of a white dove following up behind the goat, which could only be a portent of the Holy Ghost, telling her *the goat be all right; her needin' the milk and all.* And what milk! That goat's udders were bigger and fatter than any she ever laid her poor eyes on. The tits under her would strangle a calf.

The goat trotted around in circles sneezing, stamping its feets and swinging its horns in all directions, looking for something to clobber and pass on its troubles to. It was such a sight Granny Idee just stood there with her drawers down. Even her old dog Spitfire was moved to come down off of the porch and mustered up a bark or two before he remembered his rheumatism and decided he'd not like to hightail-it on his three gimpy legs and one good one, and so shut his trap.

By and by the goat stopped cavorting and stood with all four legs planted and her tail held high. The hair along her spine was bristled up, making her look grand and impressive. The nanny regarded the old woman with a long blank yellow-eyed stare and decided where to test her luck. Stiff-legged and skeptical, the goat took a step hither and asked her, "Nuh-uh-uh?"

"Well, I reckon you'uns kin stay," Granny answered her. But already she was having her doubts, thinking of her yarb garden and the bramble ketch-pen, which held the sheep just fine, but she knew as good as anyone that stickers weren't no slow-down for a goat, and if left to it, this one nanny would eat her ketch-pen back to the bent wattles and sure as shootin' her lambs would be getting out, and the wolves and panthers would be the ruination of her flock.

But it wasn't everyday a goat was delivered up like that, so she resolved to hold her peace until more was known.

One thing was for certain; Granny Idee needed another look at the privy. She pulled up her under-drawers and smoothed down her skirt and apron, and sidled up to peek in from the side. Getting close, she felt queer again and backed off until the gibber-gabbers faded. Something unnatural was still going on in there, and she was glad her thunder bucket was safe in the cabin because after this, she didn't care to ever use the privy again.

That's when she saw the haint of her long-lost Laitha. The ghost was right there in the doorway, and when the sun hit her just so, she flickered like a candle flame, part in this world, and part in the next. Laitha wore a shift like the one she died in when the fever took her, instead of dressed in the Sunday clothes she wore to her grave. There she stood, all bare-legged and unshod and unbraided and looked like a wild thing, standing betwixt this world and that, reaching out to her old mother.

"Laitha, you'uns made it back home," Idee whispered.

Laitha's specter faded when the light shifted and Granny Idee couldn't see her anymore. But gooseflesh and turning hairs and minnows darting in her stomach were evidence that she was still there.

"I'm sorry to see you'uns come up from the netherworld, 'stead o' down from heaven," Idee called out to where her daughter had faded. "I guess what the preacher said is so: We is all stained and fallen from grace. My poor lost lil' gal!" Idee dabbed at her eyes. "Ol' Scratch never figured on my Laitha, now did he? Ain't nuthin' ever could keep you'uns down. Not even yer own perdition. Haw, my eyes! I s'pose you rode that thar goat right outn' Hell." She stood a while, waiting for an answer but none came. She stood a while longer, just to be sure, squinting at every dancing shadow and flit of light.

"Like I allus told ye. Two holes in the outhouse. One fer what goes in, the 'tother fer what comes out," she tried, but Laitha did not reappear to comment.

"Well…" Granny Idee drawled the word out to close the subject, shook her head and shook out her apron, and then went looking for her good rope to stake out the goat.

All three books of the Wardenclyffe Trilogy are available on Amazon.com:

Schrodinger's Goat (http://tinyurl.com/time-travel-goat)
The Devil's Portrait (http://tinyurl.com/devils-portrait)
The Tesla Trap (http://tinyurl.com/tesla-trap)

Other books by Dana Reynolds:

Rides Eyes of Ghost (http://tinyurl.com/eyesofghost)

The Raw Materials of Miracles
(http://tinyurl.com/materials-of-miracles)

Author's Note

I hope you enjoyed this book. If so, please leave the highest rating this book deserves on Amazon.com, and share it with others. Your public appreciation is the best 'thanks' you can give any author, especially those who publish independently and rely upon their readers to promote their work.

Click here to leave your review:

http://tinyurl.com/time-travel-goat

And...

If Sergei Sunshine Tillman were in this particular plane of existence, he would ask you to consider a donation to **water.org.**

http://give.water.org/f/Water4Wardenclyffe/

Science Fiction comes true all the time. In the meantime, it takes very little to save lives and change the world.

About the Author

Time travel aside, I am guilty of 'writing what I know'. I grew up reading Heinlein and Bradbury and was certain I'd head out for a space colony somewhere, just as soon as space exploration caught up with my sci-fi expectations. In my universe at least, that was not to be. Instead, I married while still a teenager to an Arkansas farm boy. Back in 1980, my husband and I took ownership of a little valley farm near Decatur. Our house was built around a log cabin and sat atop a bluff under which flowed an abundant spring. At night we'd lay awake listening to the mice running through the old log chinking in the walls. This was our first home, and even today when I dream of home, this is where my dreams take me, so naturally, it is where I set this book. We kept dairy goats there, raised chickens and sheep and children. On the sloping back porch I had an old desk where I first began writing stories with a number 2 pencil.

Except at the usual rate and in the usual direction, I'm sorry to say I have not, as yet, traveled in time. If this work survives the distant future, let this be notice that I'm game. Come and get me! —As long as you can get me back again in time to milk the goats.

∞

Acknowledgements

All of the quotes by Mark Twain and Nicola Tesla are their actual words.

This novel also makes reference to the excellent book, *Tesla: Man Out of Time,* by Margaret Cheney, Published 2001, Simon & Schuster. This is not a novel, but an account of the life of Nicola Tesla that proves truth can be stranger than fiction.

It also quotes a line from "Antigonish", a poem by Hughes Mearns, 1899

Special thanks to Travis Folck who demonstrated peculiar interest when he learned I was writing, and actually volunteered —*volunteered!* —to read it while it was in its early first drafts. In addition to this, he showed tremendous courage in telling me what he thought, and managed to be encouraging anyway. That we are still good friends, is a tribute to his generous good humor.

Thanks to Malcolm Wood who helped me understand the value of a strong opening and encouraged me to get serious about the craft of writing.

Also, thanks to my story editor Meredith Short for the solid recommendations, and to Emily Schmid, my copy editor who is probably kicking herself for not charging me for every hyphen she had to remove. Thanks, Emily, for giving me a head-start on making my manuscript presentable.

I also want to thank Donald Harrington, who inspired me more than he ever knew, as a writer, historian and teacher. I will thank him in person when I reach the same Arcadian heaven he has departed to.

And finally, my deepest gratitude to you, my reader. When it comes down to it, I did this for only two people. I did it for me, and I did it for *you.*

Acknowledgments

∞

About Wardenclyffe Tower Books™

Wardenclyffe Tower Books™ is a micro-publisher of books that meet the following criteria: They must aspire to an optimistic vision. They must have characters that support an ideal of dignity, ingenuity, courage and perseverance of heart. And, of course, they must be fun to read.